**Abigail Gordon** lo
combination of me
in a Cheshire villag
and is even called u
annual village pantomime. Her eldest son is a hospital
manager, and helps with all her medical research.
As part of a close-knit family, she treasures having
two of her sons living close by and the third one not
too far away. This also gives her the added pleasure
of being able to watch her delightful grandchildren
growing up.

Starting with non-fiction, **Dianne Drake** penned
hundreds of articles and seven books under the name
JJ Despain. In 2001 she began her romance-writing
career with *The Doctor Dilemma*. In 2005 Dianne's
first Medical Romance, *Nurse in Recovery*, was
published, and with more than twenty novels to her
credit she has enjoyed writing ever since.

# THE SHY NURSE'S CHRISTMAS WISH

## ABIGAIL GORDON

# SECOND CHANCE WITH HER ARMY DOC

## DIANNE DRAKE

MILLS & BOON

First Published in Great Britain 2018
by Mills & Boon, an imprint of HarperCollins*Publishers*
1 London Bridge Street, London, SE1 9GF

The Shy Nurse's Christmas Wish © 2018 by Abigail Gordon

Second Chance with Her Army Doc © 2018 by Dianne Despain

ISBN: 978-0-263-93378-9

Printed and bound in Spain
by CPI, Barcelona

# THE SHY NURSE'S
# CHRISTMAS WISH

## ABIGAIL GORDON

**MILLS & BOON**

# CHAPTER ONE

THE TRAIN WAS already at the platform when Darcey Howard got to the station. As she heaved her case on board she saw at a glance that it was crowded and about to leave at any moment. Tired and harassed after the happenings of the last few days, she felt like weeping.

Under other circumstances she would have booked a seat for the journey, wanting to arrive at her destination cool and collected with an air of quiet competence about her, but instead she was overwrought and going to be standing all the way there from the looks of it as there were no empty seats to be seen at a glance.

Until a man nearby looked up from the laptop on the table in front of him and, on seeing her standing in the doorway of the carriage, moved a pile of paperwork off the seat opposite him. Pointing to it, he lifted her luggage onto the rack provided while she sank down gratefully into the empty space with a whispered word of thanks and her head bent, her gaze fixed unseeingly on the floor beneath her feet.

When he'd seated himself again Daniel Osbourne observed her briefly.

While hoisting her case he'd seen the name of the town that she was heading for and it was the same as where he lived, which was a coincidence, but he had no time to chatter about that sort of thing.

Having been away on a seminar about new treatments in the orthopaedic field he had been making copious notes about what he had seen and heard while there, and having found a seat for the pale-looking person now seated opposite, he was in no mood to talk.

Yet he couldn't help wondering what was taking her to Seahaven where he lived and worked. Was it its coastal attractiveness, its pleasant town, or like many folk a need for treatment in Oceans House with problems of the body that could make movement an ordeal in one form or another.

He was employed as top surgeon at the place and having been away for two weeks was looking forward to a restful evening with those he loved before going back to his usual work tomorrow.

It had been Alexander, Darcey Howard's eighteen-year-old brother, who had wiped out the pleasure of receiving the news that she had been accepted as a ward sister at Oceans House.

There was just the two of them, brother and sister, having been left parentless some years ago, and since then Darcey, as the eldest, had cared for Alex like the mother he had lost, while at the same time studying for a degree in orthopaedics at a nearby medical college and commuting daily from the home that they shared.

On getting her degree in nursing she had worked on the orthopaedic wards of a local hospital with reasonable contentment until seeing a vacancy for a ward sister in the beautiful coastal town of Seahaven, with accommodation available in the apartment complex at the side of the hospital building.

It had meant a move to new surroundings, living in a new environment, and she'd been happy that Alex had shown no reluctance to move there with her as he was only eighteen and keen to follow in her footsteps by studying for a degree similar to her own.

In fact, he'd been quite excited about the move at first until one night he had talked non-stop about two of his friends who were taking a year out after high school, wanting to see the world first, and had invited him to join them, much to Darcey's dismay.

She had listened painfully to the way that Alexander had put to one side as if they had never existed the long years that she had cared for him lovingly after losing their parents in an avalanche while on a skiing holiday. Darcey had always accepted that one day Alex would want to leave the safe cocoon she had made for him, but not so soon, she'd thought achingly.

At university he would be where she could see him, care for him still from a distance, whereas if he was travelling the world he could be swallowed up for ever, she'd thought, and it had hurt to know how easy it was for Alex to find freedom from life's burdens as if he had more exciting things to do, when she Darcey had given up so much over the years.

It was the first time since losing their parents that they'd had a disagreement, as Darcey, ten years older than her brother, had always been there for Alex no matter what. Comforting him when he'd cried for his mother, carefully budgeting what money they'd had, making sure Alex had everything he needed.

She had known that one day he would break free from the bonds of her love and been quite happy with the thought, but not now, as what he was planning had thrown her into confusion and deep dismay.

When she'd expressed her hurt at his change of plan, Alexander had been difficult and unapproachable, and their quarrel had made her contemplate turning down her new job. But, hurt by Alex's attitude, she decided to put herself first for once in her life, and now, tired and dejected, was travelling towards the new life she had chosen for herself in spite of the anxiety that was consuming her on his behalf, while he was involved in last-minute preparations before he and his two companions flew out to lands far away, from where he had promised faithfully to keep in touch.

He had promised to be at the railway station to see her off earlier but hadn't kept to the arrangement. Hence her late boarding of the train where she would have been standing if it hadn't been for the man opposite who had now returned to his laptop after his brief but welcome assistance, and seemed to have no wish to be involved further, for which she was thankful. Darcey was glad that the seating arrangement was for just two passengers instead of the usual four, and also the fact that she could hear the refreshments trolley trundling along the carriage.

She was more than ready for a drink and a bite and when the trolley stopped beside them, and in a mad moment she asked him if he would like a coffee or something similar as a token of her gratitude for his assistance on the crowded train.

'No, thanks just the same,' he said briskly, taking his glance off the laptop for a moment. 'Just see to yourself and if I may be allowed to say so you look as if some light refreshment is needed to combat exhaustion.' With that he turned back to what he'd been doing, leaving her to squirm at the thought of what she must look like.

She knew that her hair, a soft honey gold, looked lifeless, and many sleepless nights had left lines beneath eyes wide and blue. She'd lost weight and felt bony rather than slender, and a quick sideways glance in his direction, tanned and supple-looking with hair dark and waving, and deep hazel eyes, did nothing to raise her spirits.

As the train picked up speed, her thoughts returned to Alexander, and how his travelling companions seemed decent enough, but she still couldn't help worrying about their safety, being so far away. She would have liked to have been there when their flight left but there had been a change of plan by the three of them, causing a delay that might have meant a late arrival for her new position in hospital care. Feeling that she had endured enough misery over recent days, Darcey had decided to keep to her original arrangements for travelling to Oceans House.

She groaned softly and the man opposite observed her before asking, 'Are you all right? Not in pain, physical or mental?'

'No. I'm fine, thanks,' she said, perking up to avoid any further questioning from a stranger, and turned her thoughts to the apartment that was going to be her home from now on, and some of the excitement that had been there before Alex had decided to branch out on his own came back.

An announcement over the loudspeaker system broke into her thoughts, informing travellers that the main station on the line, and her destination, was the next stop. She rose to her feet at the same time as the stranger who had taken pity on her, and as he reached her case down effortlessly from the rack above and placed it beside her she was hoping that she might be seeing the last of him, as it was clear that he had her listed as a helpless creature, not that she could blame him.

He was closing the laptop and shrugging into an expensive winter jacket, ready for off, and Darcey wondered what he did for a living, and decided that if there was a taxi queue at the station she was going to join it with all speed to avoid further assistance from him.

There was a queue, a long one, but the man from the train didn't move towards it because someone had come to meet him. He was getting into a smart car parked a few feet away and Darcey saw him lean over and plant a kiss on the cheek of the attractive woman in the driving seat before it pulled away onto the road in the winter afternoon, and she thought wistfully that he looked like someone who had it made from all angles.

'So, Cordelia, what has it been like with me away and you landed with the brood at the Young Sailors' Club?' Daniel Osbourne was asking quizzically of his sister, who had turned out to chauffeur him home, when he caught a glimpse of the woman who'd piqued his interest on the train and wondered if she would be able to find her way to where she was going if she hadn't visited the place before.

Yet he thought he'd done quite a bit of fussing during the rail journey, so enough was enough, and, as Cordelia pulled out into the moving traffic homeward bound, he thought the odds were that the woman, whoever she was, would have seen enough of him and neither needed nor wanted any more assistance.

He'd had no doubts about her lowness of spirit from the moment of helping her with her case, and if he hadn't been so engrossed with the paperwork from the course that he'd just been on he might have done more.

'The "brood", as you describe them, have been in trouble,' Cordelia told him with an affectionate glance at the man beside her. 'They have missed you, of course, two of them especially who have ended up in Oceans House with fractures and suchlike that A and E passed on because they were too complex for them to treat.

'But I hope that you're not going anywhere near the place tonight because we're having friends round for supper and we want you with us if you're not too stressed after being away over the last fortnight.

We're letting the children stay up as the moment your name was mentioned the girls were keen to see you. So what do you say?' she questioned.

His expression was sombre after the news about what the sailing club had been up to and he commented, 'There are other doctors at Oceans House as well as me who will take good care of the injured miscreants.' Now he was smiling. 'And with regard to the invitation to supper I say, yes, of course. I've got something for the children in my luggage and if they get tired I'll tell them a bedtime story. You know how much I love your daughters.'

'Yes, I do,' she told him wistfully. 'I wish you had a family of your own, though.'

'Don't fret about me,' was the reply. 'At the time when I could have done something about it I was dumb about a lot of things, blinkered by my own concerns, such as getting my degree and providing for us both as Katrina had expensive tastes and a short fuse. She thought herself right in all things and since I divorced her I haven't seen her—which suits me fine.

'But you know all about that don't you, sis?' he questioned as Cordelia stopped the car outside a block of apartments with sea views, not too far from Oceans House and near to where she lived contentedly with her husband and two small girls who adored their Uncle Daniel.

'Yes, of course I remember,' she said gently. 'Maybe one day you'll—'

'Don't ever be too hopeful about that,' he said dryly. 'I'm content to give my time to my patients and when called upon take my place in the lifeboat. Plus getting to know the young teens in the sailing club and helping them learn how to handle the rescue safety boat. But some of them need a firm hand, and with regard to supper I shall look forward to being with you and yours once I've showered and changed.'

'Good,' Cordelia enthused. 'I wasn't sure if a gruelling fortnight away might have wearied you too much.'

'Not at all,' he assured her, with the thought unspoken that he'd also had a cheerless return rail journey on a packed train. That brought to mind again the memory of the fellow passenger that he'd taken under his wing, and he ended up with the feeling that he'd been bossy and interfering. Hopefully they wouldn't meet again.

Spending time with Cordelia and Lawrence's children was always a pleasure. Aged seven and five years, the two small girls always greeted Daniel with delight and excitement because he never arrived empty-handed, and that evening was no different.

But the memory of his conversation with their mother in the car on the way home from the rail station was lingering, and he asked himself, as he sometimes did, why he had committed himself to living alone when it would be so easy to respond to the interest that women frequently showed in him. But having made one mistake, he would never be in a hurry to make another.

Darcey had arrived at Oceans House and, having obtained the key to the small apartment allocated to her, was taking stock of the premises that, circumstances permitting, were going to be her home for some time to come.

It contained a bedroom, a shower and a cosy enough sitting room with a through kitchen adjoining. As she took off her jacket and sank down wearily onto the nearest chair the thought was there of how happy she would have been if the original arrangements that she and Alex had made regarding both their futures had stood firm.

There would have been none of the anxiety on her part because before he had developed a yearning to see the world he had been accepted at university, and been offered accommodation in the halls of residence there, which would have meant that they could have seen each other regularly. It was the kind of situation that did happen and usually parents would be involved, but theirs, hers and Alexander's, were long gone. She knew that if she didn't calm down, her own future was going to be threatened and then what would she have left?

For a crazy moment the memory of the man in the train came back, with his calm authoritarian manner and casual concern about her well-being. She could imagine him having an attractive wife and family waiting eagerly for his return to an orderly organised life while her own was a shambles, but why concern herself about that when she was never likely to be in his company again?

Her phone rang at that moment and as she fished it out of her hand luggage, Darcey prayed it was Alex. They'd barely been on speaking terms when she'd left and that had hurt the most of all. If he had just turned up at the rail station for a few moments it would have been a move towards peace between them. But there hadn't been any sign of him and she'd waited until the guard had blown the whistle to announce the train was about to depart before she'd hurriedly boarded the train, and felt like weeping when she'd discovered how little room there had been for last-minute arrivals. But someone had seen her plight and she had been less than grateful for his assistance, which was awful, she thought as the phone continued to ring.

It was not Alex who spoke when she answered. The voice in her ear was that of the overseer of the pleasant small property that she and her younger brother had just vacated, who was phoning to thank her for promptly settling all rent owing to his firm, and wishing her everything that was good for the future.

With regard to her signing the necessary forms regarding her residence in the hospital property, Darcey had been given all the details of procedure on her arrival there and been informed that the staff restaurant was open until late if she wanted a meal. As she fought back tears at the kind thought from her ex-landlord, hunger was rising. The last time she'd eaten had been from the refreshment trolley on the train, and after food she needed sleep if she was to appear on the wards the next morning with her wits about her, she told herself. But whether sleep would come to her as easily as the food she sought was another matter.

\* \* \*

As Cordelia watched her brother play with her daughters that evening, their conversation of the afternoon came back to trouble her. Was Daniel really so disinterested in a family life of his own? she wondered. A couple of her friends were present and would be there in a flash if he should show interest. Both were recently divorced and ready to try again.

But that was the difference, she thought, he wasn't. He'd made one mistake along those lines, having married the wrong woman in the petulant Katrina and was not going to make another. Yet watching him with Bethany and Katie, his small nieces, it was clear to see that he would make an excellent father to children of his own given the chance.

He went once the children were in bed and on the point of leaving told his hosts, 'I won't be seeing much of you next week. I'm in Theatre most of the time and there are going to be some staff changes due to retirement and pregnancies, so I will be hoping for no high tides.'

As Darcey was drifting off to sleep the phone call that she'd yearned for came through, with Alexander sounding awkward and apologetic, asking if she was all right, and after assuring him that she was she enquired the same of him, and was told breezily that everything was great and he would phone her again soon.

The brief conversation hadn't been exactly heartwarming but after he'd gone off the line she was too tired to think any further than at least he'd been in touch, and that tomorrow she would be starting her new life in Seahaven, which meant that she was going to have to improve her appearance after today's stresses. After that exhaustion claimed her.

She was awakened in the middle of the night by the sound of an ambulance somewhere nearby, with sirens breaking into the silence, and for a moment she was confused by the strangeness of her new surroundings, but as she gazed around the place that was to be her home for as long as she was employed at Oceans House it wasn't hard to work out that the staff accommodation where she was going to be based was the nearest building to Emergency.

As senior doctor at the place, Daniel Osbourne often did his ward rounds late in the morning depending on how much time he had spent in Theatre first thing, planned or unexpected as the case may be, so it was almost midday when he came into the main children's ward with a couple of registrars in tow to check on the progress of those he had already treated or were awaiting their turn.

On observing a different ward sister, pristine in a new uniform and immaculately turned out, with golden hair tied back from a face that was familiar from the day before, Daniel pondered if this could really be the tired and listless traveller he had taken under his wing and thought, Surely not!

The woman had been moving from bed to bed when he appeared, giving medication and taking temperatures, while members of her staff dealt with other duties allocated to them with regard to child patient care, but on hearing his voice she became still and turned slowly to meet his gaze.

Darcey had known it was the man from the train by the brisk and authoritative tone, and aware that she would be expected to accompany him on his round she went to stand beside him and introduced herself, praying that in a short space of time, namely the matter of hours that she had been on the ward, she would have remembered correctly the answers to any questions that he might have for her with regard to the young patients there.

But to her surprise what he had to say first referred to herself as he queried, 'Why didn't you say that you were coming here to work when we were on the train?'

'I had no need to, or so I thought,' she protested faintly. 'And I was so tired.'

'But of course you were,' he agreed crisply. He glanced at the two registrars, who were chatting to a girl on the nearest bed with one of her legs in traction. 'So, shall we proceed, Sister?'

'Yes, Mr Osbourne,' she said meekly, and as his companions wasted no time in joining them she smiled at the girl who'd had their attention and told him, 'Olivia seems to be resigned to her plight for the moment and I'm told that when some of her school friends appear each day in the late afternoon there is a lot of chatter and news, which helps to get the hours over for her somewhat.'

'Mmm… I'm sure that it must,' he murmured, his attention on the young patient and the state of her leg, which was supported by attachments from an overhead frame. Turning to Darcey, he said, 'The fracture of the tibia occurred during a hockey match and this is the result, the leg immobilised until healing of the bone is achieved. Have you dealt with this kind of thing before?'

'Yes, a few times,' she told him, thinking that her appearance of the day before hadn't been one to instil confidence, but surely it might now. As they moved on to the next bed she went on to say, 'I have trained and worked in orthopaedics ever since it became my specialist subject at university, and the opportunity to work in a hospital in a beautiful coastal area was too tempting to pass by.' With a sigh, she added, 'I wasn't expecting to be alone in my change of scene but far countries seem to have got in the way of my plans, and, as you saw on the train yesterday, I was at a low ebb.'

'Mmm, so it appeared,' he commented, without showing much interest, and moved towards the next bed, followed by Darcey and the two registrars.

It was over. He had done the rounds and was about to depart, and his thoroughness had been no surprise to her, with his keen observations of the slightest thing that had caught his eye, whether it be good or not so good.

Once he had left there was a buzz of conversation amongst the nurses that was centred on Daniel Osbourne and all of it was complimentary so that she was left with no doubt regarding his popularity in spite of his no-nonsense approach.

With regard to herself, Darcey was cringing at the way she'd been so free and easy with her comments that might have given him the impression that it was a failed romance she'd been hinting at when it had been far from that.

When her lunch break came round, instead of making her way to the staff restaurant, Darcey went out into the cold air of the seaside promenade that went past the hospital and stood gazing out to where a choppy blue sea rose and fell in the distance.

As she turned to go back into the warmth of the hospital a smart black car pulled up beside her at the pavement edge and he was there again, the down-to-earth doctor who seemed to be everywhere she turned. Winding the car window down, he asked what she was doing out there in the cold without a jacket.

'It is the first time I've been able to see the sea since I came,' she told him. 'When I arrived last night it was dark, and the same this morning when I reported to the ward, and I've only been out here a moment.'

Daniel was smiling and she thought that he was different away from his duties at the hospital and looking after lost souls like herself on the train, but he was right, the cold was biting and she was hungry. What did he do about lunch? she thought. Had he already eaten? He was pulling away from the kerb, giving her no time to ask, and she went inside with hunger calling and curiosity taking hold. Where did he live? she wondered, and with who, and was that his day finished?

\* \* \*

It was not, by far. Daniel was about to make a brief visit to the sailing club that he had arranged for teens with time on their hands. He usually put in an appearance in the evening but having been away, and remembering his sister's comments of the night before, he was keen to see the state of things at the place and what he observed there didn't please him.

His helper with the running of the club was an old guy called Ely, a retired fisherman who was usually to be found on the premises, but not today it seemed, and the boat that was the magnet that brought young folks to the club was in a state of repair in the harbour.

What had been going on? he pondered. When he called at Ely's cottage nearby to get up to date with the situation, his wife Bridget told him that her husband was in hospital with a heart problem, where he had been when the boat had been damaged.

'With you both not around, the would-be sailors were impatient to be out there and they took the boat without permission,' she told him, 'and came unstuck on a rocky reef, which meant the lifeboat having to turn out. Two of the lads were injured and are in Oceans House.' With that cheerful item of news to digest Daniel returned to the hospital to carry on bringing mobility to the immobile in one form or another for the rest of the day, and if Darcey had still questioned his movements after watching him drive away in the lunch hour she would have had her answer on seeing him moving purposefully along the main hospital corridor in the direction of the operating theatre in the early afternoon.

In the evening that followed, Darcey was restless. There had been no more phone calls from Alexander, no contentment at the end of her first day at Oceans House, nothing to brighten the last hours of it. Just a mediocre night of entertainment on the television screen in the small apartment that was now her home. Her time on the ward had been great, she thought, but what now?

On impulse she reached for the warm winter jacket that she'd travelled in and her knee-high boots and without another thought went out into the dark night where a moon hung over the sea that was less choppy than earlier in the day.

The promenade was well lit with a selection of bars and restaurants to choose from, but Darcey was not entranced at the thought of dining alone in a strange place where she didn't know anyone, and when she came to the teenage meeting place at the far end of the promenade that, unknown to her, was Daniel Osbourne's project she paused outside the wooden building and looked around her with interest.

Nearby was the harbour and she saw a roomy boat there in the process of being repaired, and as she looked around her she heard the sound of young voices on the night air. A short distance away was the lifeboat house, shuttered and locked until needed, and as she lingered curiously a deeper voice that was becoming familiar caught her attention as it spoke with authority into what had become silence inside the wooden building and she was rooted to the spot.

When Daniel Osbourne had finished speaking the young members of the organisation came pouring out as the clock on a nearby church tower hit the stroke of ten, and having no desire to be seen hovering outside the place she quickly hurried through the crowd of teenagers as they spread out over the promenade, breathing a sigh of relief when the staff accommodation for Ocean House came into sight. Thank goodness he hadn't seen her lurking outside while he'd been speaking to the young people.

Daniel thought whimsically that the new sister had had no cause to flee from his presence. She'd been unaware that he had been on foot amongst the kids, and short of sprinting after her in the early dark of an October night had to be satisfied with just quickening his pace. But the apartments had come into view and she'd been inside in a flash with the door locked behind her.

It was just a matter of common courtesy to make sure that a newcomer amongst those he worked with was home safely after wandering alone amongst the night crowds who drank in the bars and ate in the restaurants on the promenade, and with that thought in mind he proceeded to his own residence, which wasn't far away, where he lived in solitary comfort that was edged with loneliness.

After her speedy return to base Darcey made a hot drink and pondered on the moments that she'd spent outside the place where Daniel Osbourne and the teenagers had been meeting. He hadn't sounded pleased about something and had been making it known, she thought. The young folk had seemed chastened when they'd come filing out into the dark night.

'Young Sailors' Club' was what it had said above the door of the wooden building at the end of the promenade and next to it had been the harbour where the boat was being repaired. So was it something to do with that to blame for bringing forth his annoyance?

Daniel could have told her that it was. He had started the club to keep the kids occupied and off the streets by training them in the complexities of sailing in the rescue safety boat, which was a smaller craft than the lifeboat but just as necessary in moments of danger nearer to the shore. No members were allowed to take it away from its moorings without himself or Ely being there.

But with the old guy hospitalised and Daniel absent, some of the teenagers left to their own devices had taken it out and damaged it against a rocky outcrop. So much so that the lifeboat had been called out to get them all safely back on shore, which, as far as Daniel was concerned, was an even greater annoyance as it could have been avoided if they hadn't broken the rules.

Two of the young guys had been injured in the mishap and when his sister had informed him on his return that they were in Oceans House with fractures, his annoyance had been normal, but it had peaked when he'd seen the boat.

Hence the stern reprimand to the rest that Darcey must have heard through the open doors of their meeting place, and it hadn't improved his mood as he'd been bringing the evening to a close when he'd caught a glimpse of her through the open door on the pavement outside, alone in the winter night, which had brought forth his effort to catch her up as she'd hurried back to her own place.

And what now he thought with mild irony as he settled down in front of the fire in the sitting room of the tasteful apartment that had long been his residence.

Tonight would have been another example of him interfering in the life of the new sister on the children's ward if he'd caught her up. What was the matter with him?

If she'd seen him sprinting along behind her down the promenade she would have thought him insane when he had merely been trying to be helpful, but that was it. From now on he would keep a low profile where she was concerned. His only contact would be at the bedsides of their young patients.

# CHAPTER TWO

UNAWARE OF THE promise that Daniel had made to himself the night before, when he had finished his ward round the next day and was about to depart Darcey said, 'I am so sorry about your boat, Dr Osbourne, and I do hope that the two boys who are being treated here will soon recover. I was on the promenade last night near the harbour and saw it.' She added with a wistfulness that surprised him, 'If my young brother lived here, he would be most keen to join your sailing club.'

'So he doesn't live near, then?' he commented with the chaos of the night before still upon him.

'No. I'm afraid not,' she replied, and when a small child in one of the cots began to cry she went to him and lifting him carefully, soothed the little boy gently until he was comforted, and watching her Daniel thought that whoever had designated her to be sister-in-charge of the children's ward had got it right.

On the point of departure, he informed her, 'Needless to say, I've seen the two lads with the injuries and am treating them myself now that I'm back. We are talking about a badly fractured leg and a spinal problem at the moment, and tonight I intend to visit my old friend Ely who is in a hospital in the town centre with a heart problem and doesn't know about the boat and the sea rescue.'

His wife has sensibly kept it from him under the circumstances. As there was never really any time for chatting in his working day he turned to go, yet it didn't stop him from turning for a last look at her with the child in her arms.

The day had run its course. The night staff had arrived and Darcey and those she worked with were homeward bound. She had been the last to leave as she'd needed to discuss problems with the night sister that had arisen with one of their young patients just before the changeover, and when she left the ward the corridor outside was empty apart from a small group gathered near the exit consisting of Daniel Osbourne, the attractive woman who had been waiting for him in the car at the station, and two small girls who were cuddling up to him.

If there had been another exit close by she would have taken it, but there wasn't, and hastening past the small family group she was out in the cold winter night in a flash, her curiosity about his background satisfied after seeing the happy family group.

As Darcey walked the short distance to her apartment loneliness was wrapping itself around her. It was something that she'd only experienced since Alex had gone, and having just seen the happy family group in the corridor it had hit her even more as she thought that she had been right in her surmise that Daniel Osbourne would have an attractive wife and adorable children, and didn't begrudge him them. He was too charismatic and attractive not to have a family of his own.

Engrossed with his visitors, he hadn't seen her coming swiftly towards them and by the time it registered she was past and going through the outer doors of the hospital into the night. As he gazed after her Daniel was conscious of her solitariness and hoped that there was someone else in Sister Darcey Howard's life besides the unavailable young brother that she'd mentioned.

Cordelia and the children had been on their way home from the birthday party of one of their friends and as they'd had to pass the hospital she had taken them to see him briefly. When the passer-by had disappeared she asked, 'Who was that, Daniel?'

'The day sister in charge of the children's ward,' he replied briefly, and volunteered no further information because he had none, and once those he loved had said goodbye he didn't wait long before calling it a day and returning to the familiar solitude of his apartment, which usually replaced the day's strains and stresses with tranquillity, but not this time. He was restless, couldn't settle, but wouldn't admit to himself that it had anything to do with having watched Darcey leave without any assurance that once she had taken off the garments of her profession she wouldn't be exploring the night life of the promenade on her own, as she had done the night before.

* * *

Daniel was not to know there was nothing further from Darcey's mind. She was feeling low and lost, and after a snack followed by a shower Darcey went to bed and until drowsiness took her into sleep, she spent the time listening in vain for the phone to ring.

A fourth day had dawned with no more contact from Alex and as the three young men were staying anywhere they could with friends and relatives until flight time she was wishing she had been more adamant about him keeping in touch. But something new was appearing in her life as well as his. Alex was happy in the choices he was making, so why shouldn't she be the same?

The opportunity was there that hadn't been present before for her to experience something new in the form of a freedom of her own after all the years that she had cared so devotedly for her young brother. She had put him first in everything and suddenly that was no more, the need for it was gone.

But she still had to know that all was well with him before even contemplating anything else, and, as if he'd read her mind, just as she was about to go to present herself on the ward, Alex called. He told her that he hoped that she would be happy in her new job and that he would keep in touch when he could. To hear his voice was solace after the hours of anxiety that he had caused her.

Over recent days the smile with which the new ward sister greeted Daniel and his entourage on their arrival on the ward had been missing, but he saw that today there was a change, not totally but she was more relaxed, less pale and stressed than of late.When he stopped at the first bed in the ward, where its little occupant's condition was causing concern, Darcey was as clear and confident as she always was when doing the rounds with him and was tuned in immediately to his comments, just the same as while he was examining the young girl who had suffered a spinal injury after falling off a swing the previous day and was in much pain.

At that moment the child was in a fretful doze, unaware that she was the centre of attention. Daniel read the notes clipped to the bottom of the bed and said, 'Sister, I want this child to have a scan and some blood tests to check if there is some injury that hasn't shown itself previously and has surfaced during the night.'

'Yes, Mr Osbourne,' she said levelly, and immediately sent for a porter to follow his instructions. Then, picking up her desk phone, she rang the parents of the injured child to explain there was a new development regarding their daughter's accident, which came as a shock as they had been at her bedside until late the previous evening and had only left when she had fallen into a deep sleep that had indicated no cause for alarm.

But the little girl had awakened in a winter dawn feverish and in pain, and as the porter moved swiftly towards the ultrasound unit with the crying child on the trolley Daniel was close behind, having left his second-in-command to do the rest of the rounds in the children's ward.

\* \* \*

The doctor's name was Brendan Stokes and Darcey braced herself to spend the next hour or so being patronised by him. He had already asked her for a date and been refused because he was arrogant and pushy, and it annoyed her that on something as important as caring for sick children he was still eyeing her up and down. While Daniel Osbourne was just the opposite, this one was the opportunist of all time, she thought.

But having seen the man on her mind in the corridor with his family the other day, it was easy to understand his contentment. With a wife and children of such a kind he must be totally happy. His interest in her would be merely keeping an eye on a newcomer to Oceans House, and as far as she was concerned looking after Alex all those years had left little time to make any commitments with the opposite sex.

There had been a couple of times in the past that she'd let herself be dated by local Romeos, but always Alexander had been her main concern, which had put a dampener on every occasion.

When Daniel came back, she observed him questioningly and he said with reasonable calm, 'I was concerned that we might have missed something when the child was brought in, but there is nothing of that nature. It seems that she was in the process of developing a chest infection at the time of the accident and now it is making itself felt and causing her temperature to soar. Our young patient is on her way back to bed and I've put her on antibiotics to cope with it. So keep a close watch on her, Sister, and don't hesitate to send for me if you have any more concerns about her.'

'Yes, of course,' she replied, 'and I'll make sure that the night staff are fully informed.'

He was looking around him and questioned, 'Where is Dr Stokes? Has he done the rounds?'

'Not quite,' she told him, pointing to a small side ward off the main one.

'Right,' he replied. 'I'll join him,' and as he turned to go, 'Is all well with you?'

'Ye-es,' she said hesitatingly, and he glanced at her.

'Are you sure? I've thought that you seemed to have lost some of your zest. The kind of work that the likes of us have to cope with can be wearing sometimes, to say the least.'

His concern was quickening her heartbeat and her colour was rising as she repeated that she was fine. Partly reassured, he left her and went to find his assistant and with his departure Darcey wondered what Daniel Osbourne would have said if she'd told him the reason for the melancholy in her that he had picked up on. He would probably have thought she was crazy to be so upset at the freedom that Alexander's departure had given her.

When a couple of the nurses said they were going to go for a meal at a nearby restaurant on the promenade when they'd finished for the day and did she want to join them, she said yes, and thought that if Daniel saw her out and about he would have no cause to question her lowness of spirit.

Inevitably his name came up in the conversation

during the meal as the three nurses chatted ab[...]
working day, and Darcey commented that it w[...]
be hoped that the sailing club he was connected wit[...]
didn't meet every night or he wouldn't have much
time to spend with his family if both his days and
nights were spoken for all the time.

The comment caused her two companions to ob-
serve her in surprise and they wasted no time in informing her that Dr Osbourne wasn't married, that he
was a free agent, and if he ever decided to change that
situation there would be no shortage of would-be brides.

'It would have been his sister and her children that
you saw him with,' they told her, and Darcey listened
in amazement. 'The dishy doctor was married way
back, but it didn't work out, from all accounts, and it
seems that since then he has steered clear of matrimony with all its joys and sorrows, and gives all his
attention to his sister's children. You'll know from seeing him on the wards how good he is with young ones.'

'Er...yes,' she agreed weakly, and thanked the un-
seen fates that had prevented her from saying anything out of turn to him. She'd been crazy to take it
for granted that he was a family man that day, that the
woman and children were his, and wondered what it
was that had been the cause of his marriage break-up.

It was still early evening when Darcey arrived
back at the apartment after the meal with the two
nurses, and now, thinking back, it seemed a long time
since her brief conversation with Daniel Osbourne
after they'd done the ward rounds, but short as it had

...eness about it that had never
...n any man she'd met.

...had gone straight to the har-
...ns House Hospital at the end
...at progress the repairers were
making with the ...ged boat, and had been told by
them that it would be at least a week before it was
seaworthy again. With a grim nod Daniel had proceeded to the hospital where Ely was and had been
relieved to find him much better.

The old man's face lit up when he saw him and the
first thing he said was, 'I know about the boat, Daniel. Those young scallywags will get the length of
my tongue when I get out of here. A couple of them
came to visit me this morning and let the cat out of the
bag because Bridget has been keeping quiet about it.'

'Did they tell you that two of their friends are in
Oceans House with injuries from the accident?' Daniel questioned.

'Aye, they did,' he was told. 'They'll have to do
better than that if they want to be in the lifeboat crew
when they're older. Has it been called out at all while
I've been in here?'

'No,' his visitor said, 'for which I'm thankful, as we
both know the need for sea rescue can be sudden and
dangerous to undertake, but at the moment all is calm.'
Daniel got to his feet. 'I'm going to leave you now, Ely,
and go for a bite at one of the places on the promenade
to save me bothering when I get home. I'll call to see
you again soon and in the meantime take care.'

'Aye,' he agreed, 'and you take care too. I'm expecting to be discharged in a week or so.'

As he drove along the promenade Daniel was half expecting to see Darcey Howard, as on other occasions, somewhere along the way, but not this time, and as he ordered a meal in his chosen restaurant the memory surfaced of how his second-in-command Brendan Stokes had been trying to chat her up when they'd arrived at the children's ward that morning and how her lack of response had made him hide a smile.

But he was far from relaxed about the new ward sister's seeming lack of family and friends. Was the romance she'd mentioned still off? Was that why she sometimes seemed remote? he wondered, and had to remind himself that it was absolutely nothing to do with him. He had his own life sorted and wasn't looking for any side turnings.

The grip of winter was taking hold as October made way for November and Darcey was not looking forward to Christmas. Alexander had been in touch briefly to say that they were having a great time so far with no mention of being home for Christmas or the New Year.

When he asked what plans she had made for the festive season she was vague, not wanting to tell him that she hadn't got any and that being so had volunteered along with others to work over Christmas and the New Year to give staff with families time with their loved ones.

She was surprised when one Friday morning in early November, Daniel took her to one side when he had finished his rounds and said with a smile, 'The boat is now seaworthy again. Some of the club members with me in charge are taking it for a sail down the coast some time over Christmas, and remembering your comment about your brother's interest in that sort of thing I wondered if you would like to come with us instead as he isn't around to join us.

'Some of the young ones seem to be at a loose end on Boxing Day so I thought maybe to go sailing then if the weather is suitable. That is if you're free, of course, as I'm aware that Christmas is a busy time for most people.'

Darcey could feel her colour rising. The last thing she wanted was to have to explain to him that she was so lonely that she'd volunteered to work all over Christmas. So instead she told him truthfully that she would be otherwise engaged elsewhere.

'Thank you for asking me,' she said weakly. 'It was a very kind thought, but I won't be free any time over Christmas. I'm fully booked, I'm afraid.'

She saw surprise in his expression and thought that she could at least have explained why she wouldn't be available, but there was no way she wanted anyone to know how alone she was, least of all him.

Daniel Osbourne had probably never had anyone of her sex not want to be with him, though it hadn't exactly been for a date, she reminded herself. The other two nurses she'd been with that night had described him as a loner. There would have been a boat full of teenagers to keep them apart if she'd accepted the offer.

'That's fine, then, if you aren't going to be alone,' he said levelly, and went on his way.

When he'd gone Darcey could have wept with shame at the way she'd thrown his concern back in his face, but the fact remained that she just couldn't have admitted what a miserable thing her life was at the present time, and if Daniel Osbourne was the loner that she'd been told he was, maybe he was also going to be on his own during the festivities, which would make her refusal of his suggestion even more bizarre.

Though having seen his sister and her children briefly, and in spite of the haste with which she herself had made her exit, she had noted the affection between them that day when they'd called to see him, so it seemed hardly likely.

The day, like any other when she was on duty, was demanding her time, energy and patience, and she put the unexpected conversation they'd just had to the back of her mind until such time as when she would be free to absorb it fully, which was fortunate as at that moment a ten-year-old boy was admitted to the ward in pain and fractious with the osteomyelitis, which was more common in children than adults.

Daniel had seen Evan Roberts in his clinic and given orders for him to be admitted to the children's ward and given a course of antibiotics to clear the inflammation, and as Darcey and her staff followed his instructions and comforted Evan, there was an ache inside her at the memory of how she'd been so quick to refuse to sail in the ex-navy whaler that his club practised in.

Her reply to the effect that she was already going to be occupied on that occasion had been the truth and the reason for it had been understandable as far as she was concerned, having volunteered to work during the most important days of Christmas.

But would she have made that sort of commitment if she'd known that he was going to want to take her sailing, and what would he say should she tell him that she would love to go with him on some other occasion when she was free as long as the offer wasn't made out of pity because of her solitary state.

Daniel had referred to the lifeboat on a few occasions, a bigger and more powerful craft than his club used, as theirs was involved more in the safety of local events, and the thought of it made her keen to know more about the man who had come into her life on a crowded passenger train.

As she was leaving the ward after checking on Evan and having handed his care over to the night staff, Darcey saw Daniel glance unsmilingly in her direction as he went to speak to one of them, leaving her to make her way home with the feeling that it was going to be a miserable evening and if that was what it turned out to be, she had only herself to blame. With that thought in mind she decided to eat out at one of the restaurants on the promenade to delay enduring the gloom of the evening ahead any more than she had to and went to the nearest one, only to discover that it wasn't a good plan as just as she was about to enjoy the food put before her, Brendan Stokes appeared. Looking down at her upturned face, he said, 'Hi, Darcey. Do you mind if I join you?'

Before she could say yes, no or maybe, he was seated opposite and was beckoning to a nearby waitress who had eyes only for a customer who had just presented himself at a table at the other side of the restaurant but had paused to answer his phone, and as Darcey followed the woman's gaze she stifled a groan.

Why hadn't it occurred to her? she thought. It was to be expected that staff from Oceans House who had been working all day would choose the nearest restaurant, as had been the case on the night she'd dined with the two nurses.

'The boss just appeared,' her unwelcome companion said. 'He hasn't had much to say today, but it's clear that someone has rubbed him up the wrong way.' As she glanced over again, she saw Daniel abruptly standing and preparing to leave. 'Look, he's no sooner arrived than he's going, which I suspect will turn out to be a lifeboat alert.'

'So tell me about Mr Osbourne's connection with the lifeboat service,' she said. 'How does he come to be part of it?'

'His father was in charge at one time, him and old Ely were the main crew members, and when he died a couple of years back Daniel agreed to fill the gap his passing had left.

'He and Ely are hoping that some day new members of the lifeboat crew will come from their Young

Sailors' Club, but their antics while he's been away haven't exactly filled him with confidence.'

As he turned to leave, Daniel glanced across and saw Darcey and Brendan dining cosily together, it seemed, and his jaw tightened. Was his second-in-command the reason for Darcey's fully booked Christmas, he thought grimly, the womaniser who never missed a trick if an attractive member of the opposite sex was anywhere near? Had the apparent lack of interest she'd shown when Brendan Stokes had eyed her up on his rounds merely been a pretence?

He had entered the restaurant by another door, but in leaving he passed their table and with a brief nod was gone in answer to the request for his presence on the lifeboat, taking with him the thought that she was the first woman he had even looked at since Katrina's welcome departure, and he might have been on the way to making another big mistake.

# CHAPTER THREE

BACK IN THE restaurant Darcey was leaving the food on her plate untouched, and observing it her unwelcome fellow diner said, 'It's like I told you, the boss hasn't been his usual self today for some reason. Why don't we two make a night of it while he's riding the waves?'

She rose to her feet and said briefly, 'No, thanks. I'm going. It's been a long day and I'm tired.' And before he could comment further she had called the waitress over, paid the bill, and was on her way back to her accommodation.

On her way home Darcey heard someone say that the coastguards had been onto the lifeboat station to report that a yacht was in trouble out in the bay, and within minutes Daniel and the rest of the crew were kitted out and ready to sail into the winter night with all speed, while back in her small apartment Darcey crouched by the window that overlooked the sea and prayed that they would soon return with the boat and its occupants brought to safety, and after what seemed an eternity she saw white sails in the light of a pale moon with the lifeboat alongside, and sent up a prayer of thanks for all those concerned.

Especially for the man who had spent a busy day working in Oceans House, making good the problems of others, then had gone without the meal that he must have been more than ready for to take part in a situation that could have been dangerous in the extreme. As she closed the curtains and readied herself for bed she prayed that Brendan Stokes would not turn the incident of Daniel Osbourne's seeing them together in the restaurant into a tale of false innuendos.

The day's happenings had made her realise just how much Daniel's good opinion of her mattered to her and with that thought came the memory of her glib refusal of a sail with him and some of his club members during the festive season, giving him the impression that she would be living it up all over Christmas.

When he appeared the next morning she flashed him a tentative smile as he began his rounds but was met with a brief nod as he went from bed to bed, checking his young patients and passing on to her his requirements regarding them where necessary. Darcey felt that the only good thing to be happening was the absence of her dining companion of the night before, who, it appeared, was going to be away on a course for the coming week.

Daniel was determined to remain coolly professional towards Darcey. The sighting of her with Brendan in the restaurant the night before had made him think how mistaken he'd been about her, after seeing her ignore Brendan on the ward only to find her dining with him happily enough at the end of their working day. No doubt that was the reason why she was fully booked for the activities of Christmas.

As for himself he had almost been on the point of changing his mind regarding his solitary existence, only to discover that she had an agenda of her own that he had known nothing about. The tired traveller on the train journey of not so long ago was turning out to be anything but short of company by the looks of it.

On the following Saturday Darcey was free from hospital duty and leaving the promenade behind went shopping in the town for food and other necessities, and once that was done she went into a nearby café for afternoon tea with the idea of delaying her return to the emptiness of her living quarters.

As she looked around her a woman seated at the next table smiled in her direction and as she acknowledged the gesture from a stranger with a smile of her own Darcey felt she looked vaguely familiar, and a flashback of herself zooming down the hospital corridor where Daniel Osbourne was chatting to his sister and her family, as she'd discovered afterwards, came to her.

'Would you mind if I join you?' the woman asked.

'No, not at all. I would be glad of the company,' Darcey told her, and thought if this was who she thought she was maybe she might get to know something more about the man who was in her thoughts more than was good for her.

The woman introduced herself as Cordelia, and seated herself beside her. 'I remember seeing you at Oceans House's Orthopaedic Centre not long ago. My children and I had called briefly to see my brother, who is a great favourite with my little girls, and you went past us on the corridor, I recall.'

'Er…yes, that was me,' Darcey told her. 'I didn't want to intrude and quickly made my departure.'

'How long have you worked at the centre?' Cordelia questioned.

'Just a matter of weeks,' replied Darcey.

'And do you like it there?'

Darcey frowned slightly. 'Yes, and no. It can be quite lonely as I spend nearly all my free time on my own, which is only to be expected when one is living in a strange place, I suppose, but I love the job. When I saw a vacancy advertised for a ward sister at a coastal resort I didn't hesitate, and basically I have no regrets.'

'Would you like to dine with us one evening during Christmas to break the monotony?' Cordelia asked. 'I could invite Daniel along to swell the numbers.'

Darcey felt her face flush. 'It is very kind of you to invite me,' she said hastily, 'but I feel that Dr Osbourne wouldn't like it as he sees enough of me on the ward, without my intruding into his private life.'

'All right, if that is how you feel,' Cordelia said understandingly. 'But do let me know if you change your mind. Now I must go. My husband has taken our daughters out for the afternoon and they'll be back soon and ready for a meal. But one last thing before I go, what is your name?'

'Darcey Howard,' she said, with the feeling that she was getting out of her depth.

'Well, it has been nice to meet you,' the other woman said, and with that she was gone, leaving Darcey to visualise Daniel Osbourne's expression if he found himself thrown together with her socially after the chill he was bringing with him every time he entered the ward.

She went overboard with the shopping and as she stepped off one of the trams that ran along the promenade she pointed herself and her bags in the direction of her apartment, only to be brought to a halt momentarily as Daniel came walking towards her out of the hospital's main entrance. Observing her heavy load, he stopped to say, 'Let me take those for you, Darcey,' and as she hesitated, 'Have you started shopping for Christmas already?'

'Maybe just a couple of things,' she admitted as he took her shopping from her, 'but most of it was a weekly shop for the basics. Yet I did find time to have afternoon tea while I was out, which was nice, and while there I had the pleasure of getting to know your sister.'

She saw the dark hazel of his eyes widen, but his voice was calm enough as he said, 'You met Cordelia? How did that come about?'

'She was sitting at the next table and recognised me from the afternoon when she and your nieces called at Oceans House to see you, and the two of us had a nice long chat.'

'Not about me, I hope?' he questioned, and now his voice was cool.

'Well, maybe just a little, I suppose,' Darcey admitted uncomfortably. 'She invited me to dine with them and yourself some evening over Christmas but I felt that you might see enough of me during the day at the hospital without another appearance later.'

'That is as it may be, but aren't you all booked up over Christmas, if I remember rightly?' he said smoothly, and the moment to tell him the truth of what exactly she would be doing passed by because she was hurt to think that the man who was like no other she had ever met might be pairing her off with someone like Brendan Stokes.

'Yes, I suppose there is that. I can't let someone down at the last moment,' she agreed, with the thought in mind that it was only herself that she was letting down by not telling him the truth, that because she had no friends to turn to over Christmas she was going to give instead of take by being with the sick young ones in her care, and that an evening spent with him and his family would be something to hang onto in her loneliness.

But they were at the door of her apartment. Daniel was placing her shopping carefully on the step ready to be off and Darcey knew she couldn't beg for his company and that of his family, even if she never spoke to a soul over Christmas other than her young patients and their families.

As they faced each other she thanked him for carrying her shopping and, unaware of how much their unexpected meeting meant to her, he gave a brief farewell and was gone.

It was Ely's first night back with them after his illness and Daniel had been home to change his clothes before the evening ahead when he'd seen Darcey get off the tram and had found himself searching around for an excuse to linger and then thought better of it, but it didn't stop him from wondering what Cordelia was up to.

He knew that his sister wasn't happy about his solitary life but it was his choice, and even if he was attracted to Darcey Howard, so what? He hadn't forgotten seeing her and Brendan Stokes all cosy together in the restaurant, and he'd noted that Stokes had booked the time off way back to make sure that he wasn't caught up in the work zone during the festive season.

As Darcey unpacked her shopping the thought was there that Daniel hadn't been bursting to socialise with her at his sister's house during Christmas, which was not surprising, she supposed, if he was the loner that he appeared to be.

But what was it that he was expecting of her if she did? That she would pin him down beneath the mistletoe? Expect him to be dressed up as Santa Claus? Or that she might turn up looking like a Christmas fairy?

She'd done that several times when Alexander had

been small and crying for his mother. But none of that was likely. If he was a touch-me-not, so was she, and on that thought she resigned herself to another lonely evening.

It had been great having Ely back amongst them at the club, Daniel thought as he made his way home after the meeting, and to make it even better the first of the two injured youths had been discharged by him from Oceans House and been well enough to attend, which left just one missing member, and Daniel was hoping that soon he too would be ready to leave the hospital, having also had time to dwell on their recklessness in taking the boat out without supervision.

It was cold, frost was glinting on the pavements and rooftops, and all the eating and drinking places on the promenade were full of those seeking warmth and company on a November night. Tempted by the scenes around him Daniel decided that a hot supper would be just the thing on such an occasion with the right company if possible and his thoughts went to Darcey who he had left earlier.

Would she be in or out? he wondered. And what would she think if he was to knock on her door to find out?

It had been as she'd expected, Darcey was thinking, a boring and lonely Saturday evening with no doubt many more to come, and as she gazed out of her window into the dark night her eyes widened as she observed Daniel walking purposefully towards her front door in the light of a nearby streetlamp, and when she opened it in answer to his knock he said, 'Can I come in? I thought you might have gone to bed but it seems not.'

'Is something wrong?' she asked in amazed enquiry.

He was smiling. 'Only if you say no.'

'What?' she exclaimed. 'I don't understand. Why have you come?'

'I was walking home from the club, in high spirits I may add because it has been a great night with Ely back amongst us, along with one of the lads that I've been able to discharge from Oceans House, and I suddenly felt the need of a hot supper but didn't fancy eating alone. Knowing that you live quite near to all the night life of the area I wondered if you would like to join me?'

'But I'm not dressed for the occasion,' she protested, 'and why me?'

'I've just explained that you were the nearest person to ask. So what do you say? All you have to do is put on a warm coat and off we go.'

'Yes, all right,' she agreed slowly. 'It has been a long, boring evening so maybe I'm ready for a change of scene, just as long as you're sure.'

Unexpectedly, Daniel felt his heart lifting. 'I'm sure,' he said. 'What do I have to do to convince you? The place we go to can be your choice.' He was tempted to comment, *As long as it isn't where I saw you with Brendan Stokes*, but thought better of it as that would put the dampener on the moment, if anything did.

'Where do you usually dine?' she asked as they left for the bright lights of the promenade. 'You know the place so much better than I do.'

'Right here,' he said, pausing outside the upmarket restaurant that was always his choice, unless it was at the end of an extra busy day at the hospital.

If that was the case he went to the first one he came to as he had done on the night when he'd seen her with Brendan.

'So do you want to try it?' he questioned.

'Oh, yes, please!' she said with eyes shining at the suggestion, and Daniel thought how different she was now from the weary traveller of that day on the train. Yet he still didn't know anything about her background. The only family member she'd mentioned had been her young brother, but surely there were others?

He was rather short on the ground with relatives himself, but Cordelia and her family were joy untold to have near so what more could he ask? And as the answer to that question surged forth, he pushed it to the back of his mind.

Of course he wanted children of his own, much as he loved his young nieces, but children needed a mother, which was a gap that he couldn't ever see himself filling, and with regard to his curiosity regarding Darcey's family, maybe that was where she was planning to go over Christmas, the thought of which would be much easier to contend with than days and maybe nights imagining her with Brendan Stokes.

Darcey observed Daniel, wondering what was going through his mind, as they studied the menu, and was on the point of finding out when he spoke.

'What are your family planning for over Christmas?' he asked casually, and she hoped she'd managed to hide the raw hurt that question caused.

'If you mean my brother, he's spending some time in Thailand over Christmas with a couple of friends. It's the first time we have ever been apart at this time of year and I'm missing him. The three of them have been bitten by the travel bug, which has left me alone, and if that sounds self-pitying I can't help it.'

'So what do your parents say about that?' he enquired.

'They are dead,' she told him flatly. 'I've brought Alex up since he was eight years old. There has just been the two of us and we've been happy enough, though I've known all along that one day he would want to branch out on his own, but didn't expect that it would be so soon.'

A waiter was approaching to take their order and when that had been accomplished she said, 'And that is it, but the trouble about caring is that it can come to be a habit that isn't easily broken.'

'Yes,' he agreed, 'and a burden that one can't easily be free of. I know because I've been there. But I haven't coaxed you out into the frosty night to depress you,' he said gently, 'and, Darcey, the young folk of today should be able to cope.'

'I know,' she agreed. 'I'm the one who isn't coping and I suppose I should know better.'

He reached across and stroking her hand said gently, 'There wouldn't have been many teenage girls prepared to do what you did for your young brother, to have been there for him until he reached manhood.

'So don't have any feelings of remorse. Instead be proud of yourself and watch as he becomes the man that your parents would have wanted him to be through you.'

As the food they had ordered, a veritable feast, was placed in front of them, and the man sitting opposite seemed more like a friend than a senior medical figure, or mentor of a group of young would-be sailors, Darcey couldn't believe how much she was enjoying the unexpected invitation to join him for a hot supper in a first-class restaurant. The only flaw was that he hadn't given her time to dress up for the occasion.

It would be something to remember in the long dark nights of winter when she was alone, and she hoped that the man sitting opposite hadn't invited her to dine with him because he felt sorry for her.

'So how do you like being based in Seahaven?' he asked as she gazed around her. 'Is the absence of your young brother taking the pleasure out of it in any way?'

Her smile was wry as she told him, 'Yes, I suppose I could say that because there has been just the two of us for so long I'm finding it hard to let go, but I'm finally seeing sense, as after all the only thing I want for him is that he should be happy, and that is what he is at present.'

'And what about you? Are you happy, Darcey?' he questioned gravely.

'At this moment I'm in heaven,' she told him recklessly, and when he had no comment to make lapsed into silence with the feeling that she had overdone the rapture somewhat on the strength of a nice meal in elegant surroundings.

As they walked towards her home when the meal was over and midnight was approaching, there was silence between them. The pleasure of the evening was disappearing fast as Darcey reminded herself uncomfortably that Daniel had only taken her for a meal to fill a gap.

That from what she'd heard, he was strictly off liaisons with her sex, and when they reached her door she turned the key quickly in the lock and at the same time thanked him for the meal, then was gone before she made any more unwanted comments.

They were there again when Daniel opened his door some minutes later, the silent rooms, the lack of a woman's touch that he'd never had any problems with since Katrina's departure. But now he was wanting it gone, and of all things that he didn't want at that moment was for the phone to ring with a message for the lifeboat crew to tell them to be on the alert for a turn-out call to a stranded pleasure steamer that was having problems that it might be able to sort out, or it might not. When all he wanted was to sit quietly and remember the moments he'd just spent in the company of a woman who, it seemed, had got her priorities right.

How much had she given up, he wondered, in caring for her brother over the years? There were no rings on her fingers, wedding, engagement or otherwise, he'd been relieved to see. But was he getting carried away by her sense of duty to a parentless youngster, or was it the attraction of the sexes that he had avoided ever since the nightmare of Katrina that was out to snare him?

The phone rang again and there was good news. The pleasure steamer had arrived safely in the harbour and after some repairs would soon be on its way again. Relieved, he went slowly up the stairs to bed but not before he'd glanced to where not so far away there was still a light on in Darcey's apartment.

He wondered if she, like him, was going to put the evening down to a one-off, not to be repeated. There was still the memory of the hurt that a broken marriage brought with it as a warning and with that thought in mind he lifted the bedcovers and sought sleep.

In her own small abode Darcey was cringing at the thought of how she'd been so over-enthusiastic in her comments about the occasion that she'd found herself in, but it had been true. It had been heavenly to be wining and dining with a man for whom she had much respect for his work at Oceans House, and who was extremely attractive too, as that kind of situation had been almost non-existent before she'd changed her job for the delights of Seahaven.

Her position of ward sister in a local hospital had been just as demanding as the present one, and the rest of the time she'd spent trying to make up to Alexander for the loss of his parents, so that wining and dining with members of the opposite sex had been a rarity, hence her enthusiasm when she'd replied to Daniel's invitation.

But now she was wishing she hadn't been so forthcoming in her enjoyment of the occasion. It had made her sound naïve and had caused his lapse into silence that had continued until he had wished her goodnight on her doorstep and gone on his way.

The next time they met would be on the ward and she decided that when that happened she would show a restraint in her manner that couldn't possibly offend.

She was on duty tomorrow but Daniel Osbourne was only on call on Sundays for emergencies that only he could deal with, so it would be Monday before they met again and the job would come before anything else as they nursed and healed the young ones in their care.

On his way to his usual Sunday meeting at the boathouse, Daniel halted as Oceans House came into sight, and with sudden determination he pointed himself towards its main entrance, knowing that he was about to act totally out of character, but he had to see his dining companion of the previous evening, if only for a few moments in which to tell her that he had enjoyed her company.

His assurance might sound trite after he'd ignored her pleasure on the occasion but, sweet and vulnerable, she was hurting from the lack of her brother's company and he hadn't helped by withdrawing into his shell to combat her enthusiasm, which had brought him onto the defensive.

Darcey was with a trainee nurse when he arrived at the ward, showing her the facilities available for the care of the young with orthopaedic problems and as the two of them moved to the bed nearest to the door she saw him standing there and her eyes widened in surprised dismay.

She appeared to be waiting for him to speak first and, taking the hint, Daniel said, 'Just a word before I go to the Young Sailors' Club, Sister Howard,' and with a glance at the trainee nurse at her side, added, 'It will only take a moment.' Beckoning Darcey to follow, he went into the ward office and waited for her to come in.

When she'd closed the door behind her and was observing him warily he said, 'I've stopped by for a moment to thank you for your company last night. I requested it without giving you any warning and have since felt that I could have been more sociable, so I do apologise. I feel sure that you would have been much happier in the company of my colleague, who is due back amongst us in a week's time.'

Darcey wasn't ready to present her new personality of restraint in his presence. He was a day too soon, and the vows that she'd made the night before when he'd gone on his way after their silent walk home from the restaurant were not going to see the light of day, she thought, not after that comment. She told him, 'I am here to work, Mr Osbourne, not to find myself a man friend or lover, and if I were, the person you just mentioned would not be of my choosing. So now, if I may be excused, I am spending some time this morning with a trainee while the rest of the staff carry on as usual.'

Daniel stared at her, then nodded. 'Fine,' he said. 'Proceed, by all means.' As he watched her return to where she had been occupied he was aware of what he was missing in his determination never to be hurt again by a woman, and added to that Darcey Howard must think him an interfering bossyboots into the bargain.

But he had other matters to deal with in the next few hours that were separate from everything else in his life. They were different from any other thing he had ever done before and were in memory of his father, who had perished while saving the lives of others in a terrible storm.

He had lost his mother some time previously and he and his father had been very close, with both of them having a love of the sea, and he was getting used to the idea that the lighthouse just a mile up the coast and no longer in use, having served its purpose in bygone years, now belonged to him for whatever purpose he had in mind. It stood on a clifftop like a lonely guardian angel and there was the desire in him to bring it back to life in some way, which he hadn't yet decided upon, that would be a tribute to his father.

Up to the previous night he'd thought that a woman's perspective might be worth seeking with regard to his plans for the derelict building, but the opportunity hadn't materialised so far, and now that he and Darcey were at odds with each other, he felt it would be better to avoid the issue and stick to their doctor-nurse relationship. But it wasn't going to prevent him from being curious with regard to her fully booked-up Christmas if she wasn't chummy with Brendan Stokes after all.

# CHAPTER FOUR

IT WAS OLD and neglected, Daniel thought as he surveyed the lighthouse keenly, but in a beautiful position. It had promise, and with some thought and expense could be transformed into a few things in its position high up on the cliffs.

He was going to rename it after his father Mark Osbourne, who had put the safety of others before his own, and he took detailed notes regarding the repairs needed as he walked slowly back along the top of the cliffs deep in thought, until he came to where the Sunday afternoon meeting of the Young Sailors' Club was in progress and put the challenge of the lighthouse out of his mind for the time being.

As the day progressed Darcey was finding it hard to forget their brief exchange of words in the ward office but she was not repentant. She'd had very few friendships with the opposite sex because of her responsibilities to Alexander and had never been bowled over by anyone she'd met.

But from the moment of their meeting on the train

she'd been so aware of Daniel Osbourne it was like a bright light in the midst of darkness, and that he should have coupled her with someone like Brendan Stokes had been mortifying, to say the least.

Maybe she'd been expecting too much in her new-found freedom from caring for Alex, she thought. Daniel was the top orthopaedic surgeon in the hospital, she was a ward sister, and they lived very different lives. But as the last few moments of a busy day presented themselves she thought rebelliously that she didn't need to have someone to take her to a nice restaurant if she wanted to dine there.

She decided she would go to the place where they'd dined the previous night on her own and if by any chance the man on her mind turned up, she would give him a Mona Lisa smile and continue to enjoy the food brought to her in all its excellence.

That thought died a death when a friendly waiter stopped by her table and commented, 'Your friend the doctor won't be joining you tonight, will he? We've been told that the lifeboat is out there and it's mighty rough.'

'And Daniel Osbourne is on it?' she questioned with her mouth dry and the food on her plate losing its appeal.

'Well, yes,' she was told. 'He's taken his father's place and in spite of all the demands of his work at Oceans House he never hesitates when he's asked to turn out with it. He is highly respected in these parts.'

'Yes, he must be,' she murmured, and asked for the bill with the urge to be some place where she could be alone while it registered how much she cared about him. Their skirmish earlier in the day was as nothing when she faced up to how much he was always in her thoughts.

She'd never been in love before and wasn't sure she really was in love now, or so she told herself as she went out into the cold night and pointed herself towards her small residence.

But once inside she couldn't settle and within moments was out again and was battling against strong winds towards the harbour, where relatives of the lifeboat crew and interested spectators were gathered with their gazes on the distant skyline for a glimpse of any sign of activity, but as yet there was none, and a group of Daniel's young trainees were huddled together in silent apprehension.

An elderly woman, with a calm that spoke of many such occasions, was passing round hot drinks that were being gratefully accepted by the watchers, and when she stopped beside Darcey she said, 'You have the look of somebody who has not seen this kind of thing before. Am I right?'

'Yes,' she said slowly. 'I'm a nurse from Oceans House and it is terrifying.

'What kind of situation has the lifeboat been called out to?'

'A couple of yachts with inexperienced crews have been caught unawares. If they manage to bring them back you might find some of them brought to the hospital if Daniel sees the need.'

At that moment a crew member who had stayed behind to keep in touch with the coastguard called,

'They've been spotted! Our crew have found them. One of the yachts has sunk and two of its crew were in the water when they got there, but they've hauled them aboard the lifeboat and are towing the one that's left. If they have no further problems they should be here soon.'

A couple of ambulances had arrived with their crews at the ready for possible casualties, and there were agonising moments that followed with Darcey not wanting Daniel to see her amongst those waiting for their return, but neither did she want to leave the scene until she had seen for herself that he was safely back on dry land.

So she waited until a cheer went up and as the rescue vessel came into sight, towing the remaining yacht behind it, with Daniel in full view she went, walking fast along the promenade where some of the restaurants and bars were still serving customers, unaware of the drama that had been unfolding at the end where the harbour was situated.

Darcey hadn't wanted to leave the scene there, yet neither had she wanted Daniel to see her amongst the crowd after their early morning exchange of words that had still been rankling. But as she went inside and locked the door behind her there was a great well of thankfulness inside her that was wiping out every thought except relief.

The ambulances had gone, taking both crews of the yachts to the town's main hospital to be checked over, and their arrival hadn't caused a great deal of surprise

as the bay where Oceans House was situated was the
source of a popular yachting competition every spring
and those intending to enter were out in all weathers,
practising before the event.

Back at the harbour there was the relief for the lifeboat crew of returning safely to hot soup, specially
made by Bridget, to take away the chill of the last
few hours, and on Daniel's part amazement to hear
from her that one of the nurses from Oceans House
had been there tense and concerned for their safety
and his in particular.

'What was she like?' he asked. 'Did she say who
she was?'

'Er...no, and I didn't think to ask,' Bridget told him.
'She was blonde with blue eyes that were filled with
horror at the seriousness of what was happening, yet
she went as soon as she knew that you were all safe.'

'I see,' he commented thoughtfully and asked himself if it was wishful thinking on his part that the first
name that came to mind was that of Darcey Howard,
though he had been so abrupt with her earlier that
morning it was highly unlikely that she would have
been concerning herself about him.

Unlike the night before, there was no pleasure to
be had in knocking on her door. Neither was there
any at the thought of returning to the peace of his
apartment with its quiet comforts, as along with his
verbal trespasses in her life he was tired.

It had been rough and dangerous out there in the
bay, and on their return he'd been the only one of the
crew who hadn't had an anxious relative waiting to

welcome them back to safety, as he kept his lifeboat excursions as private as possible from Cordelia and her husband. Having lost the father she loved, he had no wish to cause his sister any further grief.

The only happy occasion that the day had brought had been his visit to the lighthouse that now belonged to him, and Daniel's last thought before he slept was that if she would let him, Darcey would be the first person to know about his recent purchase and it would be interesting to see her reaction.

On Monday morning Darcey gave Daniel a tentative smile that was tinged with the relief she was experiencing on seeing him his usual businesslike self when he was on the wards. She could cope with that where waiting for his return from the turbulent sea had been torture, especially so as she'd had no experience of that sort of thing before.

She'd gone before he had actually stepped on dry land because the last thing she'd wanted had been for him to think that she was making a nuisance of herself, and all the way back to her flat Darcey had been questioning silently how the families of the lifeboat crew coped on such occasions. The elderly lady stoically handing out refreshments to those who waited anxiously for their return had been very welcome.

There had been two fresh admissions to the children's ward that morning, a small boy with a fracture of his elbow and a teenage girl who had become unseated while horse riding, and as Daniel examined them Darcey felt that her world was righting itself after the traumas of the day before.

'Looking at the X Rays that have been taken, it is plain to see that young Harry's elbow is fractured so I'll get that sorted first as he has more damage to contend with than Ruby. Hopefully her neck will react to massage and heat to take away the pain. And, Sister, if we manage to get a lunch hour there is something I'd like to show you.' And off he went, leaving her to wonder what on earth he had meant by that.

She was more nervous in his company now than at any time since their meeting on the train that first day. She was so aware of him when he was near that she could hardly breathe and she had no idea what he could possibly want to show her.

It was a busy Monday morning for them both with regard to the children's ward, with Daniel setting Harry's elbow and then stabilising it in a cast, and afterwards instructing the nursing staff with Darcey in charge regarding the treatment for Ruby.

She had given up on finding time for a lunch hour, even though everything was in control on the ward, and was not expecting to see Daniel again, but he surprised her by appearing at the ward door and beckoning her across.

'Have you eaten?' he asked.

'Er…no, not yet,' she told him. 'I was just going to have a sandwich that I brought with me.'

'Would you be happy to eat it in the car?' was his next question.

'We need only be gone for a short time and after

such a busy morning the staff will expect you to take a break.'

'Yes, all right,' she said, mystified, and went to get her coat.

They had driven past the harbour and the Young Sailors' Club and were now moving along the road at the top of the cliffs, with Darcey completely bewildered by what was happening, until Daniel stopped the car outside a disused lighthouse that incredibly had a sign outside that said 'Sold'. As she turned to face him in complete disbelief he said, 'You are looking at the new owner,' and glancing at his watch he added, 'There is just time for me to show you round before we return to Oceans House.'

As she walked slowly around the derelict building Darcey was speechless as she observed its condition, until finally, on the point of leaving, she gasped, 'Why?'

Daniel smiled. 'I can understand why you ask me that. A lot of other folk will be doing the same thing and the answer is that I'm going to have the whole place renovated in memory of my dad.'

'Ah, yes. I see,' she said gently. 'That I can understand. I think it's a lovely idea. If I can help in any way you have only to ask.'

'You were the one whose comments I wanted to hear,' he told her, 'as from what you've told me of your life so far it would seem that it has been one of giving rather than taking. And now I'm going to drive you back to where we belong.'

He wanted to ask if she had been amongst the crowd awaiting the return of the lifeboat the night before, but felt that today's gesture had been enough.

There was no way he wanted to give Darcey any wrong impressions.

But Darcey had a question to ask as they drove the short distance back to the hospital, and it was to be expected. 'Do your sister and her husband know about your plans for the lighthouse?' she asked.

'No,' he said firmly. 'I will tell Cordelia and Lawrence when it is done and ready for viewing. She wouldn't approve of its present condition one bit, but when she sees that it is named the Mark Osbourne Lighthouse she will be pleased, so I'd be obliged if you don't mention what I'm up to if you should happen to be in conversation with her again.'

The fact of their absence together during the lunch hour had been noted on the ward and there was a comment passed in Darcey's hearing to the effect that Daniel would be a hard nut to crack for anyone with hopes of becoming the second Mrs Osbourne, that he was content in the life he had chosen, and no one seemed to want to disagree with that.

As far as she was concerned, Darcey had no hopes whatever of someone like Daniel even noticing her, but it didn't stop her from rejoicing to have been asked for her opinion about his decision to buy the old lighthouse.

She could live with that and the fact that it was her that Daniel Osbourne had invited out to supper when he'd been on his way home from the sailing club, and if as a result she was falling in love with him she would just have to accept it and suffer in silence.

But that evening alone in the apartment, with not the slightest yearning to venture forth as she had been doing of late, Darcey began to think about Christmas. It was early December. All along the promenade were decorations celebrating the event and it was going to be the first time she hadn't spent the occasion with Alexander.

Instead she would be working during both Christmas Day and Boxing Day, and solitary in the evening, and if Daniel Osbourne came across her in such circumstances what was he going to think about her refusal to go sailing with him and his club members?

Yet the fact remained that when he'd extended the invitation she had already committed herself to working during the festivities, and somebody had to do it so why not her with no family ties or suchlike to prevent her? And she would make sure that her small patients who had to spend Christmas in Oceans House had as happy a time as possible under the circumstances.

She knew she had to keep her feelings for Daniel Osbourne strictly under control to avoid making a fool of herself, as every time she thought about their lunchtime trip to the lighthouse she felt tearful because he was so special and so out of reach.

In the meantime, she needed to shop for a special Christmas gift for Alexander to be presented whenever he chose to return. It was her day off and the shopping didn't take long, with only two to buy for, and as Darcey waited to be served at the till in one of the stores in the town centre, Cordelia Mason appeared laden with parcels and wanting to know if she felt like joining her for a coffee.

She didn't hesitate to say yes because she liked Daniel's sister and felt that being in her company was the next best thing to his.

'We haven't seen much of Daniel for a while,' Cordelia said after they'd chatted about various small matters, 'which usually means that he is very busy at Oceans House, or with other things that he knows would upset me if I knew, such as taking Dad's place in the lifeboat, which he insists on doing, and pointing out that he has no wife or children of his own to concern himself over and that my two are safe and happy with Lawrence and me. So it wouldn't hurt anyone but himself if one time he didn't come back to dry land and safety, ignoring the fact that he would have made a fantastic husband and father if he hadn't married Katrina.'

As she listened to what Cordelia had to say, Darcey thought that he was wrong. There was someone else who would die a death if anything happened to Daniel even after so short an acquaintance, but she was in no position to make any comments to his sister, especially after his lovely gesture with regard to their father and the lighthouse.

'He is very busy most of the time at the hospital,' she said, without admitting that she had actually been present on a recent occasion, 'but he does sometimes get called out to help man the lifeboat, so I'm told.'

'Can I ask you to let me know if he is ever in any grave danger that I may not be aware of?' Cordelia asked anxiously, and with a reluctant nod Darcey prayed that such a day would never dawn.

His sister was checking the time and commented, 'I'm going to have to leave you, I'm afraid, Darcey. I'm due to pick the children up from school, but before I go just one thing, the invitation to visit us still stands whenever you can manage it. I hate to think of you all alone over Christmas. If you do find that you can spend some time with us, Daniel will give you our phone number and will drive you to where we live whenever the occasion arises.'

Darcey swallowed hard. There was no way she could get involved with those kind of arrangements. There was the minor matter of her opting to work every day over the Christmas period, and he would take a dim view of the fabrication of the truth that she'd resorted to when he'd invited her to sail with him and some of the young sailors on Boxing Day, and then discovered what her plans were with regard to that.

On the strength of it the last thing he would opt for would be taking her to share her lonely evenings with his family and himself. She would rather exist without seeing a soul than gatecrash Daniel's time with those he loved, having checked the work rotas for the period and seen that he was only available for extreme emergencies. The day-to-day running of the

hospital would be in the hands of two junior doctors
and an elderly retired consultant who was volunteer-
ing his services to give Daniel a break.

When the two of them met up the next morning for
their usual ward round Daniel said amicably, 'I believe you saw Cordelia again yesterday. It seems that
she is still keen for you to visit some time during
Christmas in spite of you being sorted. But I must
warn you that she will have her matchmaking hat on
as she longs for me to give up my bachelor status.'

Darcey felt the colour rise in her cheeks but her
voice was cool as she told him, 'Thanks for the warning, but as I mentioned previously I will be booked
up for most of the Christmas period.'

'With whom, might I ask?' he enquired abruptly,
and her eyes widened at his sudden interest in her
affairs.

She looked around her at the collection of cots
and beds and their young occupants and told him,
'I'll be with those I care for. What more could I ask?'
And when their gazes held, his was wanting to know
more than that, and hers was holding back the tears
of her loneliness.

His rounds of the ward had been done without any
further stresses and Daniel had gone to his own part
of the hospital where he had his office and held his
twice-weekly clinic, while Darcey and her staff went
about their duties as usual.

But beneath her normal competence the ward sister was miserable and unhappy to have been warned off accepting Cordelia's invitation to dine with them because his sister was anxious to see him as married and happy as she was with her husband and children.

It was as if Daniel had warned her to keep her distance and it hurt as there was no way that she was going to seek his attention under the guise of visiting his family. She had more pride than that, was aware that if she hadn't devoted her life to her young brother she might have found love long ago. But she had no regrets about that. Alexander's needs had always come first.

Back in his own quarters at Oceans House Daniel was cringing at the way he'd made himself sound such a catch instead of a loner in the matrimonial stakes.

Since meeting Darcey Howard he'd been unsettled. His solitude was lying heavily upon him instead of being a comfort, and he'd just made sure that she wasn't going to want to be in his company outside hospital hours. Better to mention that to Cordelia and tell her to lay off the matchmaking as it could only make matters worse.

At the end of the day he stopped off at his sister's on his way home and found her in the kitchen, preparing the evening meal, and was immediately invited to share it with them.

'No, thanks just the same,' he told her gently. He cared for her too much to quarrel, but nevertheless wanted to make it clear that if ever he decided to involve himself in marrying again he would make all the moves and the proposals without any assistance from anyone else, and introduced the subject with the comment that Darcey had told him that they'd met up again and that Cordelia had repeated the invitation to join them some time over Christmas.

'Yes, I have,' she replied, 'because she is so lonely, Daniel.'

'That is not so,' he told her firmly. 'When I asked Darcey if she would like to sail with me and some of the kids on Boxing Day she was quick to explain that she was fully booked up all over the Christmas period. How, I don't know and wasn't prepared to ask. Maybe she could be planning to share it with her young brother if he will be back from abroad in time, but I really don't know. What I do know is that she has got Christmas sorted and is not the lost soul that you see her as.'

'All right,' she agreed. 'Maybe my imagination has been running riot, but if Darcey does decide to accept the offer, promise me that you will make her welcome.'

'Yes, of course!' he said, feeling rather affronted. 'What would you expect? That I would ignore her presence? Insist that she stand in a corner without speaking?'

He was hardly likely to inform Cordelia that Darcey Howard had captured his imagination ever since that day in the discomfort of a crowded railway carriage, and as he'd got to know her better the more she was in his thoughts, yet not to the extent that he was ready to give up his freedom from matrimony.

Young voices could be heard coming from up above, and putting the discussion they'd just had on hold Cordelia said laughingly, 'Your fan club have been watching television and will be down shortly. Are you sure that you don't want to stay?'

'Not this time,' he said. 'I have some business to attend to.' And to make up for leaving before the children appeared, he offered, 'How about I have them for the day on Saturday so that you and Lawrence can have some time for just the two of you during the day?'

'That would be lovely!' she exclaimed. 'But are you sure? You are always so busy.'

'Yes, I am sure,' he told her smilingly. 'I'll take them for a short sail in the club boat on Saturday morning and to a children's matinée at the cinema in the afternoon, as there is no meeting of the Young Sailors' Club this week. Its members have arranged a dinner dance in the evening at a large hotel on the promenade instead to help raise funds to pay for the repairs to the boat.' With an upward glance to where the children were playing, he gave his sister a quick kiss on her cheek. 'And now I must go.'

Daniel wasn't sure how good a case he had made with his sister regarding his private and public lifestyles, and as he pulled up outside the place that he used to call home minutes later, he couldn't resist casting a glance in the direction of the hospital apartments to check if Darcey's light was on. Seeing its bright light glowing in the early evening darkness, he went inside feeling content.

# CHAPTER FIVE

DANIEL WASN'T TO know that in the late afternoon after he had left the hospital to call at Cordelia's on the way home, some members of the sailing club had gone to Oceans House selling tickets for the event of the coming Saturday and that Darcey had bought one to brighten up her quiet life away from the hospital, with her first thought after making the purchase being what she was going to wear.

There was nothing suitable amongst the clothes she'd brought with her and the event was only days away, so she needed to move fast in the form of some late-night shopping. After a quick snack, she caught the promenade tram and went into the town centre in a frame of mind that was willing to be appealed to by what she saw, and appealed to it she was by a dress of turquoise silk that accentuated her golden fairness and the soft curves of her body. With shoes to match and a faux fur jacket to hold off the winter chill she was very pleased with her purchases.

Daniel had seen that Darcey's place was in darkness and, imagining her on the promenade on her own somewhere in the winter night, was unusually fraught and irritated at the thought, so instead of relaxing in the warm comfort of his apartment he drove along there a couple of times. After no sightings of her, he checked the nearest restaurants to make sure that she wasn't anywhere to be found.

Then, deciding that if he lingered any longer he might be accused of loitering, he was on the point of departing when he saw her moving fast towards her apartment building with a carrier bag from one of the boutiques swinging from her wrist. The question of where was she going to wear what she'd bought came immediately to mind with a vision of her somewhere in another man's arms.

Usually he didn't give a damn who he saw in those sorts of circumstances but every time he was near her the attraction of who and what she was brought back desires long dead, so he pointed his car homewards without letting her see him hovering nearby. As he drove the short distance the thought uppermost in his mind was, Who and what was she going to be occupied with all over Christmas?

When he arrived back at the apartment there was a message from the architect who was in charge of the renovation of the lighthouse, wanting to discuss various matters, and by the time Daniel had returned his call there was, as expected, a light where there had been darkness in her apartment, and for what was left of the evening he refrained from glancing in that direction.

The dinner dance was to be held at a large hotel in the town centre and tickets had been selling fast as the townsfolk were always ready to support any event connected with safety on the sea that surrounded Seahaven.

·   It was an event that Daniel was keeping a low profile on, which was perhaps as well because he was late arriving due to an accident victim with a spinal injury being brought into the hospital as he had been on the point of leaving, and he had stayed to perform the necessary surgery, followed by going home to change into evening wear.

Darcey, stunning in the new clothes she'd bought, and unaware of the reason for his non-appearance, was trying to keep Brendan Stokes, who had returned from his refresher course, at a distance with the thought in mind that without Daniel the event would mean nothing.

He came at last and she felt that her bones would melt with longing, but when he saw her he smiled briefly and went to talk to the elderly woman who had been handing out hot drinks on the night of the lifeboat rescue, and an elderly man she presumed was the lady's husband. On seeing her expression, her unwelcome companion commented, 'If the boss ever decides to tie the knot again, I wouldn't count on it being someone at the hospital.' And sauntered across the room to where a group of young women doctors was gathered.

Darcey watched him go and wished herself far away from the cheerful gathering of locals. She was a stranger in their midst, lost and lonely, and was contemplating a speedy departure when Daniel appeared beside her and said, 'Don't let Brendan Stokes upset you, Darcey, he's not worth it. As all the tables are full I came to ask if you would like to share with Bridget, Ely and myself?'

'I'd love to,' she said, smiling her pleasure, even though Bridget might remember her from the night when she'd been one of those frantically hoping for the safe return of the lifeboat and those it had gone to rescue.

When Daniel took her to be introduced to his friends Bridget did indeed remember her from the night when Darcey had stood white faced on the edge of the crowd, waiting anxiously for the return of the lifeboat. And now, seeing her with the man that she herself had much respect for, Bridget made no comment regarding that, just shook her hand and welcomed her warmly, while Ely looked on in disbelief at the sight of his friend with someone of the opposite sex. When Daniel took her onto the dance floor his surprise peaked, though not as much as Darcey's.

Darcey was so conscious of his touch and so aware of the surprised glances that were fixed on them as they moved around the floor that she was speechless, and he said with dry amusement, 'I just thought I'd give them something to talk about, the ones who would like to see me with a woman just out of curiosity.'

Daniel felt her stiffen in his arms and knew he'd hit a nerve, but he wanted some response from her, be it good or bad, and he was getting it as she broke away from his hold and went to join a group of nurses from Oceans House who were sitting at tables near the bar.

'What did you do to the lass?' Ely asked in amazement when Daniel rejoined his friends.

Bridget commented, 'Darcey was the nurse that I told you about who came to join those of us that night when the lifeboat had been called out. I recognised her when you brought her to meet us tonight. Do you remember me telling you?'

'Yes, vaguely,' Daniel replied, 'though I've got to know Darcey because she's the sister on the children's ward. But there's nothing going on between us. I brought her across to our table because she was on her own, that's all.'

'That's a disappointment, then,' Bridget told him. 'I'm always ready for a new outfit should I hear wedding bells.'

Daniel was only half listening. Darcey looked lovely beyond belief in the turquoise dress. Was that what was lacking in the empty life he had chosen with the break-up of his marriage? Someone like the caring nurse who had appeared out of nowhere on a crowded train?

He had wanted to hold Darcey close and would have continued to do so if he hadn't been irritated by the stares and smirks coming in their direction. Now the opportunity had gone and he had only himself to blame.

Looking across to where she'd been sitting, he saw that the place was empty and when he went into the hotel foyer he saw her in a taxi that was in the act of pulling away from the pavement outside, and as it drove off he flagged down the next one to arrive and told the driver to follow the vehicle in front.

Darcey was in the process of paying the taxi driver when the second vehicle pulled up behind it, and to her surprise she watched Daniel climb out. He said to her driver, 'I'll settle that,' and to his own driver, 'And yours too in a moment.' She observed him with a stony-faced expression as he dealt with the two fares. Once the vehicles had departed, he turned to find her putting her key in the lock with the intention of leaving him on the step.

'May I come inside for a moment?' he asked, and without speaking she stepped to one side to let him pass and then closed the door behind him.

'I just want to say I'm sorry if you felt I was using you to suit my own ends when I took you onto the dance floor,' he said as they faced each other in the apartment's small entrance hall.

'The reason was because you looked so beautiful in the dress and as we are both free spirits it felt like the right thing to do. But for some reason the fact of my having no desire to make a commitment in the marriage market is of interest to some people and irritates me more than somewhat. Someone once told me that when I do appear with a member of the opposite sex they place bets on whether it will last or not. So will you accept my apology for what happened back there, Darcey?'

'You don't have to apologise, Dr Osbourne,' she

said stiffly. 'I have no wish to be involved in your private life and neither do I want to be made a laughing stock by those who are so interested in it.'

He groaned softly and reaching for the door handle ready to depart said, 'I can hardly blame you for feeling like that. My sister has yearnings to see me at the altar every time a possible candidate appears, but she knows how small the chances are of that happening, and if she hadn't, I would have soon put her right.'

Darcey thought if that was the case, what was it that she had done to deserve so much attention?

To make it even more upsetting, he went on to say, 'It would seem that you have already got Christmas lined up with friends past and present on the occasion of your first time of celebrating it by the sea, and if that is so I wish you a happy time amongst them.'

With a wild desire to tell him the truth about what she would be occupied with she moved towards him, but the door was swinging open, he was gone and no way was she going to chase after him, which left the next morning on the wards looming ahead like a pit of embarrassment.

Having no wish to make any further upsets for anyone, Daniel went straight home and sat gazing towards the light in Darcey's window. She was a sweet, kind woman, he told himself, and deserved better than such as himself, so the less he saw of her away from Oceans House the bigger the favour he would be doing her. Unaware that not so far away she was gazing across at the light in his window with a yearning to be with him, in his house, in his arms, in his life.

Darcey was spared the dread of meeting up with him again on Monday morning because Brendan Stokes was doing the ward rounds, Daniel having been called out to join the lifeboat crew on another mission to rescue some teenagers who were way out past the coastguard station, and when she discovered where he was and what he was engaged in, the stress of meeting him on the wards was as nothing compared to knowing that he was out in dangerous waters, fighting the elements again, and she loved him for it, just as she loved him for everything he did.

This time she couldn't be present when the lifeboat came back to base and was frantic to know if and when all concerned were safe, until Bridget stopped by the ward in the lunch hour to report that another stressful situation had been resolved. Grateful for the elderly woman's thoughtfulness, Darcey thought that she wasn't the only one who loved Daniel. So did Cordelia, and so did Bridget in a motherly sort of way, and with that thought came another.

She had made a reluctant promise to his sister that she would tell her if Daniel was involved in anything dangerous or stressful with regard to the lifeboat and today was the second occasion when she had failed to do so, not wanting to distress Cordelia.

With a few moments of her lunch break left, she went into the office on the ward and rang the number that his sister had given her, but got no answer and tried a few more times without success. Finally she gave the operator the number and asked to have it checked in case there was a problem on the line as now she was more than ready to talk to Cordelia as it would be only good news that she had to greet her with.

But the operator reported that the line was being investigated and it could take some time, and as Darcey replaced the receiver, Daniel was there framed in the open doorway, observing her unsmilingly and asking, 'What's wrong? Everyone is back safely. No cause for alarm, and that was Cordelia's number. Why? What goes on?'

'Er…your sister asked me to get in touch if ever you were hurt or in danger,' she said haltingly, 'but there has been no need, and in any case I would have hesitated to do anything of that nature, which was against your wishes, but I saw no harm in letting her know that you are safe after today's occurrence if she is aware of it.'

'I see,' he said tonelessly, and went on to inform her, 'The last thing I want would be to cause Cordelia grief on my account. She has already had to face up to us losing our father. I don't want any other sorrow coming her way because of me.'

'So why do you do it if that is how you feel?' she questioned.

'Because it is what he would have wanted of me.'

'Yes, I see,' she told him, and thought that Daniel was already doing his share of saving lives at Oceans House and many of them were young ones, which would be enough for most people, but he wasn't most people.

Around her the staff on second lunch were disappearing and as he hadn't eaten since breakfast he followed them and left her to thoughts that were not happy ones.

After lunch Daniel went to take his Monday afternoon clinic with the feeling that he had been needlessly abrupt in his conversation with Darcey, especially after the fiasco of the night before, and the thought came that flowers, roses maybe, with a note of apology attached, might clear the air between them without creating any more situations that she might have misunderstood.

As soon as the clinic was over he rang a florist and arranged for flowers to be delivered the next day, as the following morning he was due to fly out to America for two weeks, where he would be speaking to medical staff in various hospitals about orthopaedics, with the intention of arriving home on the day of Christmas Eve, when he had arranged to go straight to his sister's for the festivities, while Darcey was enjoying her first Christmas in Seahaven in what had sounded like a full programme of events when he'd suggested taking her for a sail and had had the offer turned down.

It was six o'clock the next morning and as the taxi that was taking him to the airport was driven along the deserted promenade for his flight to America Daniel was wishing that he wasn't going to be without sight of Darcey for two whole weeks.

There had been no signs of life as he'd been driven past her apartment, which wasn't surprising considering the hour, and his reluctance to be away from where she was going to be increased. In an hour or so the florist would do as he'd asked and deliver the flowers before she began her day's work, and what she would think of that he wasn't going to find out as she would have no way of knowing that they were the first flowers he'd sent to anyone of the opposite sex since his marriage to Katrina had fizzled out in a cloud of misery.

At the time of arranging the visit to various American hospitals he had been keen and raring to go, but now the thought of being away from Oceans House meant being away from her, and when he returned on Christmas Eve she was sure to be well into the Christmas festivities that she had planned, which could mean only one thing, that away from the job and in so short a time she had created a good social life, which was more than he could say for himself.

When there was a knock on the door of her apartment just before eight o'clock, Darcey paused in her preparations before heading for the children's ward for the day, and was presented with an assorted display of beautiful roses and lily of the valley with a card attached that said briefly, 'Sorry I was so unfriendly yesterday, Daniel.' Her heartbeat quickened at the comforting thought that in the middle of his last-minute arrangements for his departure he had taken the time to want peace between them, and her step had a lift to it as she walked the short distance to where she would be spending the day with her young patients.

On the Saturday in the middle of the fortnight of his absence, when she'd done her shopping Darcey went into the café where she'd first met his sister in the hope that they might meet again, and was happy to find Cordelia seated at one of the tables and beckoning her across to join her.

Desperate for news of Daniel, she was quick to accept the invitation and heard how he was enjoying his visit to one of America's largest cities and being entertained socially every evening by those he was working with in the daytime.

The name of Mallory, a medical colleague over there, cropped up a few times and Darcey's pleasure in receiving the flowers that he'd sent on that last day shrivelled into nothingness.

But Cordelia had not forgotten her liking for the young nurse seated opposite and asked anxiously, 'Are you sure that you have a good time planned for Christmas, Darcey? You are most welcome to share it with us if you are short of company.'

'Yes. I've got it sorted,' she replied with false confidence, 'but thanks for the thought. You are very kind, Cordelia, and all my good wishes to you and your family.' On the way home afterwards she looked down at the shopping she was carrying and thought how it was just the usual weekly things with a box of chocolates as her only sign of festive fun, but that thought was followed by a vision of anxious parents beside the beds of their precious little ones at Christmas. Rather than feeling sorry for herself, she knew that to be there for them would be a privilege.

It was Christmas Eve a week later and Daniel was homeward bound in a taxi that would shortly be arriving at Seahaven, and much as he had enjoyed his visit to America he was eager to be back in the place he loved the most.

What would Darcey have planned for the evening? he wondered, as the promenade came into view with Oceans House at the far end. Whatever it was, it would not include him, from the sound of it, and as far as he was concerned if he hadn't been staying with Cordelia and her family over the festive break he would have gone straight home and to bed after the long flight.

But to the two small girls who loved him, his presence on Christmas morning added greatly to the excitement, so that he would never disappoint them willingly. And as for the nurse who had been in his thoughts more than was good for him while he'd been away, he supposed he should be happy for her to have settled into Seahaven so well that her Christmas was fully booked.

It would prevent him from stepping into something that he might regret afterwards, and with that thought came the memory of Darcey's eager response when he'd asked her if she was enjoying being taken unexpectedly to dine in his favourite restaurant that night.

It could have been the beginning of something special and precious if he'd responded with similar enthusiasm, but the barriers had been up, the warning signs had been there. He'd sat there poker faced as Darcey had made no secret of the pleasure that his unexpected invitation had created in her lonely life, and now he was wishing that he'd responded.

An attractive medical administrator called Mallory had accompanied him on his visits as he'd moved from one hospital to another. They'd also dined together in the evenings, and it had become clear that she'd been romantically interested in him.

But Daniel had thought grimly that, as pleasant a person as Mallory was, she was coming onto the wrong sort of guy as far as he was concerned, and in her place would come a vision of Darcey soothing a fretful toddler in the children's ward at Oceans House, and on another occasion gazing wide-eyed at the old lighthouse he'd bought in memory of his father with complete understanding of his need.

As the hospital came into view at that moment, with her small living quarters close by, he was tempted to pay the taxi driver and call on her if she was there, but the opportunity didn't arise. The place was in darkness. It seemed as if her busy Christmas was already under way.

In the two weeks that Daniel had been away, the friendship between Darcey and Cordelia had strengthened and they'd met for coffee a couple more times, with Cordelia inviting Darcey to the party that she and her husband were hosting on Christmas Eve.

But as Darcey had remembered the glib pronouncement that she'd come up with when Daniel had offered to take her sailing, and imagining his expression if he arrived back and saw her at the party, she had said, 'It is kind of you to invite me, Cordelia, but I really don't want to cause any difficult situations that could be avoided.'

'The party will finish at midnight,' her new friend hastened to tell her, 'and Daniel won't be back until the early hours of Christmas Day. I know you are concerned that he might think you are invading his privacy, but it should be long over before he puts in an appearance, so do come, Darcey. One of our daughters is keen to become a nurse when she is older, and will be asking you all sorts of questions about it before she goes to bed.'

'Yes, all right,' she'd agreed, unable to resist being with company on Christmas Eve, even if she was going to be alone for the rest of the holiday period, and if she would be well gone by the time Daniel put in an appearance there couldn't be any harm in having a happy evening for once, instead of another empty one.

There was just one snag to that arrangement, though. The last two weeks had been filled with the longing to have Daniel back where she could see him, but she wouldn't see him on Christmas Eve, according to Cordelia, and as he wasn't on the staff roster for over the holiday it could be some time before they came face to face again, unless she sought Daniel out with some excuse.

Darcey went to the party in the turquoise dress that had bowled him over on the evening of the effort to raise money for repairs to the rescue boat, and was feeling good to be socialising with a group of friendly folks at Lawrence and Cordelia's house.

But, like Cinderella, come midnight she had to leave, and with just a few moments to spare Darcey went round saying her farewells to her hosts and their friends, and then she was gone, striding purposefully along the brightly lit promenade to where her small dwelling awaited her, having refused the offers of a lift home from some of the party guests who would have liked to get to know her better.

As the taxi driver drove along the coast road on the way to Seahaven, the old lighthouse was silhouetted against a pale moon and Daniel felt a rush of tenderness at the memory of how Darcey had understood immediately how much it would mean to him to have a memory of the father so near and so dear to him.

The two weeks he'd been away had seemed like two years and once he was home there was no guarantee that she would be where he could see her if she had the Christmas break all planned, as it had seemed to be from what she'd said.

Ahead the promenade had come into sight and as the taxi moved nearer to his destination Daniel was observing groups of revellers out there, celebrating the midnight hour and the arrival of Christmas Day.

He had caught an earlier flight than previously arranged and within minutes would be back amongst his family and friends, but the one person he wanted to see the most would be doing her own thing somewhere else, and he would so like to know where.

No sooner had the thought crossed his mind than his wish was granted.

Darcey, wearing the lovely turquoise dress that he'd seen before and been enchanted by, under her coat, was walking briskly along the opposite side of the promenade, and he asked the taxi driver to stop for a moment. Flinging himself out of the vehicle with all speed, he followed her quickly on foot.

When she heard his footsteps behind her, she turned and stared at him in amazed dismay as he said with cool calm, 'What are you doing out here alone at this hour? Where are all the friends you're spending Christmas with?'

Seeming to recover from the shock of his sudden appearance, she told him, 'It's tomorrow that my busy time starts.'

'So where have you been?' Daniel asked with quiet impatience, wishing their reunion after an empty fortnight could be more ecstatic.

He could see the desperation in her eyes as she told him, 'I've been to a party at your sister's house on the promise that you wouldn't be back for a couple of hours, as I knew that you wouldn't want to find me there when you returned.'

'So you read my mind, do you?'

'Yes, up to a point,' she told him defiantly.

'I doubt it,' he said with silky slowness. 'Otherwise

you would know what is coming next.' And as she gazed at him wide-eyed he pulled her into his arms and kissed her until she was limp and trembling, and only then did he let her go.

'Merry Christmas, Darcey', he said in a low voice, and beckoned the taxi driver to bring his vehicle to their side of the road. 'Get in,' he ordered, and as she obeyed, he told her, 'I'm going to see you safely home, and then will depart just in case you have any worries on that score.'

Daniel had asked the taxi driver to wait to take him the way he had come to his sister and brother-in-law's house a short distance away because his baggage was on board, but first he wanted to see Darcey safely inside. As she turned the door key of the apartment in the lock he said tonelessly, 'Have a good Christmas, Darcey. You're young and beautiful so should have no trouble with that.' Before she could reply he turned and hurried off into the night.

Sitting in the waiting taxi, he groaned softly and the driver asked conversationally, 'Was that your girlfriend, sir?'

'Er…no,' he told him. 'She is just a friend that I was expressing my good wishes for Christmas to,' and as the other man nodded understandingly Daniel lapsed into silence with the thought uppermost that he had just made a prize fool of himself.

Darcey was weeping, hunched beside the small gas fire in what served as her sitting room. Worries, he'd said! As if she would have any worries about Daniel's intentions, she thought tearfully. Longings, hope, yes, but not worries. It was a situation where Daniel was way out of her league and for the first time in her life she was in love, hopelessly, totally in love with a man whose failed marriage had left a bitter taste behind, so much so that a stray kiss of the kind they had shared would be the limit of his trust.

The moment she had longed for had just taken place. Daniel had kissed her long and meaningfully but without a word of love, and it had turned what might have been a moment of joy into something hurtful.

Or was she making a big thing out of something small? she asked herself bleakly, because her experience of such things was limited due to the burden of care she had carried for so long with regard to her young parentless brother?

Whatever the reason, she was relieved that after what had happened she would be tucked away at Oceans House during the days of Christmas, and in the evenings would find a way to pass the time somehow or other, even if it meant eating out on her own, and with that cheerful thought in mind she went to bed and was drifting into a restless sleep when the phone rang. When she picked it up, Alex's voice came over the line.

'Darcey! I've been trying to get through to wish you a merry Christmas for ages,' he said. 'Where have you been?'

'I've been to a party,' she told him, 'and haven't been back long. I rang you a couple of times and had the same problem. Everyone is so busy at this time of year, I'm afraid. Where are you ringing from?'

'We're still in Thailand and I'm just returning to the hotel after having a great time. It's early morning here,' he informed her. 'We will be moving on after Christmas as we want to see as much of this country as possible before we come home, and the money won't last for ever. We'll probably be back by Easter.'

She was smiling, her loneliness forgotten for the moment as she told him, 'I'm so glad that you've been in touch and are well and happy. I've volunteered to work during Christmas to give staff who have young families some time with them, so if you need me for anything you will know where to find me. Now I have to say goodnight as I have to be on the ward at eight o'clock in the morning with all of Christmas Day to follow, so take care and have a good time with your friends.'

'I love you, big sister, and I'm sorry I was such a pain before you left,' he said in parting, and when Darcey lay back against the pillows again, the frustrations of earlier in the night didn't seem so hurtful. Maybe she'd been wanting too much from Daniel. Been longing too much to see him back in her life, and he'd had no such yearnings, so that the kiss out there on the promenade had just been a 'nice to see you' sort of gesture, and on that thought sleep came at last.

When Daniel arrived at his sister's house Cordelia and Lawrence were busy clearing up after the party, ready to bring down the children's Christmas presents from wherever they were hidden, and she exclaimed, 'Daniel! Did you get an earlier flight?'

'Yes,' he told her wryly, 'and who do you think I met on the promenade moving at a similar speed to Cinderella when she left the ball that time?'

'I have no idea,' she replied.

'Oh, yes, you have,' he protested gently, and as Lawrence turned away to hide a smile, 'You match-maker! Didn't I tell you that Darcey had her Christmas fully arranged as from tomorrow? She will have been working today and then will be off for the rest of the festivities.'

'I invited her to the party because I thought you wouldn't be there,' Cordelia protested, 'not because I thought you would. And it was only when I told Darcey that you weren't due home until quite a while after twelve o'clock that she accepted the invitation to join us. What did she have to say when you met up like that?'

'Not a lot, just the usual pleasantries,' he told her casually. It was hardly the moment to explain that Darcey's lack of conversation had been due to the fact that she'd been unable to get a word in edge-ways as he'd been kissing her most of the time. For what had seemed like a delightful eternity he'd held a lovely woman close and had got it all wrong. Was he so out of practice?

Climbing the stairs to the immaculate bedroom that was always his when he stayed the night at Cordelia and Lawrence's house, Daniel's train of thought moved to the next day when his two young nieces sleeping across the landing would awake to the excitement of Christmas morning, and if they found him less than cheerful they would be disappointed. So smiles would be called for at breakfast-time and lots of fun.

# CHAPTER SIX

THE SAME APPLIED to the children's ward, even more so for young ones in a strange environment away from all the things they were used to, and parents had been given extra visiting hours to make up for the change of circumstances so that they could bring some of the things that Santa and his reindeer had brought for them.

For any who had not received any toys, for whatever reason, the nurses, at Darcey's suggestion along with the hospital facilities, had brought toys and nice things for them, so that no child was missed out, and as she walked the short distance to the ward the next morning it felt more like a joy than a duty to be there for them.

She had put the happenings of the night before to the back of her mind until the day was over and the night was ready to unfold on her, except for the memory of her brother's phone call, which had brought back how it used to be with them, and to have that feeling again after the stresses she had endured before moving to Seahaven was relief untold. What she had faced before moving to Seahaven had helped to put the moments she'd spent in Daniel's arms into perspective.

When she arrived at the ward parents and friends were already arriving, and to give the day staff time to see that their young patients were washed and given their breakfast, followed by whatever medication had been prescribed for them, the hospital had provided breakfast for their families in one of its restaurants.

It was to be a short respite for them in the midst of their anxiety, and much as she had tried to put Daniel out of her mind Darcey couldn't help thinking that the day lacked his presence there just as much as she missed him.

Her return to her accommodation at the end of her working day was just as drab as she had visualised it would be. There was brightness all the way along the promenade but none where she lived, and as Darcey went inside it was there, the loneliness that she dreaded.

On a sudden impulse she showered and changed into evening clothes beneath a warm winter coat and set off along the seafront to find a restaurant that wasn't booked up for the occasion, and wasn't finding it easy when she saw Bridget and Ely coming towards her and there was no avoiding them.

'Hello, there,' the elderly boatman said. 'Surely you're not on your own on Christmas Day?'

'Yes, I'm afraid so,' she admitted uncomfortably.

'Then you must dine with us!' Bridget exclaimed. 'Everything is ready for our Christmas meal. We just came out for a breath of air, choosing to eat at home, and you are most welcome to join us, my dear.'

'I couldn't intrude like that,' Darcey protested weakly.

'You wouldn't be intruding,' Ely told her. 'Any friend of Daniel's is a friend of ours.'

'I am very interested in the Young Sailors' Club,' Darcey admitted. 'I would love to hear more about that.'

'So come and eat with us and we'll tell you all about it,' Bridget said.

'You are too young and bonny to be spending the evening of Christmas Day on your own. How have you passed the rest of it?'

'I'm Sister on the children's ward at Oceans House,' she told her, 'and I've been working there all day.'

'But Daniel wasn't, I take it,' Ely commented. 'He will have been with his sister's children. He loves those young ones. Pity he hasn't some of his own.'

And Darcey found herself thinking that she could do something about that if he would let her, but he would have to want to first.

Bridget and Ely lived in a neat fisherman's cottage not far from the harbour and made her most welcome in their small property where cooking smells lay on the night air and a log fire in the hearth took away the chill of the night outside, so that Darcey's loneliness disappeared as they answered all her questions about the Young Sailors' Club and Daniel himself, who they were obviously very fond of.

But Bridget was concerned that as well as his work at the hospital he was committed to turning out with the lifeboat when required, and although she made no comment Darcey agreed with her sentiments wholeheartedly.

There was no mention of the old lighthouse in the conversation. Clearly Daniel was intending that the repairs and renovation of it were to be a surprise and her amazement that he should have shared his secret dream with her surfaced again.

As the clock's hands began to move towards midnight she got up to go, with the thought of going back to Oceans House in the morning, and as she thanked them for their hospitality Ely said, 'I'll see you safely home, my dear.'

Bridget chipped in with, 'You are welcome any time, Darcey. It has been a pleasure to have you with us.' Tears pricked at their kindness and almost overflowed when the elderly lady went on to say, 'It is a shame that you are on duty tomorrow, or you could have gone sailing with Daniel and some of the young ones, it being Boxing Day.'

When she arrived back at her small residence and Ely had gone after seeing her safely inside, Darcey sank down by the window and, looking out into the Christmas night, gazed at the brightness of the stars and the moon above, while the kindness she had received from Ely and Bridget kept at bay the loneliness that she'd been dreading.

The only trouble with that was they would be sure to mention in Daniel's presence how they'd met her all alone on the promenade and he would want to know the reason why. But she would worry about that tomorrow, she decided, and with another day on the ward ahead put the thought of sailing with him to the back of her mind.

There might come another chance for that, she thought as sleep crept over her, and if it didn't happen she would always have the memory of the time he'd taken her to see the lighthouse.

It was good weather for sailing the next day. So much so that Daniel had taken one lot of the young would-be sailors out in the morning and another group in the afternoon as the sea was calm and the sky blue and cloudless, which made Darcey's absence even more disappointing, but he understood.

She'd been new to Seahaven and had probably thought he'd been in a rush to get to know her as she hadn't been aware of his reputation for steering clear of her sex, so he needed to slow down, give her some breathing space.

When Ely had mentioned casually how he and Bridget had met Darcey all alone on the evening of Christmas Day he'd been horrified. Was he so unlikable that she'd lied when telling him that she was booked up for the Christmas period, and if so how was she going to get the days over?

He had his answer when he popped into the hospital to meet up with the elderly consultant covering for him over Christmas, a man who'd been his tutor when Daniel had been a student. As they chatted over coffee in the cafeteria, James Collins said, 'I was impressed with the children's ward on my first shift when I took over.'

'Yes,' Daniel agreed. 'Darcey Howard, the regular sister, has taken time off during the Christmas period and will be pleased to hear that the rest of the staff are how she would want them to be.'

The other man was looking at him in puzzlement. 'She has been there all the time ever since I arrived. I met her on my first morning on the wards, and even caught a glimpse of her as I was arriving this morning. It would seem there has been a change of plan perhaps.'

'Yes, maybe,' Daniel agreed, thinking grimly that he had his answer to where Darcey was hiding out over Christmas. Was he such a monster that she had to resort to that sort of thing to avoid him?

It was further proof of what Ely and Bridget had said. Darcey wasn't going anywhere other than Oceans House. Wasn't spending Christmas with anyone except the nursing staff, and had been so desperate to avoid him after what he'd said about Cordelia's matchmaking that she'd concocted a story about a busy social life to keep him at a distance, so he could imagine how welcome his kiss on the promenade on Christmas Eve had been.

But he had to see for himself that she was there,

and the only way to do that was to visit the children's ward. So while the other man continued with his rounds Daniel made his way to the ground floor, where she would be if what he had just heard was correct…and it was.

Darcey was seated at the desk in the office, talking to the parents of one of her young patients, and he felt sick at the thought of how determined she'd been not to spend any time over Christmas with him.

The visitors were getting up to go and when she saw him observing her from the doorway of the ward he saw the colour drain from her face. But she didn't falter as she repeated the reassurances that she'd been able to give to the concerned parents about their child as they said their goodbyes.

Once they had gone he was beside her in a stride and, shutting the office door behind him, asked without preamble, 'So this is why you didn't want to come sailing with me, you would rather be here. I might applaud your self-sacrificing gesture if I didn't know that it was aimed at avoiding me.'

'I'm here because I told you a lie and then found I had to make it believable,' she told him tonelessly.

'I'm not with you,' he gritted. 'What has being here to do with you not wanting to come sailing with me?'

'I'd already put my name down to work over Christmas because I dreaded how awful it would be if my days turned out to be as empty and lonely as my nights,' she told him in a low voice.

'When you asked me to go sailing with you I was already committed to working over the holiday and had to think of a reason to refuse the invitation so I pretended I was booked up over Christmas because I didn't want you to know how lonely I am most of the time and start pitying me.'

'And that was it!' he exclaimed.

'Yes, that was the reason why, pathetic as it is,' she admitted wearily.

'And to think that I convinced Cordelia that you were booked up for the whole of Christmas!' he said tightly, and then with his tone softening added, 'She and Lawrence are going to be partying again tonight and I know they would love to see you again. Suppose I pick you up when you've finished here and take you to their place? How soon could you be ready?'

*Faster than the speed of light*, she wanted to tell him, but instead said casually, 'About an hour after I leave here, which will give me time to shower and get changed into something appropriate.'

'Such as the lovely dress that you were wearing on Christmas Eve when we met on the promenade?'

'Er...no, not necessarily,' she told him. 'I've worn it a couple of times now and I do have other clothes to choose from.' With her glance on the ward that awaited her presence, she said, 'Will you forgive me for lying to you, Daniel? I really did want to go sailing with you and the club.'

'Yes, of course,' he said gravely. 'Perhaps we could make up for that disappointment by driving out to the lighthouse sometime to view what the firm that I've commissioned to do the repairs has done so far.'

'I would love to!' she cried, and as he turned to

go was unable to refrain from asking what was up-permost in her mind, and it didn't concern the light-house. 'Will you always be on call for the lifeboat?'

'Yes, I am totally committed. They need me,' he replied. 'Although I suppose there might come a time when someone else is willing to take my place, but until then I shall follow in my father's footsteps as long as the need is there.'

On that promise he went, with a last reminder that he would call for her as arranged once her commit-ment to the children in her care was finished for the day.

Darcey was ready when Daniel came for her in the evening but not exactly sparkling due to an extra-busy day on the ward without his brisk expertise. And she was having doubts about letting him foist her onto his sister and her husband after they had already made her so welcome on Christmas Eve.

But most of all at the back of her mind was his reply to her question about his commitment to the lifeboat. She couldn't question it, understood totally. But would she want to spend the rest of her life in Seahaven praying for its safe return, that their chil-dren still had a father in the knowledge that the man she loved had only the bricks and mortar of an old lighthouse to remind him of his father?

Unaware of her fears on his behalf, Daniel's only concern on arriving was to reassure her regarding his intention to take her to his sister's once again, and when she mentioned her concerns on that score he just smiled and commented that Cordelia had mentioned she was looking forward to talking with her again, and that also there would be the chance for Darcey to chat further with the elder of his two young nieces about anything she wanted to know about nursing.

'Will that make you feel less of an outsider?' he asked, and Darcey swallowed hard at the thought that she must have sounded weak and whining when he'd come into the ward office that morning.

'Yes, hopefully,' she told him, and smiling at her reticence he brought the colour to her cheeks with his next comment, which was, 'Am I allowed to tell you that you look very beautiful?'

She was laughing now. 'Oh, yes, please do! I need something to boost my morale and I do like to wear black occasionally, although the dress isn't new.'

'It is to me, though,' he replied, and taking her hand he took her out into another Christmas night. He drove her the short distance to his sister's house and hoped that nothing would go wrong in the evening ahead.

Daniel had been right about the young would-be nurse. No sooner had they arrived than Katie was ready to check their general health once they had been introduced to everyone there, and as Darcey watched him playing the part of the patient to the full there was an ache around her heart at the thought of how much he had missed by letting a stale marriage separate him from a family life of his own.

Daniel saw her expression and wondered what was causing her to look so solemn, but before he could

ask, Cordelia came to chat while their friends watched
football on television, and it was all relaxing until
he saw tiredness fall on Darcey like a cloak as a reminder that hers had been a long day, with others to
follow, and tenderness washed over him as they said
goodbye to the only family he had with the thought
uppermost that she had even less.

They had to pass the apartments where he lived
on the way home, and glancing across at her sitting
quietly beside him in the passenger seat Daniel said,
'I seem to be in and out of your place all the time,
Darcey, but you have never seen mine. Are you too
tired to come in for a coffee?'

She smiled across at him. 'No. I would like that. I
imagine it is quite sumptuous.'

'I don't know about that,' he said laughingly. 'It is
more like an empty shell that I use to eat and sleep
in, a boring place really.'

He was driving into the parking area, which was
well lit, and Darcey became silent as the difference
between their two residences became apparent, yet it
stood to sense that it would, and did it matter? They
were only socialising like this because it was Christmas.

She had already weighed up the pain threshold of
loving him with the memory of losing her parents
still starkly clear, and tonight was not going to be a
stepping stone in that direction, she prayed as Daniel
settled her into a comfortable sitting room while he
went to make the coffee. When he came in with it,
as if he'd read her thoughts he said, 'It is midnight,
Darcey, and you are already exhausted after a busy

day at Oceans House, so much as I would like your company for longer, once we've had the hot drink I'm going to take you home.'

If he'd told her the truth it would have been that he longed to carry her up the stairs and make love to her in his lonely bed, but that would be a poor show of caring about her tiredness, not how he wanted it to be at all, and short of offering her his guest room there was no way he could keep Darcey near until morning when she would require an early departure to get changed into her uniform, and might not thank him for that.

Darcey gazed at him above the rim of her coffee cup but said nothing, the memory of her fears of losing him to the sea feeling as if it would be a similar tragedy to that of her parents lost in the snows, and knowing that Daniel would always honour his father's devotion to the mighty ocean so near the town, no matter what. She could see nothing ahead but pain if he ever loved her as much as she was beginning to love him.

He was getting to his feet as she put her coffee cup down and he held out his hand. As she rose to face him he said quizzically, 'Can I take it that tonight you haven't been lonely?'

She flashed him a tired smile. 'You can indeed,' she said softly. 'I envy you your delightful family, Daniel.' Reaching forward, she stroked his face gently with her fingertips and said, 'Thank you for sharing them with me on this occasion.'

'It was a pleasure for all of us,' he said gravely, as if her tender touch wasn't making him long for more.

'And as for our young would-be nurse, don't be surprised if the next time you see me I'm covered in bandages and plasters.' Taking hold of her wrap, he draped it around her snugly and led her out into the night once more, where the warmth of the car awaited them.

When they got to her apartment Daniel saw her safely inside, and with Darcey's work routine as familiar as his own he didn't linger but had one last thing to say regarding her almost non-existent social life. 'I don't like to think of you alone on New Year's Eve,' he said sombrely.

'My two young nieces go to the birthday party of one of their friends on that occasion every year and stay overnight, which gives the rest of us—Cordelia, Lawrence and myself—the chance to go to the ball at the biggest hotel in town.

'This year I have a spare ticket that I got in case the doctor who is filling in for me at Oceans House would have liked to have gone, but he has another engagement for that night. So if you would like to join us you will be most welcome. I would pick you up at seven thirty.'

'Daniel, it is very kind of you to offer, but I'm afraid that I have something special planned for New Year's Eve,' she explained awkwardly, and cringed at his expression.

'Fine,' he said briskly, 'just as long as you won't be alone.' And during the short drive home he decided that maybe Darcey found him too overpowering, but if that was the case why didn't she say so?

Back at her apartment Darcey was going over

those few embarrassing moments in her mind and cringing at the way she'd handled them. But she reasoned that, however much she would have liked to have gone to the ball with Daniel, her yearly pilgrimage to a church on New Year's Eve, wherever there might be one near, had to come first in remembrance of the deaths of her parents on that long-ago New Year's Eve, and during the week that followed the new closeness between the two of them that Christmas had brought seemed far away.

A nearby church was almost full when she got there on the night but she found a seat near the back and when she looked around her Darcey saw that Bridget and Ely were sitting nearby, and when they saw her and smiled across for a moment it was as if those she had lost were there in the friendly older couple.

Both were wearing winter coats, but as it was quite warm in the church they had unbuttoned them, and she could see that they were dressed in evening wear, which made her heart sink.

They must be going to the ball, she thought, and when they got there would be sure to tell Daniel that they had seen her elsewhere in the town, and a dampening thought was that if they were attending the church service first they must be confident that when it was over they would be in time for the ball.

But once Daniel had spoken to Bridget and Ely it would be too late for any afterthoughts on her behalf. It was an hour to midnight and Darcey was alone, as she had expected to be when she had refused Daniel's suggestion that she be his guest at the ball, but she had seen his friends since then and if they had met him earlier it hadn't sent him to her.

So maybe he'd had his fill of what he might see as her playing hard to get, as after seeing Bridget and Ely she was not likely to have gone to the ball without a ticket and risk being sent away if he didn't see her arrive.

The minutes were passing, soon it would be a New Year, a time to make a fresh start for some, or make the best of what they had for others, and neither suggestion was appealing.

It was ten minutes to the hour when Darcey heard a car pull up outside the apartment and her mouth went dry. What now? she wondered, and as she opened the door to him she had her answer. There was no sweeping her into his arms, just questions needing answers.

'Why are you so secretive, for heaven's sake?' he asked as he stepped over the threshold, 'Or is it only with me that you are like that, such as hiding your loneliness from me when I was able to do something about it once I knew, and it was a joy to make you happy for a while.

'Yes, I have spoken to Bridget and Ely, and they told me that they saw you in church. What you did after that I have no idea, but when you said that you had something special that you had to do tonight, why didn't you say what it was so that I could have driven you there, or maybe even been present at the service where they saw you?'

'It was just something that I always do on New Year's Eve wherever I happen to be,' she told him, 'and it is a very private thing, Daniel, that is all. My parents lost their lives in an avalanche when they were skiing on New Year's Eve many years ago, and it was in their memory that I was unable to go to the ball with you.

'If I'd had the opportunity to check the time of everything properly I would have realised that I could have managed to get to both the church service and the ball, which I do so regret missing, but I wouldn't want to become a burden in your busy life because I'm new here in Seahaven,' she told him awkwardly.

He groaned inwardly at her enchanting honesty and thought she was one burden he would carry with him for ever if she would let him, and what could have been a more suitable occasion for them to get to know each other better than in the last hours of the old year and the first hours of the new one?

When Bridget and Ely had told him about seeing her in the church, he hadn't wanted to intrude into whatever need had taken her there until midnight was almost upon them, but he knew that he needed to be with her like he needed to breathe.

He held out his arms and, unable to help herself, Darcey moved into them, but the night was not to be theirs. A greater force than their attraction to each other had different plans for them as Daniel's phone rang, and as he listened to the voice at the other end his hold on her slackened.

'Yes, all right,' he said flatly. 'But I'll have to change first. I'm still in the clothes I wore to the ball and will change into the spare outfit that Ely keeps for me at his place. See you soon.' Disconnecting the call, he said, 'The lifeboat has been called out, Darcey. Some folks on a pleasure boat have come unstuck in the same place as where our young ones almost scuttled theirs not long ago.

'They've hired it for partying but have run into very high seas and the only one of them capable of bringing them safely back to shore has been drinking ever since they set off, so is totally out of it.' His hand was already on the door catch. 'Make sure that you lock up after me.' As an afterthought, he added, 'I'm due back on my usual routine at Oceans House in the morning, so I will see you then if all goes well with this callout.'

'And if it doesn't?' she questioned raggedly.

'It will, don't fret,' he informed her briskly, and was gone, and as she heard his car engine start up outside Darcey sank down onto the nearest chair and thought miserably that it could have turned out to be one of the most special moments of their lives, but if Daniel didn't return safely it would be the worst and she couldn't live the sort of life again where someone she loved was snatched away in a moment.

It might not have been so hard to cope with if he hadn't shown her the derelict lighthouse that he was having restored and told her the reason why.

At the time she had been moved by his acceptance of what must have been a terrible loss, but at that time she had been merely a sympathetic bystander, not a woman in love.

It was turning out to be a painful beginning to the first hours of the New Year, the two of them being on the brink of something magical that had fallen apart.

# CHAPTER SEVEN

BRIDGET CALLED TO let Darcey know the lifeboat was
out there, and after Darcey hung up, all she could
think about was that when Bridget was gone, would
*she* be expected to take the elderly woman's place,
providing hot drinks and sandwiches for those who
waited anxiously for the return of their loved ones?

No! She would want her life to be wrapped around
children that she could love and adore with a fantastic father, but she was moving too fast. How could
she be sure that it wasn't just a quick hug that Daniel
had been about to bestow upon her? That saving lives
on the sea came before even his expertise at Oceans
House, and that love and marriage were a poor third
after what had happened to his father.

The time was almost one o'clock in the early morning of New Year's Day and her main concern had to
be with the sick and injured children who were in her
care, Darcey thought as she lay sleepless beneath the
covers, but at the back of her mind there were still
Daniel's comments about her refusal to let him take
her to the ball and the mix-up of the timing. What

else could go wrong? she questioned miserably, and turning her face into the pillow felt the dread from earlier return like a hand grasping her heart.

He had said on leaving that he would see her in the morning as he was back on schedule from then, and the thought of how she would cope if he didn't arrive was beyond thinking of. But there could be various other reasons that might delay him and with that frail comfort to hold onto she finally drifted off to sleep, until the alarm clock beside her bed awoke her to reality once more in a winter dawn with no phone calls to draw comfort from or messages of a safe undertaking on the mat. This could mean that the lifeboat was still out there, or that Daniel had got back and rather than disturb her had gone to bed knowing that they would be meeting up first thing in the morning.

Then again, there was a third possibility that had occurred to her when he'd received the phone call the night before. It was that of expecting her to be as easygoing about the danger involved as he was, and if that was the case he couldn't be more wrong.

There was no sign of him when she arrived on the children's ward, or anywhere else for that matter. No one had seen anything of him so far, which made everything that she'd felt so definite about seem unimportant.

His absence had to mean that the lifeboat was still out in dangerous waters, she thought frantically, and began her rounds with dogged purpose to stop herself from weeping, until magically she heard the voice that she longed to hear.

He was there, observing her from the doorway of the ward with dark hazel eyes red-rimmed, his face unshaven, and when he beckoned her she went to him as if in a trance.

'I've only just got back,' he said, 'so I'm going to have a shower in the en suite bathroom adjoining my office and then ask one of the hospital's restaurants to bring me some breakfast. Once all that has been accomplished, I will start my rounds, with the children's ward first as I usually do.'

As their glances held, Darcey thought there was no mention of what he and the rest of the lifeboat crew had been facing during the long hours of a stormy night and maybe it was just as well. She was concerned enough without a blow-by-blow account that would make the kind of life she dreamed of seem even less likely to ever be hers.

But for the present there was the exquisite relief of seeing Daniel back in familiar surroundings, and when he appeared later, looking scrubbed and clean and ready for action, she was content until he said, 'When are you due for a break after being on duty all over Christmas?'

'I've got a week off, starting tomorrow,' she said awkwardly, as they approached the first small bed in their line of vision.

'And have you anything planned?' he asked.

'No, not especially,' she told him. 'Why do you ask?'

'I'm intending going to see how the work on the

lighthouse is coming along and thought you might like to join me for the day, as it isn't quite as isolated as it appears. Often in years gone by one would find a manor house and a cluster of cottages that housed the lighthouse keepers not far away from it, along with a small church. All of which are still there but no longer lived in, and I might decide to change all that by buying the manor house.'

Darcey was gazing at him in disbelief, but they had reached the bedside of Luke, a ten-year-old boy who stared at them unblinkingly and asked how long it would be before he could play football again after a serious leg injury. As she listened to Daniel explaining gently that it could be some time, but it would happen one day, Darcey knew beyond doubt that he was the man that she wanted to father any children she might have, and if he couldn't be for any reason she would do without.

As they moved on to the next bed their private lives were shelved to attend to the needs of their young patients, and by the time that was accomplished Darcey was due for her lunch break and Daniel would proceed to the adult wards that had still to be visited due to his late arrival.

'So what do you think of that for an idea, buying the manor house?' he said as they were about to separate. 'I've had it in mind for some time and would like your opinion.'

'Why me?' she croaked.

'Why do you think?' he said softly. 'I want you to be the mother of my children one day.'

'And that's it?' she questioned flatly. 'Expecting me to be the mother of a one-parent family if you don't come back from a lifeboat callout? I've endured that kind of thing for over ten years with Alexander after our parents went in a flash and left us alone, and I can't bear to make another commitment of that kind, Daniel.'

'Yes, of course, I understand,' he said levelly. 'But my father's sacrifice was a willing one, as my mother had already gone and Cordelia and I were adults in charge of our own lives.'

'And what would your decision be if you found yourself in a similar position to his?' she questioned.

'If I had a wife and children I would only risk my life in the most extreme circumstances, I can promise you that, but whether it would be enough is up to you, Darcey.'

'I don't know,' she said painfully. 'I just don't know. You haven't said that you love me, have you? Just that you would like me to have your children.'

He was observing her with a twisted smile. 'I've loved you ever since you let me put your luggage up on the rack in the train, though I don't know why as when I saw you on the ward the next day and saw how really beautiful you were I realised that you had been sad and exhausted, far from your best on the journey.'

'But I must go, Darcey, I'm way behind in my routine today after my late start. Do you think we could meet up again this evening and finish what we were discussing earlier?'

'Yes, I suppose so,' she told him weakly. 'Although

I don't see what it can achieve. Our needs are too different, our lives too far apart. We work together. It's not a good idea for us to get involved.'

He was laughing. 'I'm not sure I would agree with that, so what about tonight? I'll take you for a meal, but do you want to change out of your uniform first?'

'Yes, it won't take long, about half an hour?' she said hesitantly.

'That's fine and, in the meantime, while you're getting ready I'll call briefly on Bridget and Ely as my being in America for the last two weeks meant them having to cope with the club members, who can be a handful at times.'

Turning towards the stairs that would take him to the floor above where adult patients were being treated, he said, 'I'll call for you half an hour after you finish, Darcey, and no need to dress up for such an occasion if the answer to my suggestion is going to be no.' And on that cheerful comment he left her to a brief lunch in the staff restaurant with the feeling that she was out of her depth, in love totally for the first time…and not coping.

Daniel had booked a table at a different restaurant from the one he'd taken her to the last time to avoid casting any more shadows than there were already in their relationship, and he could tell that Darcey read his mind.

'I suggest that we eat first and talk afterwards,' he said gently, and she nodded mutely.

The food was excellent but she ate it mechanically

with no enjoyment and when the meal was over he looked around him and said, 'It's too crowded in here, Darcey, to be having a serious discussion amongst all these folks. There is no privacy and too many of them know who we are. We'll go to my place, if that's all right with you.' When she nodded once again he called the waiter over and settled the bill.

There was no conversation between them as Daniel drove the short distance to his apartment, or when they were inside for the first few moments, but when she took off the winter coat she was wearing and went to stand by the fire it came like a rushing wind, the chemistry between them, and when he held out his arms she went into them like a homing bird, with his every kiss a magical moment, but when at last they drew apart and he said softly, 'So can we start arranging a wedding?' he felt her withdrawal like a knife wound.

'I thought you'd brought me here to discuss both of our points of view,' she told him flatly, 'but it would seem that it is only yours that matters.' Before he could reply she had flung her coat on and was whizzing through the front door like a rocket, and by the time he had gathered his wits she was out of sight. He thought, so much for that, he'd made a mess of the whole thing.

He had meant what he'd said to be gentle teasing before telling her that since their discussion that morning he had been in touch with the authorities who were in charge of appointing the coxswains on the lifeboats and would have to await their decision with regard to his request.

Obviously he should have told Darcey that first, instead of mentioning marriage and teasing her about a wedding, as if that was all he was bothered about. But her reaction to what he'd said had been so abrupt that he'd been taken aback, otherwise he would have gone on to tell her that he had wasted no time since that morning in considering her needs, and now there was no sign of her on the road outside.

Yet there was no way he was going to leave it at that so he drove onto the promenade, his concern increasing until he saw a taxi that she must have flagged down pulling away from the front of her apartment and went weak with relief. Not wanting to cause any further upsets, he drove back home the way he had come in sombre mood and it didn't lighten at all when only seconds after his return a frantic Cordelia phoned to say that his younger niece had suffered a spinal injury in an accident and was being transferred by ambulance straight to Oceans House so could he meet them there? He was on his way almost before she'd finished speaking.

When he got there the ambulance was just pulling up in the space provided for such vehicles and as Bethany was carried out on a stretcher, with the rest of her family close behind, Daniel thought grimly that this was the punishment he deserved for his thoughtless treatment of Darcey. As if she'd read his mind, she appeared beside him, having seen the ambulance arrive and witnessed his grave concern from the window of her apartment.

'What's wrong, Daniel?' she asked anxiously.

'I don't know until we get her inside,' he said bleakly. 'From what Cordelia said when she phoned, it sounds as if Bethany has had some sort of accident and it has affected her spine.'

'Oh, no!' she exclaimed. 'Poor little one! Can I do anything to help? I'm sorry for my outburst earlier. It was just that—'

'It's all right,' he said levelly as his young niece was lifted carefully out of the confines of the ambulance. 'Save it for another time, Darcey, if there ever is one.'

As Cordelia and her family followed the stretcher he stepped forward to greet them and, feeling unwanted and in the way, Darcey moved to one side and waited to see if he would take her up on her offer of help as there would be night staff to assist if he needed them.

'So put me in the picture,' Daniel said to Lawrence as the two men strode beside the hospital trolley with Bethany's sister Katie holding the sedated young patient's hand. With her arm supporting her friend in the rear, Darcey listened patiently as Cordelia explained tearfully what had caused the accident that had injured their daughter.

'We were going skiing at half-term,' she said, 'and had gone late night shopping for suitable clothes in one of the big stores when Bethany lost her footing at the bottom of an escalator and fell backwards onto the metal steps. She was screaming with pain as we lifted her off and unable to stand, so the store sent for an ambulance, which brought us straight here to Daniel.

'When I rang to tell him what had happened he'd just got in from somewhere and didn't sound very happy, but when I told him about the accident he was back in the car and wasted no time in meeting the ambulance on its arrival, as you saw.'

'He will be sending Bethany for X-rays first,' Darcey reminded her, 'so that he can assess the damage to her back, and your family will need you near, Cordelia. So if you go ahead with the two men, I'll wait here as I don't feel Daniel will want me around unless he has a use for me, which is not likely.'

If her friend had been less traumatised she would have wanted to know what was meant by that cryptic comment, but with all that she had on her mind taking first place she hurried off and Darcey was left to wait until there was a result from the X-rays before any further communication with the man who she thought achingly loved the lifeboat more than he loved her.

Why hadn't Darcey stayed with Cordelia? Daniel wondered as he waited for the X-rays. If she didn't want anything to do with him any more, so be it, but why take it out on his sister, especially in her hour of need? They were his family and he would move heaven and earth to save them pain if he could. His venture into romance had been a step too far, it seemed, if Darcey didn't want to be in the same room as him.

But the X-rays were ready for his scrutiny, and as he studied them relief washed over him in a thankful tide.

There was severe bruising and bleeding of his little

niece's back but no spinal damage or broken bones. With gentle nursing while in Darcey's care, and his expertise available at a moment's notice, she should make a full recovery.

When he looked up to where the little one's loving parents were waiting to hear what could have been so much worse, Daniel was smiling as he said, 'No broken bones, just a lot of soreness that will disappear with tender care. But no skiing at half-term, I'm afraid, and I would recommend a few days in the children's ward with Darcey in charge, just to make sure that our small patient is progressing satisfactorily.' As he gazed at those he loved, there was just one person missing, but what was new about that?

'I must go and tell her,' Cordelia said as if she'd read his mind. 'I wanted her to be with us when you gave us the verdict, whether it was good or bad, but she seemed to feel that she would be intruding and said she'd wait in the corridor.'

'Go and tell her by all means,' he agreed, 'and when Darcey joins us I will confirm what I said about having Bethany stay here for the next few days, where Darcey will be in charge. There is no one better.

'Lawrence and you will be able to visit for as long as you like as there aren't any restrictions, and I will be around to keep my professional eye on things, so please feel free to explain that to Darcey when you see her.' As she listened to his instructions, Cordelia wondered what had gone wrong between them.

When she found Darcey still waiting in the cor-

ridor, her friend asked worriedly, 'Have the X rays
come through?'

'Yes, thank goodness,' was the reply. 'There is
bruising but no broken bones and Daniel wants Bethany to stay in the children's ward for a few days, or
as long as it takes for her to recover. He is not pleased
that you weren't there when he announced the results.'

'Yes, it would seem that he and I are not as com-
patible as we thought,' Darcey said flatly as they went
to join the others.

Daniel was on the phone to the night sister when
they appeared, explaining that they would be bringing another small patient to the children's ward in a
few moments and that he was going to stay there for
the time being to watch over her during the night.

'I've persuaded Lawrence to take you and Katie
home once Bethany is settled in there,' he told Cordelia when he'd finished the call, 'and I will be in touch
immediately if there are any further problems.' And
with his glance on Darcey, who so far hadn't spoken, he continued, 'I shall stay until you arrive in
the morning, and when I've left will expect to be informed at the slightest sign of anything you are concerned about.'

'Yes, of course,' she said levelly, and wished he
wouldn't speak to her as if she was a stranger.

Even worse, she was being dismissed as he said,
'And now I suggest you get some sleep, knowing
that I shall be with Bethany until you take over at
eight o'clock tomorrow.' After that pronouncement
he turned and held Cordelia close and at the same

time put his arm around Lawrence's shoulders while a tearful Katie snuggled close, telling them gently to go home and rest and he would be in touch in the morning.

When he turned to say goodnight to Darcey she'd gone, hurt that Daniel could change so quickly when she loved him so, but a sweet little girl who had slipped on hard metal and hurt her back was going to be her first concern in days to come, not whether anything was left of their brief relationship.

Seated beside Bethany's bed in the children's ward, Daniel watched over his little niece with ragged calm, alert to every sound or movement that she made in spite of the medication she'd been given at the time of the accident, and when he wasn't reliving the moment of Cordelia's horrifying phone call he was remembering Darcey's hurt and anger at his suggestion regarding a wedding when he hadn't told her about him having already asked for someone to take his place on the lifeboat.

The magic of those moments before she'd flung herself out into the night in hurt and anger had gone, and if he were to tell her now about his request for someone to take his place on the lifeboat it would seem as if it was a quick afterthought and he was no lover of that sort of thing. So he needed to let it lie for a while. Maybe until Darcey had seen the manor house near where his father's memorial was going to be.

Yet knowing her, she would be happy in one of the

cottages that had previously housed the lighthouse keepers if she knew that he really loved her, let alone the manor house, and that was the problem. How was he going to convince her of that?

If he told Ely what he was proposing to do, he knew the man would be grieved to see him go and so would Bridget, but hopefully they would understand, and there was no doubt about what Cordelia would say as all she had ever wanted was for him to be happy. It was when it came to his own feelings that he faltered.

In Darcey he had found the love of his life, but she was hurt and bruised by what life had done to her so far, and he didn't want her to be hurt even more because of him.

There was a little cry of pain from Bethany and when she opened her eyes and saw him sitting there, a big tear rolled down her cheek as she said, 'I fell and hurt my back, didn't I, Uncle Daniel?'

'Yes, you did, my little love,' he said softly, 'and I'm here to watch over you and make sure you get better very soon.' He smiled as he gazed at her. 'Would you like a drink and something to eat?'

'Can I have an ice-cream cone?' she asked weakly. 'My mouth is very dry.'

'Yes. I'll ask one of the nurses to bring one from the café upstairs, which is the only place open at this time where they have that sort of thing. But you will have to let me hold it while you lick it because of your sore back. OK?'

'Yes, please,' she said, and he wondered if he had

botched his chances of being a father to children of his own by upsetting Darcey like he had. Would she want to be left alone after the evening's earlier catastrophic mix-up? But the ice cream was on its way for his niece and he had a job to do.

Once the treat had been enjoyed to the full, Daniel checked her temperature and was relieved to find it normal, and when two of the nurses on his instructions had gently turned his little niece onto her side he was able to inspect the damage to her back, which, although sore in parts, he knew could have been much worse, and by the time a fresh application of a soothing ointment had been applied again, Bethany had gone back to sleep.

# CHAPTER EIGHT

IT WAS TWO O'CLOCK in the morning and Darcey was sleepless because the happenings of the evening were too fragile and hurtful to be put out of her mind.

First there had been Daniel's marriage proposal that had sent her back home like a rocket because there had been no mention of her fear of the sea claiming him as it had his father, and when later they'd met up at the hospital and she'd apologised for leaving so abruptly earlier in the evening, he had been the one who had indicated that the subject was closed.

With Cordelia and Lawrence totally distraught, Daniel had persuaded them to go home for a few hours while he watched over their daughter, and hadn't even noticed when she had gone home to rest, to be ready for the coming morning in the children's ward, where she and her staff would take over when Daniel took a break from his loving vigil.

It was all logical thinking but not sleep-producing, she thought. Even as it registered, she was dressing quickly and hurrying out into the night to the hospital.

'Darcey!' he exclaimed tonelessly as she appeared

in the dimly lit ward. 'What are you doing here? Go back to bed.'

'I came to see how Bethany is,' she told him, 'and to ask if you would like me to bring you something from the restaurant.'

'No, thanks, I'm fine,' was the reply. 'The nurses are keeping me fed and watered.'

Looking down at the sleeping child, she asked softly, 'And what about your small patient? How is she?'

'At this moment content,' he said levelly, 'having just had an ice cream and the dressing on the soreness of her back dealt with, but once all that wears off she will still be in a lot of pain, which is why you should be bedded down for the night instead of here.'

'Yes, maybe I should,' she agreed, aware that it was the day she was due to go on leave and was now not intending to do any such thing until Bethany's condition had improved.

Cordelia and Lawrence had been kindness itself to her over the lonely days of Christmas. The least she could do in return was to be there for them at such a time, and as for her replacement, the staff nurse who was to have covered her role for the coming week would be happy to be relieved of the responsibility as she was heavily pregnant. Without further comment, Darcey went, with the hurtful thought in mind that Daniel's passion had been short-lived.

Daniel groaned softly when she'd gone, having wanted to hold her close and tell her how much she meant to him, but the day's happenings had taken their toll. His concern for his small niece had to come first, and as if the thought had transferred itself to her, she awoke, began to cry, and it was a case of another gentle application of the soothing ointment and a cool drink before she went back to sleep.

Back at the apartment Darcey was doing what she'd been told to do, settling down for what was left of the night, but it wasn't to sleep, she thought bleakly. Daniel was very much mistaken if he thought she could switch off the nightmare happenings of a day that would soon be drawing to a close unresolved.

For one thing, she was most concerned on Cordelia and Lawrence's behalf that a shopping trip should end in their small daughter being hospitalised, but Daniel being who he was had been there for them, so at least one of the day's catastrophes had not gone unattended, and as for the other, the rapture it had also brought with it had disappeared.

He had said that he wanted her to be the mother of his children, and as she'd watched him with his small niece she'd thought there were two sides to that. Children needed a father too and he would have been all that she could wish for them when the time came, but the give and take would have had to be equal, not all on her side, although now it didn't matter. The divide that had appeared between them was too big to be treated as a lovers' tiff.

It was only after Darcey had returned to her apartment to obey his instructions that Daniel had remembered that she was due for time off during the week to come, after being on duty all through the Christmas period, and he had just messed it up again, as if his needs came first. But why hadn't she reminded him, for heaven's sake?

The problem of Bethany's care would have to be resolved like that of the other young patients after he had apologised and transferred his instructions to whoever would be taking her place, and then maybe the two of them could allow themselves a fresh start to their relationship.

But he wasn't relishing having to account for another misunderstanding after omitting to tell Darcey that he had wasted no time in trying to find a replacement to take on his lifeboat duties.

When she appeared later, looking heavy-eyed and pale, he was quick to apologise for his memory lapse. 'I'm so sorry for making my demands of you last night with regard to you taking Bethany under your wing during working hours,' he said, 'as that doesn't apply to the coming week, does it? You are on leave and that is how it must stay after all the time you put in during the Christmas break.' With a glance at the sleeping child, he added, 'The person who is due to take your place will manage very nicely, I'm sure, and what is more Cordelia and her family are here. They arrived at six o'clock and have gone up to the restaurant to have a quick bite before I leave them to it, as I have a very busy day ahead in Theatre and on the wards.'

'Which makes me all the more intent on being here,' she told him. 'They are good friends and have

shown me much kindness during my solitary existence over Christmas.' She gently reached out a hand
and stroked Bethany's hair before saying, 'I will need
to know your wishes regarding Bethany's treatment
before you sign off. And, Daniel, with regard to us,
maybe we were too hasty in allowing a commitment to
form between us that we are not capable of fulfilling.'

'So that is what you think, is it?' he said with steely
calm, restraining the urge to demonstrate how mistaken she was about that. Collecting the paperwork
that he had been working on during the night as his
young charge had slept, he passed her the sheet on
top and said, 'Those are my instructions regarding
Bethany's treatment. If you have any problems, you
will find me somewhere in the building.'

Then he had gone and she did so wish that he
hadn't. When his sister and her family appeared
some seconds later Cordelia exclaimed, 'Darcey!
We thought you were due for some time off? This
can't be right.'

'It is very right indeed that I of all people should
be here for my friends and their hurt little one,' she
said gently. 'I had nothing planned for the coming
week and if I had I would have cancelled it. Daniel
has given me all the details for Bethany's treatment
and her progress so far before he went to start on his
usual Monday morning clinic, with instructions to
seek him out immediately if the need arose.' She sent
a smile in Katie's direction. 'When you come next
time, bring your nurse's outfit and you can help us
on the ward.' She was rewarded with a cry of delight.

At that moment Bethany awoke and as Cordelia helped her daughter eat, Darcey went to check on the rest of her young patients and wished that Daniel was there, doing his rounds with her as he would normally be, while instead his presence had been restricted to the night hours that were going to be followed by a very busy day.

Yet typically he managed to call at the ward for a few moments in the lunch hour and was satisfied to hear that the soreness of Bethany's lower spine was decreasing, she was in less pain and that a second X-ray had shown no further complications.

'When will we be able to take her home?' Lawrence asked, while Cordelia plied her brother with a sandwich and a mug of tea and Darcey stood by silently.

'In a few days, I would think,' Daniel told him, and with his glance on her continued, 'But I don't want to rush it as I did with something a few days ago that went all haywire.' He got to his feet, ready to depart, and she knew that she didn't want him out of her life ever, no matter what happened.

By Friday Bethany was well enough to go home. The damage to her back was healing well. She was able to walk slowly around the ward, getting to know some of the other children, and when Cordelia and Lawrence came for her she was almost reluctant to leave, but the thought of being able to play with Katie again and sleep in her own bed sorted that problem.

Daniel had been to see his small patient on her last morning in the children's ward and as Darcey watched them together it was there, as if only said a moment ago, that she was the one he wanted to give him children, which she would have been so happy to do, if only he had been equally willing to calm her fears regarding his commitment to the lifeboat, because there was always the memory of how she and Alex had been left young and parentless amongst the snows that day.

He appeared at her side when she was having a coffee and a sandwich in the staff restaurant during the lunch hour and asked, 'Have you sorted out the free time that I denied you when Bethany was brought in?'

'Yes,' she told him levelly. 'I'm having next week off. I haven't planned anything so far, but thought I might go and see Alex for a few days.' Alex had emailed to let her know he'd run out of money, so had come home and was staying with friends. He was working in a bar to get enough money to go travelling again. 'It will mean staying in a hotel somewhere near where he's staying, but as long as he's around so that we can meet during any free time he has, it will be fine.'

'So he's home, then,' he commented. 'When did he get back?' Without waiting for an answer, he commented, 'I could drive you there if you want. If you recall, the trains were very busy on the day we found ourselves going in the same direction and to the same place.'

'Oh, yes.' She recalled it all right, Darcey thought weakly, and to be next to him for a couple of hours in the closeness of the car in the present circumstances, which had arisen only a week ago when Daniel had wanted her to marry him, would be an ordeal she didn't want to have to face.

'I shall make sure that I don't travel in the rush hour,' she said hurriedly, 'but thanks for the offer.' And with a complete change of subject that came from her love for him, and knowing how much he achieved with regard to the burden of care for others that he coped with all the time, she asked, 'Have you had time for some lunch?'

'No,' he said, 'but I'm going to do something about that in the next few moments.' As she arose hurriedly, her lunch break at an end, he wished that someone, somewhere would want to take over from him on the lifeboat. In the meantime, he was hoping that the lighthouse he had bought in memory of his father would soon be ready to be unveiled for all to see.

When Darcey phoned her brother to say that she intended to pay him a short visit during the coming weekend he was highly pleased. 'I've missed you,' he said. 'It was fabulous while we were away but no one will ever take your place, big sister. Shall I book you in somewhere?'

'Yes, please,' she told him. 'From Friday morning to Sunday evening somewhere close to you.'

'Will do,' he'd promised buoyantly. 'I'll ring back as soon as I have that sorted, and if I'm not working when your train is due, I'll meet you at the station.'

When they'd finished chatting Darcey sat back and gave some thought to how she was going to occupy herself for the rest of the week, and a vision of the derelict lighthouse came to mind. She had never seen it since the day that Daniel had taken her there when she'd viewed it in its dilapidated condition.

Now from what Bridget and Ely had told her when she'd dined with them on Christmas Day, the alterations were almost complete. Soon there would be a public dedication of Daniel's tribute to his father, and with the burden of their quarrel about the lifeboat raw and hurting she did not intend to attend that occasion.

But in her free time during the coming week there was nothing to stop her from visiting the scene on her own while he was occupied at Oceans House, she thought, and the following day she caught the promenade tram as far as it went in that direction and walked the rest of the way beneath a wintry sun until the lighthouse, resplendent in a fresh coat of white paint, came into view, with the words *In Memory of Mark Osbourne* on a brass plaque fitted centrally.

There were still workmen present and one of them stopped next to her and said, 'You are the sister from the children's ward at Oceans House, aren't you?

'Our little boy was in there a few weeks ago after a bad fall off his bike, but he's all right now.'

Darcey managed a weak smile, knowing the fact that she'd been seen at the site of the lighthouse renovation was sure to be mentioned to Daniel the next time he came there, and he would want to know the whys and wherefores of her visit.

But she would explain all that when the time came, and in the meantime the light of the winter afternoon was fading and the tram that had brought her there would be arriving soon to take her back, along with the bulk of the workforce, but she had yet to see the empty manor house and the other unoccupied properties that Daniel had described to her, which were vaguely visible on the horizon a mile or so away.

So, pointing herself in that direction, she walked briskly towards them, and the moment she was level Darcey understood Daniel's yearning to do two things, live in a house within sight of the memorial he had chosen for his father, and bring life back to the remote yet amazingly beautiful village where he had wanted to bring up their children when they arrived. But could she live with the thought always there that she might lose him to the sea, as she had lost her parents to the snow, and if he didn't understand her reasoning, could they have a happy life together?

Lost in her musings, she turned to make her way back to the lighthouse and was horrified to see the tram disappearing into the distance with not a soul in sight as it transported the workforce home on their last journey of the day.

Within minutes the winter dark fell on the empty houses behind her and with it came heavy rain, slashing against doors and windows as she ran from one to the next, desperate to find shelter. Until the heavy oak door of the manor house swung back on creaking hinges and she moved slowly into its unexpected shelter.

The most sensible thing would be to stay there until the rain cleared, she told herself, and then set off in the dark on the long walk back to her apartment, being careful to stay clear of the cliff edge where the lighthouse stood.

A depressing thought was that she wasn't going to be missed as no one at the hospital knew where she had set off to, and as she was on leave, neither Daniel nor Cordelia and Lawrence would expect her to do something as crazy as getting lost and having to shelter in a big empty house before starting on the long walk back to Seahaven in the dark.

It seemed that her phone wasn't working in the isolated place that she found herself in, and along with panic came the thought that there was someone who might have noticed that she was missing from the tram on its last journey of the day.

The man whose young boy had once been in Oceans House for treatment might have realised that she was not to be seen on its return journey and act accordingly.

It had been a really busy day and Daniel was on the point of leaving the hospital when one of the men he was employing to work on the lighthouse appeared and asked if he could spare a moment. Hoping that it would be something minor, Daniel took him into his office and waited to hear what he had to say. Surprisingly, it wasn't about work.

'I might be fussing about nothing,' his unexpected visitor told him, 'but felt I had to tell you that the sister on the children's ward here must have been off duty today and came to view the progress of the lighthouse renovation.' As Daniel observed him in amazement he went on to say, 'We chatted for a few moments and then she wandered off in the direction of the manor house and the other empty properties not far away, and when the last tram of the day came and we all piled on it, I didn't notice that she wasn't there until it had reached the promenade, and I felt that I must mention it as the weather up there left a lot to be desired.'

'You felt right,' Daniel told him with a sick feeling inside. He was already on his feet, reaching for his top coat, and asked, 'So there wasn't anyone there who might have given Darcey a lift home by car at all?' The other man shook his head. 'No. Sometimes we get the occasional motorist curious to see what is going on but not today, and the rest of us use the tram all the time.'

'Thanks for taking the trouble to let me know,' Daniel told him, tense and tight-lipped at the thought of Darcey lost in the dark of a winter night. If she'd gone to view the manor house after him mentioning it, he would be to blame if Darcey was lost out there in the cold, he told himself grimly, and when he saw the whiteness of the newly painted lighthouse at the top of the cliffs he leapt from the car in the hope that for once the workmen might have left it unlocked to provide some sort of shelter, but all was in order, there was nothing to make one want to linger there.

With his anxiety peaking, he took a lantern out of the car boot and once it was lit headed swiftly towards what had once been a thriving small village and was now dark, still and unlived in, but not as empty as he'd thought it would be if Darcey was lost in there.

The rain had stopped and in what was now a clear sky the moon shone down onto the place where Darcey had been sheltering, cold and lost for what had seemed like a lifetime, and she was now about to leave for the long walk back to civilisation, until she heard a twig snap under someone's foot not far away. The door swung back slowly to reveal the one person she had longed to be with in the dark silence that lay all around her.

'Daniel!' she sobbed, as tears of relief ran down her cold cheeks. 'I was praying that the workman that I'd chatted with earlier had noticed that I wasn't on the tram!'

He was taking his warm winter coat off with all speed and wrapping it around her, and only when she was snugly inside it he said softly, 'Your prayer was answered, but only when he was back home and stopped off at the hospital to inform me of his concern about you. I have to say I was amazed as after our last misunderstanding I would have thought that the lighthouse and the manor house that I'd thought of buying would have been the last two places you would want to visit on a free afternoon in doubtful weather.

'Having seen it in this condition, I imagine that your doubts regarding it must have multiplied, but I need to get you back to the car where the heater is, and I've got a flask of coffee that I coaxed out of the hospital snack bar before I left.' Giving Darcey the lantern to hold, he swung her up into his arms and carried her carefully back to the car.

Once inside he kissed her gently and said, 'Don't ever scare me like that again, no matter what our disagreements are.' And out came the flask with the coffee, and the car heater was serving its purpose delightfully, but she wanted to weep because nothing had changed regarding their different points of view about the lifeboat but she loved him too much to ever contemplate life without him.

For his part, Daniel was overwhelmed with regret for not making it clear to Darcey that he had done as promised and asked that another coxswain should be found to replace him on the lifeboat.

If Cordelia knew he was on the point of finding true happiness with Darcey and was hesitating, she would think he was crazy, but so far no one had come forward and he didn't want her to think that she meant so little to him that he wasn't bothering.

When they reached the promenade and her apartment was in sight he said, 'I think you should come to my place for the night. It will be warm in there and I can make you a meal and be there in case you suffer any side-effects from your ordeal.' But she shook her head.

'No, thanks just the same,' she told him, and getting out of the car she took off his coat and passed it to him.

His patience faltered. 'Fine, suit yourself!' he said in clipped tones. 'You know where I am if you need me.' And he drove off into the night.

When he arrived home there was a message from Cordelia to say that she hadn't seen Darcey for a while and was she all right? So before settling down for what was left of the evening he returned the call and explained that he had just left her, having driven her home from getting lost in a strange place that she'd been exploring because she was due some free time from the hospital.

'What a shame that you weren't both off together!' she exclaimed, ever hopeful, and left him to the solitude that once had been enough and now was the last thing he needed.

There was a note on his desk in a sealed envelope from Darcey the next morning. Brief and to the point, it said that she wished to apologise for her lack of gratitude for his kindness in bringing her home safely after her foolishness in getting lost like she had, and it went on to explain that she wouldn't be around for the next few days as she was going to see her brother while she had the opportunity.

Daniel groaned when he'd read it. First, because he wanted her in his arms, not a brief message on paper, and, second, much as he understood Darcey's need to see her brother, his days were going to be long without her being near.

Cordelia was due in with Bethany for another X-ray during the morning, hopefully the last, and if all went well she would be able to go back to school after the weekend with the damage to her back having healed satisfactorily. If that was the case, her older sister was also going to be denied the wearing of her nurse's uniform at every opportunity, unless another small patient appeared from out of nowhere.

There had still been no further callouts for the lifeboat, which was unusual for the time of year, and Daniel was hoping that it would stay that way until a replacement was found to fill his position, and once that was sorted the way ahead should be clear if Darcey loved him as much as he loved her, but until his place was filled there was no way he could betray his father's trust.

If Cordelia knew the situation he was in, she would be sure to say that their father would understand and would want him to be happy, but he had no intention of bringing his sister into the confusion of his thoughts. When he had given Bethany a clean bill of health he sent mother and child happily on their way without mentioning his own problems.

He had never shirked a callout for the lifeboat. It was as natural as breathing to all of them to risk their lives, along with himself whose father's name was revered amongst sea folk and many others besides.

But knowing how Darcey had lost her parents and taken on the heartbreaking task of caring for her young brother for many years, he understood her fear of the fates taking him from her with the kind of loss she had endured, and he couldn't let her live with that sort of dread always present if she married him.

# CHAPTER NINE

WHEN THE TRAIN pulled into the station of her home town, Alex was waiting and Darcey's spirits lifted at the sight of him. He looked happy and relaxed and greeted her with a big smile of welcome.

As they walked the short distance to the small hotel where he had made her a reservation he had lots of questions to ask about Seahaven at the first opportunity.

That night, as the two of them sat in the hotel lounge after the evening meal, Alex said, 'I'm keen to see where you live and work, Darcey, in this place that is so near the sea, and I thought of visiting you over Easter, which isn't so far away. Would that be all right?'

'It would be lovely,' she said happily. 'Just as long as you wouldn't mind if I have to work the odd day or so if the ward is extra-busy. My place is very small and on hospital premises unfortunately, but I will find you somewhere nice to stay.'

'I don't mind where it is,' he said, 'and if some days you aren't around there will be plenty for me to explore in what sounds like a super place to live, with the sea top of the list.'

'Right,' she agreed, omitting to mention that it wasn't the top of her list at the moment, and told him, 'Let me know how long you want to come for and I'll make a booking for you somewhere. It will be just the two of us,' she said, happy at the thought of Alex for company when she was so miserable and lonely. She ached to have Daniel's arms around her, longed for him to find someone who would take his place on the lifeboat, but he hadn't mentioned it since their serious disagreement, which had to mean that he wasn't prepared to bend to her wishes.

But for the rest of the weekend she put those sorts of thoughts to the back of her mind, enjoying her time with Alex, and it wasn't until she was on the last train of the day in the dark night that was ending her short stay with Alex that Darcey allowed herself to think of the only man she would ever love. Amazingly, as if he'd read her mind Daniel was on the platform when she arrived back in Seahaven, his keen gaze scrutinising the faces of those for whom it was journey's end, and in seconds he was by her side, taking charge of her weekend case and smiling at her surprise.

'It's just a guess, my being here,' he told her. 'I was passing your apartment, saw that it was all in darkness, so decided to meet the last three trains of the day in case you were on one of them, as always at this hour the last tram has gone and taxis are in big demand.'

'Thank you for that,' she said awkwardly, as her hopes of good news about him having found a replacement for himself on the lifeboat didn't seem to be on his agenda, and she thought that it was as if she had asked him to do more than his love for her was capable of.

As they walked to where his car was parked he knew what she was thinking and could have explained that it wasn't for the want of trying. But so far no one had been found to replace him and, not having explained the situation to her in his first instance, he was torn between his love for her and his care for those whose lives were in peril.

When they reached her apartment and he was ready to drive off, Darcey didn't want him to go. She needed his arms around her, his kisses to set her on fire, yet didn't feel she could be as cruel as to ask those things of Daniel and not understand where his commitments had been before they'd met.

Yet she'd had responsibilities too, years of living with just Alexander in a much smaller house, and making sure that the love he had been denied by the deaths of their parents was always there, coming from her instead of them.

As she put her key in the lock he was ready to go and said briefly, 'Do I take it that you are back on the ward tomorrow?'

'Yes, you do, and I'm looking forward to it,' she said with a wry smile.

'I'll see you then,' he told her, and was gone.

'I don't remember thanking you for coming to meet me last night,' Darcey said the next morning on the ward. 'It was very kind.'

Kind! Daniel thought grimly, and fought back the

urge to tell her that it was longing that had brought him to meet her at close on midnight, and a need to see for himself that she was back safely from just the few days when she had been out of his sight.

He'd been hoping that she wouldn't ask if he'd found himself a replacement to leave him free of his commitment to the lifeboat and she hadn't, which in its way was worse than if she had as it made the huge obstacle that separated them seem even more insurmountable than ever.

But there were young ones needing him with hurt and aching bodies, just like his young niece had been, and with Darcey beside him Daniel went from bed to bed, doing what he did best, and wondering whether he would ever have a child of his own.

As she watched Daniel talk to his small patients, Darcey's heart melted with tenderness, but it didn't wipe away the fear of being left totally alone this time as Alex didn't need his big sister any more, and she could tell just how reluctant Daniel was to leave the crew of the lifeboat, especially with the memorial to his father about to be revealed. In fact, she doubted whether he had even mentioned a replacement to anyone, and why should he if sea rescue meant more to him than she did?

When they'd finished the ward round and he had gone to the next group of patients needing his orthopaedic skills, Darcey looked around her and pondered if staying the course was the lesser of two hurts or not, or would it be better to make a clean break away from the situation in which she found herself. But what then?

Live the rest of her life in a cocoon of sadness away from the man she loved because she wanted him for herself, instead of having to share him with an assortment of risk-takers who thought they had the perilous sea under control and found they didn't?

At that moment a hospital porter appeared with a little girl called Bonnie, who had just been admitted, and all other thoughts were shelved in the needs of their newest patient.

Having had no time for food shopping since her late return from her weekend with Alex, Darcey went to the nearest of the promenade restaurants at the end of her working day, expecting nothing more than some hot food and a chance to unwind after the usual stresses of the ward, but found Brendan Stokes back in the area after a secondment at a hospital similar to Oceans House.

He was seated at a table for two, and pointing to the empty place opposite asked, 'Not with the boss or anybody, are you?' And Darcey thought grimly that he hadn't lost his unique brand of charm.

'No,' she told him. 'I'm going to get a sandwich from the restaurant's take-away counter as I intend to have an early night.' Without giving him the chance to comment further, she pointed herself in that direction and said goodbye to eating somewhere warm and cheerful.

Back inside her small residence, with the dark night closing in, she found a printed poster on the mat, announcing that the reopening and dedication of the lighthouse in memory of Daniel's father was to be on the coming Saturday, and on a slip of paper attached he had written:

> *I don't expect you to be there for various reasons, Darcey. One being your nasty experience not long ago when you were lost in that area, and another your aversion to all matters of this kind, but it would help to know that you are there in spirit on Saturday.*
> Love, Daniel

She would be there in more than just spirit, she thought tearfully. Her dread of more loneliness wasn't Daniel's fault, and as it seemed he wasn't prepared to pursue her plea of retiring from his position on the lifeboat, the future was going to be an empty thing no matter what.

The next morning when they were about to start the usual ward rounds she said to Daniel, 'I will be thinking of you on Saturday. Your father must have been a very special man, from what you say. What of your mother when she was alive, how did she cope with the constant fear of losing him?'

'With difficulty, like any other woman who loves a man who cares about the lives of others,' he said sombrely, and went on to say, 'I called to see Cordelia and Lawrence last night to inform them about Saturday's event before it became common knowledge, and she was so happy to know that our father is never going to be forgotten in this place and many others.' Then, as if he felt he had said enough on the subject, Daniel indicated the occupant of the nearest small bed in the ward and said, 'Shall we proceed?'

It was Saturday and a chill wind had not kept those who had known and respected Mark Osbourne from making the journey to the clifftop to pay their respects to the memory of a brave and fearless man.

Daniel searched the crowd for a sight of Darcey but had no luck, until the latest tram-load of spectators arrived and she was the first person to alight amongst them, which gladdened his heart, knowing that at least she understood his feelings regarding the lifeboat.

But when the service was over and he looked for her in vain amongst the crowd again, it became obvious that she had left, that nothing had changed between them. His sister came up to him and said, 'I thought I saw Darcey. Has she gone?'

'It would appear so,' he replied, and as Cordelia glanced at him questioningly he explained, 'We have a problem, the two of us. I've asked her to marry me, but she is too aware of the perils of the lifeboat to say yes, for a very good reason. Darcey lost her parents in disastrous circumstances when she was in her early teens and had to bring up her young brother on her own, so now she dreads having to do the same with any children we might have, if the same happened to me as it did to Dad.'

'That is so sad for both of you!' Cordelia exclaimed. 'A chance of happiness away from old sorrows being blighted by your pasts.'

'I'm waiting to see if the powers that be can produce someone suitable to take over from me on the lifeboat,' he said, 'but so far there's no news from those quarters, and in the meantime the two of us are keeping a low profile regarding our love life, such as it is, so I'd be obliged if you would say nothing to anyone about it for the time being, Cordelia.'

Back at the apartment, after her brief appearance at the dedication ceremony, Darcey was wishing that she hadn't been in such a hurry to leave the proceedings. But the occasion had been more than she could bear, with the reason for it such a close reminder of her dread of loss and loneliness, and with those thoughts still uppermost there was the rest of Saturday to face on her own.

As she was digesting that thought the doorbell rang and when she opened it, Daniel said gravely, 'Thanks for attending the dedication ceremony, Darcey. I can imagine what an ordeal it must have been, and have come to take you for a meal if you are agreeable, leaving our differences and despair to disappear for a while.'

She smiled. 'I would like that very much.'

'So get your coat and off we go to the place that you liked so much the first time, if I remember rightly,' he commented, and thought they were acting as if there wasn't a cloud in their sky when in truth it was full of them.

He left his car in the hospital car park and as they

walked the short distance to the restaurant he said, 'Cordelia was asking after you. She was disappointed not to have had the chance for a chat.'

'Yes, I know,' Darcey said regretfully. 'That was my fault entirely. I'll get in touch during the week.'

Changing the subject, he said, 'Easter will soon be upon us. Have you made any plans so far, or are you on duty on the ward? Only we never did go out for a sail with the Young Sailors' Club after the Christmas mix-up of your working hours, did we? Or are references to such matters taboo?'

'No, of course not,' she told him, so aware of his nearness she wanted to reach out and hold him close. But she hadn't forgotten the time when she'd thrust him away as he'd taken the call from the lifeboat house to say he was needed and spoiled their wonderful moment of desire. Everything had changed since then and she knew he was trying to avoid any further upsets between them.

The restaurant was busy but a table was found for them and as they waited to be served, various people who had been at the lighthouse dedication service in the afternoon stopped by to say how appropriate a gesture it had been in memory of such a man, and when they had gone she said chokingly, 'You must be very proud of your father.'

'Yes, I am,' he agreed unsmilingly, 'but I'm not looking for any of that sort of thing for myself.' And when the food arrived at the table just then, he made no further comment and neither did she, but both were conscious of the moment that had come out of nowhere.

* * *

When the meal was over they walked slowly back to the apartment and on arriving Darcey said, 'Would you like to come in for a drink before you go?'

'Er…yes, that would be nice,' he said, aware of the message in the last three words of the invitation, but reluctant to miss the chance of spending more time with her. Inside her apartment, he couldn't help but glance through the open door of her bedroom as she hung up the winter coat that she'd been wearing, his gaze falling on the neat single bed that she slept in. With the thought of his luxurious double bed, which he so much wanted to share with her, and with the weight of the moment heavy upon him, he said, 'I think I'll give the drink a miss, if you don't mind. I've got a busy day in the operating theatre tomorrow.'

'Yes, of course,' she said flatly, and as he turned to go she added, 'The meal was lovely, Daniel. Thank you so much.'

'It was a pleasure, as is anything that we do together,' he replied, and with a brief goodbye quickly headed off into the night. When he'd returned to the silence of the empty rooms of his apartment he groaned inwardly, and once the door was locked he climbed the elegant staircase to the master bedroom and stood looking down at the bed that was so much more attractive than the neat, white-sheeted, single one he'd observed in Darcey's bedroom, which was still making his blood warm.

Would he ever have the joy of carrying her up here as his bride? he thought. There was a determination in her that came from her fear of loss and loneliness that he understood and wished he didn't, and with regard to finding another coxswain to replace him on the lifeboat, it was proving to be much harder than he had thought it would be, but there was no way he would ever leave the crew short in number. He had expected to have heard from the authorities before now with regard to his request for someone to replace him as when it eventually occurred it would leave him free to marry Darcey, which he longed to do, but there would always be the feeling of loss in his life that came from a lack of contact with the restless sea.

The last thing he did before settling for the night was to check whether her light was still on, and when he saw that the apartment was in darkness Daniel visualised her sleeping alone in the small white bed and his heart ached at the thought of the hurt he was causing her by wanting to hang onto his grim resolve.

For a long time Darcey had lain awake, wondering what would happen next, and how long they were going to continue the cat and mouse charade that they were playing out. With those thoughts running around her head, sleep had eluded her until at last she'd slept fitfully, though not for long, as the strident sound of her bedside alarm clock had soon brought her back to reality and the agenda of the day ahead.

With morning came a hint of spring. A pale sun shone in a cloudless sky and the sea was the calmest Darcey had seen since coming to Seahaven. Soon it would be Easter and Alexander would be here, she thought, and when he met him, Daniel would realise how special he was to her, the young brother that she had cared for, and maybe would understand how now she wanted children of her own with him, Daniel, as their father, but needed to know that he wouldn't be placing his life at risk.

It was Sunday and sometimes she was on duty on the children's ward, but not today. With that first glimpse of spring from the pale sun above she had the urge to be out and about, and as she was debating how and where, in the middle of the morning Cordelia rang to invite her to lunch if she was free.

'Yes, I am,' Darcey said. 'I would love to come. I owe you an apology for not seeking you out after the ceremony, Cordelia.'

'You don't owe me anything,' came the reply. 'The girls are looking forward to seeing you and so are Lawrence and I…and Daniel would be too if he knew you are joining us. But he has that pleasure to come when he arrives to have lunch with us, which is usually after his Sunday morning with the young sailors.' Into the silence that followed, Cordelia commented, 'But today he will be showing a possible applicant for his position on the lifeboat what sort of a set-up we have with our rescue facilities.'

'Yes, I see,' Darcey said, as light dawned that Daniel had been keeping to his side of the agreement that she'd demanded of him so forcibly, and now might be free of his commitment to the lifeboat service.

'I'm not so sure it will be as easy as that,' she told her flatly. 'The two of us aren't in agreement about the future because my past was a joyless thing once I lost my parents, with my young brother to care for and a living to earn, and if anything should happen to Daniel while on the lifeboat, I would be lost for evermore.'

'I understand how you feel as I worry too, but I should also say that it is rarely that a life or lives are lost under those conditions,' Cordelia said gently. 'However, obviously there is an element of risk that has to be accepted in the process, and if he does have to stay on the lifeboat crew, it will be for you to decide how much of that you can cope with on a long-term basis.'

'I've known that from the start,' she told her friend. 'I carry the thought around with me all the time, which is why I asked Daniel to be free of the perils of the lifeboat service when we marry, and he has agreed. But I am conscious of the strong ties he had with your father with regard to saving the lives of others as if what he does at Oceans House isn't enough.'

'Yes, maybe,' Cordelia agreed, 'but don't stay away from having lunch with us, Darcey. He will be disappointed to have missed you if you do.'

But not so upset that he had told her what he was going to be involved with during the morning, she thought tearfully. Yet she treasured her friendship with his sister, didn't want to upset her, and so she said, 'No, of course not. It will be lovely to see you all.'

When Daniel arrived at his sister's house just before lunchtime, he found Darcey swathed in bandages with the small would-be nurses in attendance. Laughter replaced the morning's traumas momentarily, but having spent most of it reluctantly showing another coxswain around his boat, with the thought of what it might mean in the long run, his amusement was short-lived.

'I called at your place earlier to let you know what I was going to be involved in during the morning, but there was no answer. Where were you?' he questioned.

'The spring sunshine had tempted me out and I'd gone for a stroll along the promenade,' she told him. 'When I got back Cordelia phoned and invited me to have lunch with you all.'

'So you already know where I've been?'

'Well, yes. Why didn't you tell me before?'

'Because I only got the message that this guy was coming a couple of hours before he was due.'

'And?' she breathed.

'He liked everything, except the fact that it would mean him having to move house, and he wasn't prepared to accept that.'

'And he's the only one?'

'Well, yes, of course! Do you think I've been holding them back to suit my own ends, Darcey? The answer to that is I am deeply committed to what I do now regarding the lifeboat service, but as there are very good reasons why I don't want to cause you pain or hurt I shall leave the service when the right moment presents itself. But under the current circumstances I think we should let things cool down for a while, don't you?'

'Whatever you say,' she said raggedly, and if Cordelia hadn't appeared at that moment to say that lunch was ready, she would have made her apologies and left after being made to feel so unwanted. But she cared for her friend too much to spoil the occasion and chatted mostly to the children while Daniel and Lawrence discussed sport and their hostess smiled at them all, unaware of the tense conversation earlier that had taken place between their guests.

As the sunny afternoon changed to gathering dusk Darcey explained to her friend that Alex was due to phone in the early evening regarding him visiting Seahaven in the near future, and said her farewells, but as she prepared to walk the short distance home, Daniel said, 'I'll take you in the car. It isn't a good time to be out on your own, before the streetlamps come on.'

'I'll be fine,' she said quietly, and for his ears alone added, 'I thought we were going to have a cooling-off time?'

'Yes, we are,' he agreed. 'But not at this moment.' He called to his sister, who had gone to fetch Darcey's coat from the cloakroom, 'I'm taking Darcey home and will be back shortly.'

Cordelia nodded with the thought in mind that she had longed for him to find someone to love and cherish and prayed that Darcey would be the one, but there were bridges to cross and long-ago hurts had to heal for both of them first. Only then would it come right.

# CHAPTER TEN

No words passed between them until Daniel stopped the car outside the apartment and then he broke the silence to say, 'Give my regards to your brother, Darcey. Why don't you suggest to him that he come to live here? He could join the Young Sailors' Club.'

She smiled for the first time since they'd left his sister's house and told him, 'He is already having yearnings. Maybe his visit here over Easter will help him make that decision. But it would mean going to a different university in September.'

'Yes, of course,' he said thoughtfully as she bade him a brief goodbye, and as he drove back to his sister's house it seemed strange that he, Daniel, should have the kind of family that Darcey and her brother had never had due to losing their parents, and it had to be why she so longed for a marriage that was free of worry and loneliness.

If he could give her that there would be joy in the giving of it, but the gift of life that he had given to so many caught in the ocean's grip would have to be passed on to someone else and he was going to miss that.

But first a new coxswain had to be found, and until that was done there was going to be no change in the situation in which he found himself, and added to that Easter was drawing near, with lots of would-be sailors on the seas around Seahaven, thinking they had the upper hand and coming unstuck. Maybe the fates would be good and give him one last time to copy his father if his replacement still had to be found. But no way did he want anything that he might be called on to do to cause Darcey hurt or sorrow.

With regard to his love for Darcey, he had wanted her from the moment of their meeting, had known that she was the answer to years of emptiness after a dead marriage, and when she'd responded to his feelings with similar delight it had been fantastic, until her memories of the past and his involvement with the lifeboat had taken away the joy of their romance.

Back in the solitude of her apartment, Darcey was on the phone to Alex confirming the date of his Easter visit, which was going to commence in three weeks' time on the day before Good Friday until the middle of the following week, when he was planning to fly out to Bangkok to continue his travels.

'I'm really looking forward to being near the sea,' he said. 'There is a lake near here where some of us spend all our free time between shifts and it's great, but is nothing compared to the sea. I can't wait to see it. How often do you go sailing?'

'Never have so far,' she told him flatly, with the memory of the times that Daniel had wanted her to join him and the crew from the Young Sailors' Club and been unsuccessful. 'Maybe you'll be able to show me how.'

'Sure, it's easy-peasy,' he promised, and when the call was over and the usual silence fell over the apartment, the thought was there that the safest place where Alex could sail would be as a member of the Young Sailors' Club under Daniel's guidance, instead of wherever with an overdose of confidence.

The next morning Easter seemed far away. Mondays were always busy after the weekend when young members of the population had been out and about and been less than careful during their weekend activities, which had brought them to Oceans House.

As Darcey and Daniel did the rounds of the children's ward there was little time for any other matters than the health of their young patients, and it wasn't until he was done and ready to move upwards to where the older folk awaited him that he asked, 'Are you all right after yesterday's twists and turns?'

'Yes, I suppose so,' she said. 'I ask too much of you and I'm sorry, Daniel.'

'Don't be,' he chided gently. 'Just be yourself.' Then he was gone, leaving her to question what his real feelings were.

The days were getting longer and lighter. The sun no longer preferred to hide behind cloud so much, but still there was no one to replace him, Daniel thought.

It was a situation that the rest of the lifeboat crew were totally happy with, and probably also with those who trained and staffed the boats, from the look of things, as no changes of crew were being considered, which left only Darcey with any reservations regarding the situation. He braced himself for the day that had to come sooner or later, but which was a long time in coming.

At last on the following Sunday morning Daniel took Darcey sailing in the boat that had been a wreck the first time she'd seen it, and was now back to its normal performance with a full crew of trainee mariners on board, along with themselves and Ely, and she thought that Alex, when he came in two weeks' time, would enjoy this sort of thing, with others of a similar age. They sailed closer to home than the lifeboat due to their youth, but were just as welcome when needed.

When they arrived back at their headquarters next to the harbour, Bridget provided lunch, after which the group would hold their weekly meeting with Daniel in charge. Darcey was aware of how much the young folk owed him for the time and patience he had for them, which was bettered only by his devotion to saving the lives of those who might lose them without him and others like him.

He was watching her expression and as their eyes met it was there again, the feeling of rightness that was all wrong when she tried to be sensible. On that thought she thanked him for taking her out in the sailing club's boat and went back to what was left of another free Sunday, which was an event, and would have to be made up for soon.

Daniel stared after her, wishing that she hadn't been in such a hurry so that he could have taken her somewhere after the meeting for a few moments on their own. But maybe Darcey wanted to avoid that sort of thing with their relationship up in the air and each of them having their own kind of longings.

In the days that followed, Darcey marked each one on the calendar as Easter drew nearer and with it Alex's arrival in Seahaven, and always was the thought that just for once she would have someone of her own to be with for a short time of togetherness, as her love for Daniel had become a cloistered thing due to the circumstances of it, but the need was still there.

Her brother's arrival was due to take place at midday on Thursday, and Darcey thought glumly that she wasn't going to be around to meet him until the evening as she was on duty for most of that day. So much for the two Sundays of free time that she'd just had. But it didn't seem to worry Alex much when she phoned to tell him.

'No problem,' he said airily when she told him. 'Once I've taken my gear to the place where you've booked me to stay I'll find plenty to do. Just looking at the sea will be great. I'll be waiting for you outside the hospital when you come out in the evening, and then we'll live it up, eh, sis?'

'Er…yes,' she said laughingly. 'Am I going to be allowed time to change out of my uniform?'

'Sure,' was the reply.

She hadn't seen much of Daniel socially since he'd taken her sailing with the young people in their boat. It was as if he was avoiding her but he'd also mentioned he was looking forward to meeting her brother, or so he'd said, which she supposed was better than nothing, and perhaps she could take the two of them out to dinner one night.

'Yes, maybe,' he agreed when she suggested it, with the thought in his mind that chance might be a fine thing if the lifeboat was called out as often as it usually was at such times.

At the end of her working day on the Thursday there was no Alex waiting to greet her, and as her apartment was only feet away Darcey hurried home, but he wasn't waiting there either, and when she tried to phone him there was no answer.

Yet she knew that he had arrived safely that afternoon because he'd rung her to say that he'd settled himself into the small flatlet on the seafront that she'd found for him and was going to spend the rest of the afternoon down by the sea until she'd finished work, so where was he?

Hopefully it was just bad timing and she walked on to the seafront and looked around her from there. She saw a crowd gathered to watch something that was causing much interest and her heart skipped a beat. The lifeboat had been called out and was speeding in the direction of the far end of the bay in what was one of the roughest seas for some time. She could just see the form of a young guy at the mercy of a rough sea, being swept up against rocks and then thrown back into the water helpless against its force, and she froze with fear.

The lifeboat had just reached him and she saw Daniel and another of the crew go over the side with lifebelts. They pulled the seemingly lifeless body out of the water and she just knew it was Alex who was going to be taken from her this time as anguish turned her bones to chalk.

But they had him, one on each side, before the next onslaught of the sea came back upon them, and as Daniel and the crew worked on their charge, the lifeboat ploughed its way back to safety amid cheers from those who had watched, while Darcey ran frantically to where it had been launched to await its return.

Bridget was there and on seeing her said, 'They've radioed from the boat that he's unconscious. Don't know who the lad is, but he can't have a better chance than with our team. They'll be here any moment and he will be taken straight to Oceans House where Daniel will examine him, and if he needs further treatment he'll be taken to the hospital in the town centre.'

'He's my brother,' she said chokingly, 'and is all I have in the world. But in just a matter of moments it doesn't feel like that any more.'

'It's here, the boat. You'll be able to see him in a moment and go with him to hospital,' Bridget said consolingly. 'There's an ambulance waiting to take him to Oceans House with Daniel on board, which is the usual procedure on this sort of occasion, and if you ask he'll take you with him.'

Darcey didn't hear her last comment. Her fears were confirmed as she watched the crew stretchering Alex off the boat with Daniel supervising, and when he saw her he said raggedly, 'When I saw him close to I was horrified. I couldn't believe it, you are so alike, and I knew that he was coming to stay.'

'Is he going to live, Daniel?' she croaked, as she looked down at her brother's still form.

'Yes, if it is anything to do with me,' he gritted. 'He's breathing more levelly now and I've given you enough worry and heartache. Hopefully there won't be any more once we get Alex to Oceans House.' He nodded at a signal from the ambulance driver. 'In you get. It will be just a matter of minutes before we're on home ground.'

At that moment Alex opened his eyes for a fleeting second and mumbled, 'What have I done, Darcey?'

'Fought the spring tide and lost,' she told him, 'and Dr Osbourne and I are taking you to Oceans House to be sorted out.'

'Sounds good,' was his only comment before he drifted back into semi-consciousness.

Daniel said, 'We need to go straight into X-Ray when we arrive and deal with it from there. I am so sorry this has happened to your brother, Darcey. It must have heightened your fear of lifeboats even more.'

She managed a smile. 'That isn't so, Daniel. It has made me realise how fortunate are they who are served by the lifeboat in their hour of need. I'd got it all wrong, and I don't want you to change anything regarding what you do. Without you and your team out there, Alex would have died.'

The ambulance was pulling into its parking space at Oceans House and as her young brother was carried carefully inside and straight to X-Ray, with Daniel and herself in attendance, Alex regained consciousness again and said, 'I was playing a game, dodging the big waves when they came, but they got too fast for me, and now am I going to have to spend Easter in hospital?'

'It all depends on how much you have hurt yourself,' Daniel told him. 'The X-rays are going to tell us that, and in future remember that the sea isn't always a friend, far from it.'

The results they were waiting for after a session in X-Ray were a mixture of good and not so good, as Darcey observed them issuing forth in the form of a fractured arm and massive bodily bruising in most areas. But both she and Daniel were aware that it could have been much worse, and when Alex asked what it all meant he listened in silence to what they had to say and then asked again if it was going to mean him being kept in the hospital for a while and couldn't he stay with Darcey until he was well again?

'Her accommodation isn't big enough for someone else to stay with her,' Daniel told him, 'neither would it be allowed, and it would not be wise for you to continue staying alone in your flat on the promenade until you are well again, but I do have a suggestion.

'How would you like to come and stay with me?

I have a spare bedroom, so would be able to keep an eye on you during the night, and bring you with me for the day each morning where you could get better by resting and watching your sister and myself performing our daily tasks.'

'Wow!' Alex said weakly. 'That would be great!' His gaze went to Darcey, who had stood by speechless as Daniel got to know his prospective young brother-in-law. 'What about that, sis?'

'Yes, what about it,' she replied, smiling through her tears, and she turned to Daniel. 'He can stay here tonight while we sort out our arrangements for the future, don't you think?' she asked him.

'Absolutely,' he said. 'But first let's get that arm set and put in a cast.'

Once that had been accomplished, Alex was taken to the men's ward and Daniel and Darcey made sure that he was safely settled with all details of his injuries given to staff for that night.

Then they left him in hospital care with an arrangement that they would call back soon, and went to Daniel's apartment where he showed her the guest room that would be occupied by her brother for as long as he needed it, and then took her into the main bedroom. As Darcey gazed at the empty bed he said gently, 'There has always been a place for you beside me, still is for that matter, but the ideal time for a beginning would be on our wedding night in the manor house, don't you think, with the vows we have made like stars in a cloudless sky. Will you marry me, Darcey?'

'Yes,' she said. 'I understand everything better now. As I watched you save Alex's life it was as if a blindfold had been removed from my eyes.'

'So where do you want to live when we become as one?' he said gently, and was surprised at the reply when it came.

'In the manor house near where you have preserved your father's memory for all time,' she said softly, and he observed her in amazement.

'You want to live in the place where you spent hours in the dark and the cold!'

'Yes, I'm afraid so,' she said with a smile, 'because it brought you to me, and we can make it lovely, Daniel. Also maybe sometime Cordelia and Lawrence might decide to join us in one of the other houses, or Alex could be a regular visitor once it has been brought to life again. We can make it beautiful and once we are settled there we can turn the rest of the village into a place that our children and those of others will love to live in.'

'Either of those things would be fantastic,' he said gently, holding her close, 'but first I want you to myself for a while. So before we go back to check on our young patient, can we fix on a date for a wedding and decide which local firm is going to be given the task of transforming our future habitation?'

'Yes, please,' she said, starry-eyed, and he kissed her long and lingeringly before they retraced their steps to Oceans House to check on Alexander, who was now sleeping after his frightening experience of earlier.

# EPILOGUE

IT WAS CHRISTMAS again in Seahaven and snow was gently falling as an event was taking place not far from the refurbished lighthouse and the now elegant manor house, where a twinkling Christmas tree was already in place to welcome the bride and groom, who would be returning for a wedding breakfast, along with their friends and relations after the ceremony in the village church.

Cordelia, the bridegroom's sister, was hostess for the event and delighted to be so, while her husband Lawrence was to give the bride away, and Alex, on top form, was greeting friends and neighbours as they arrived for the service in the small church, which was decorated with holly and ivy for Christmas and which hadn't seen a wedding in a long time. When Daniel heard the music change to welcome the bride he turned slowly and she was there with her eyes sparkling and mouth tender, his beautiful Christmas bride in a long white gown carrying a bouquet of red roses, and his heart sang with joy.

* * * * *

# SECOND CHANCE WITH HER ARMY DOC

DIANNE DRAKE

**MILLS & BOON**

To soldiers all around the world who came home only to find the greater battle was still ahead of them. And to Bill, who lost the battle.

# PROLOGUE

*THE SAND BETWEEN her toes tickled, and the moon was so bright it was as if someone had hung it on the beach just for them.*

*Carter always had these romantic ideas—seeing the vineyards of Napa Valley from a hot air balloon; a resort spa weekend when they'd have grapeseed massages and sip champagne in a hot mineral spring tub on their private patio, separating their world from everything else; joining in a celebration of light with a Chinese lantern inscribed with their names, sent into the nighttime sky along with hundreds of others.*

*And tonight, dancing on the beach in the moonlight. Feeling the gentle lapping of the water on their ankles as the tide trickled in. Seeing the far-off harbor lights twinkle against the black sky. Listening to the night birds searching for their evening meal.*

*"Are you chilly?" Carter asked.*

*"No, I'm fine," Sloane replied, snuggling even closer into his arms.*

*She was always fine when he held her like this. In his arms—that was where she was meant to be.*

*"Maybe we should leave?"*

Maybe they should, but she didn't want to. Not yet.

These opportunities with Carter were scarce, due to conflicting work schedules, and she wanted every scrap of every minute right where she was, before they had to go back.

*"Or, maybe we should stay,"* she countered, her body rocking so sensuously against his she knew that even when they got to their room the night would be far from over. *"Just for another few minutes."*

Carter chuckled as he pushed the wild copper hair from her face, then bent to kiss her on the neck. *"Are you sure?"* he whispered, just above a kiss.

The goosebumps started immediately. They always did with Carter. And she shivered...

*"See... I knew you were chilly."* He gave her another kiss in the same spot, leaving a trail of butterfly kisses along her neck, ending at her jaw. *"But I know where it's warm..."*

In his arms. Anywhere. Anytime.

*"Maybe we should go back,"* she whispered, a little sad that their dance had ended.

She loved Carter's spontaneity—loved the way he would simply push everything aside just to spend what little time they could together.

Last weekend a climb in the canyons. Before that scuba diving. Restaurants. Vineyards and wine-tasting. Bicycling at dusk on a coastal boardwalk, then stopping for coffee and watching the sunset.

Their moments together were so few, and yet when they did find those moments nobody else in the world existed. It was just the two of them, making the most of what they had.

"It's warm right here in your arms," said Sloane, her voice breathy with desire. She didn't want to change a moment of this, but she also didn't want to change a moment of what Carter had planned for the evening. "So one more dance, please?"

"One more," he said, then bent to her ear. "Then it's my turn to dance my way."

More goosebumps. Another shiver.

"Maybe we should save the dance on the beach for another time and go see what your dance is about."

"You know what my dance is about," he said as he scooped her up into his arms. "It's the dance that's as old as time."

She loved it when he carried her. While she wasn't particularly large, he was all muscle. Built ruggedly. Built just to fit her.

"Will there be wine?" she asked.

"If that's what you want."

There would also be white rose petals and candles, and strawberries dipped in chocolate. The reason she knew this was that she'd peeked at the bill. She hadn't meant to, but he'd left it on the dresser when he'd gone out for ice, and she hadn't been able to help herself.

Carter was always full of so many surprises—all of them for her, even if she did cheat a little in her excitement to find out. But he always made her feel like Christmas—the anticipation, the build-up of excitement, the dreaming of what he would do next.

Yes, even on the few instances she'd taken a peek,

*like she just had, and like she'd done when she was a little girl. Only then her dad had hidden packages of dolls and games and princess crowns, where Carter hid the little romantic things that caused her heart to beat faster—coupon books redeemable any time for kisses, hugs, making love...poems he'd written—not always good but definitely from his heart—and selfies of the two of them he'd had blown up and framed. There were at least three dozen of them on the hall wall leading to their bedroom.*

*But tonight there would be no selfies for what he had in store. Or maybe just one, with the two of them cuddled in the sheets. Yes, that would be nice—if she remembered. Because Carter had a way of making her forget everything but the moment.*

*"Are you going to be a brute and kick the door in?" she asked as they approached their room, she still in his arms.*

*"Oh, I'm going to be a brute—but it has nothing to do with the door."*

*Of course he wasn't going to be a brute. He was gentle in every way a man could be gentle, and as he lowered her to the bed and she held out her arms to him...*

Sloane gasped, and bolted up in bed. Tears were streaming down her cheeks. She was actually crying in her sleep for him. For them. And tonight had been no different from when she'd had the same dream before. Night after night of it, then week after week, in one version or another.

Sometimes they'd make it to their room; sometimes they'd never even get off the beach. But there was never an ending—just the way she and Carter hadn't had a real ending.

Six years together and all she had left of him was a small jar of shrapnel from his injuries.

Dr. Sloane Manning swiped back angry tears, painful tears, then reached for her phone and punched in a number. "Yes," she said, when the party on the other end answered. "I'd like to make a reservation for one."

*One.* She almost choked on the word. She was going alone to a place she and Carter had always planned to explore together when they had the time. Well, *she* had the time, and most of that time was about to be invested in moving on.

"I'll be in sometime tomorrow. Best room you've got, please." Next came her credit card number, then she was set. Maybe a good hike in the desert and some nice, hard rock-climbing would snap her out of her funk.

Or maybe it wouldn't. In any case, she was going once she'd cleared her schedule with her dad, who would make sure she was covered for the next few days. Or weeks. Either one. Because right now the last thing on her mind was surgery—which wasn't the best situation for her patients. They deserved all of her, and she wasn't even sure that if she was put back together she'd all be all there. So maybe going out and trying to find some of those missing pieces of herself was exactly what she needed. Because she couldn't go on like this: not with the dreams, the tears, the broken heart…

# CHAPTER ONE

"So, AFTER YOU left Sloane, then what?" Matt McClain asked his old Army buddy Carter Holmes.

Carter cringed at the memory of how he'd left her. With a text.

Sorry, I can't do this any longer. I've got to go find myself on my own.

Sloane Manning had done everything in her power to help him. She'd come to Germany for his surgeries and stayed at his bedside for days, until he was well enough to be shipped home. Then, at home, she'd put aside practically every aspect of her own life just to help him through.

She'd found different treatment options for PTSD, and she'd stood by him when her father had hired him back at Manning Hospital, even though he clearly hadn't been ready for the stress. And she'd stood by him again when her father had suspended him for any number of the little infractions he'd incurred in his first six months back.

He'd done nothing to jeopardize a patient. Quite the opposite. He'd done everything to jeopardize his career. Insubordination. Tardiness. Bad attitude all along.

"I found a program that seemed like it might work for me. Sloane's idea was something more traditional—like seeing a counselor or group therapy. But, that's not me. So, I looked for something else."

"And…?" Matt asked.

"I completed the first part. Did pretty well, all things considered. And my counselor there said there was excellent hope for my future. So now they've put me on a waiting list for the next part of the program, and with any luck I'll be called within the next couple of months. They give you a little time off between parts one and two, to make sure part one has taken. So…that's why I'm here, asking for a job. I need to keep myself busy until I go back to Tennessee. I need to keep my mind on the things I can control, and not on the things I can't."

"Sounds like it's working," Matt said.

"It is. It's a slow process, but little by little it's helping me define who I am again."

He and Matt had been trapped in a cave in Afghanistan when, for whatever reason, he'd snapped. Left the cave and run head-first into gunfire. He'd got hit pretty hard. Lost a kidney and a spleen as a result. Damaged his other kidney as well. Matt had risked his life to leave the relative safety of that cave to save him.

"It's a bear rescue facility. I'll work with bear cubs—rescue them if they're abandoned or injured, take care of them and, if they're able to return to the wild, get them prepared to do that. That's the hands-on part of the program. The first part was doing pretty much the same thing for myself—retraining for life in the world again. Making sure I have what it will take to work with the bears later on. It's an amazing program. Gives you a different kind of responsibility and helps you find yourself *inside* that responsibility."

Matt whistled. "Bears... I would have never guessed."

"Just the little black bear variety. Not ready to tackle the grizzlies yet." Carter chuckled. "And I'm the one who never even had a dog."

"Well, it seems to be agreeing with you."

"I hope it is," Carter said in all seriousness. "I can't live my life never knowing when something's going to trigger me. It's hell. It's also why I had to leave Sloane. She was always there, ready to help me. Maybe too much. Plus, I was breaking her heart."

Carter looked over Matt's shoulder, out the roadhouse window to the vast expanse of desert beyond them. So big, so empty. So—lonely. That was how *he'd* felt most of the time. Especially in the early days. Now, while he still wasn't better, he could see clearly enough to make distinctions about the reality of his situation. It wasn't great, but with another year or so in therapy it would improve. That was what he was aiming for, anyway.

"Anyway, I'm hoping that you can give me something to do for a while."

They were sitting in a corner booth at the Forgeburn Roadhouse, Matt drinking a beer, Carter drinking fizzy water. Booze had become a real problem in the last year. So had drugs. And while that was part of his past now, since falling off the wagon meant getting kicked out of the program, there'd been a few times he'd come close. But so far he hadn't indulged in those things since he'd left Sloane.

What was the point? Getting drunk only drove him deeper into depression. And getting high, while it may have caused him to forget momentarily, always sent him crashing back to reality, usually feeling worse than he'd felt before. It was a horrible feeling, always knowing how close to the edge he was and afraid of what might push him over.

"I don't come with a lot of guarantees these days, but I'm still a damned good doctor. That's probably the only thing I can count on."

"It's what I'm counting on too, Carter."

"Anyway, if you still think I'm worth taking a chance on, I'm yours until I get the call from The Recovery Project. And, like I mentioned when I called you last week, if I graduate from the program and you want me back, I'll be here."

No, it wasn't general surgery. But he wasn't up to that yet. Too many things to go wrong. Too many lives depending on his wavy blade. But being a good old country doctor would keep him in the profession and, hopefully, keep him out of trouble.

"Do you really think you can make the transition from being a surgeon to being a GP?"

"There are a lot of things in my life I have to

change—including my attitude. And while in the long term I don't know how well I'll adjust to life outside the OR, in the short term I know I can't go back to that right now. Maybe never again. I don't know yet."

"You've come a long way," Matt said, tilting his mug back for the last sip of beer. "Last time I saw you, you were yelling at Sloane because you couldn't find your boots. It was pretty intense."

"She took a lot of abuse from me."

That was something he couldn't forgive in himself. He'd loved that woman more than life itself, but because she'd always been there she'd become the target for all his pent-up emotions. The anger would build up in him, and Sloane would be the one who took the impact of it.

"And it kept on getting worse."

"Any chance you two could get back together?"

Carter shook his head. "PTSD is a life sentence. I may learn how to cope with it, even divert it, but there's never going to be a time when it's not waiting just below the surface. I can't take the risk of hurting her more than I already have."

"But you feel confident you can take on the part of my practice we've discussed? Because I can't keep an eye on you all the time. Like I told you before, my practice is growing, and I have a family to take care of. You're like a brother to me, but I can't look over your shoulder every minute of every day. So I need to feel good about turning you loose on the tourists, because that whole part of my practice can be a problem. You won't be treating permanent patients but rather patients who are here for only a few days. You won't have medical histories on them, and you might run into pre-existing conditions that they haven't divulged to you. There'll be all kinds of obstacles in taking on the tourist segment of my practice, and everything's going to be up to you. I'll be around if you need me, but for the most part you'll be on your own. Can you manage that?"

Doctor to the tourists in the many resorts near Forgeburn, Utah. He'd never been a GP, so it was going to be a challenge. But since he never backed down from a challenge this would probably work for him. He hoped so. Because he was ready to turn his life around. This living from moment to moment was killing him.

"My counselors think I can, or they wouldn't have sent that recommendation to you."

"But what do *you* think, Carter?"

"That I'm going to try my damnedest. Like I've told you already, I can't predict anything—can't even make any solid promises. But I want this to work, Matt. For you, because I owe you my life. And for me, because I want some kind of life back. A lot of people with PTSD don't get the opportunity you're giving me, and I don't want to mess that up."

"And what about Sloane? I know you two aren't together now, but have you talked to her about any of this?"

"No. The less involvement she has with me, the better it is for her."

That was the half-truth he always used to convince himself he'd done the right thing in leaving her.

She'd taken care of him in the early days. Or tried, when he'd let her. She'd been patient and kind. But he'd given up. Backed away. He hadn't left her any choice other than to accept what he'd done—which was to leave.

"After she waited all those years for you, you're not going to try and get her back? Because, next to my Ellie, Sloane is probably the best woman I've ever known. I can't believe you can simply walk away from her the way you did and never look back."

"Oh, I look back—but all I can see are regrets. Mine. Hers. I can't go back, Matt. She deserves better than that. Better than me."

"And she's told you that?"

No, she had not. But it was what he'd known almost from his first day home.

"I was beating her down. You could see it in her. Day by day, piece by piece, I was taking everything she had away from her. I mean, she's a brilliant heart surgeon, and such a good person, but I was sucking the life out of her and I *hated* that. But for Sloane it was like the poet Poe said in his *Annabelle Lee*: 'And this maiden she lived with no other thought than to love and be loved by me.' That's all she wanted, Matt. To love me and have me love her back. But it wasn't in me anymore."

"Sorry to hear that."

"Me too—in more ways than I probably even know."

And in so many ways that he *did* know. Ways that kept him awake at night. Ways that reduced him to tears when his thoughts wouldn't be shut off.

"So, like I said, she's better off without me."

"And you? Are you better off without *her*?"

"It doesn't matter, as long as she's not part of my life anymore."

"What *is* your life, Carter? Other than the job I'm giving you here, what is your life?"

"Damned if I know. But when I figure it out, you'll be the first to know."

"That bad?" Matt asked.

"That bad," he said in earnest. "Hopefully getting better, though."

"Because of your bear rescue program?"

Carter smiled. "Because of what I hope I can do to make my little part of the program successful."

"Well, that's the attitude I'm looking for." Matt extended his hand across the table to Carter. "So, welcome to Forgeburn's only medical practice."

Carter took Matt's hand, wondering if this was too much, too soon. He was still on a high from the success he'd seen in the first part of his recovery program, but would that be enough to the job that needed to be done here?

For a while he'd ridden the crest of the self-confidence wave, but now he was underneath it. That was PTSD, though, wasn't it? Always trying to rob you of yourself. Always chipping away at the bits and pieces that seemed to be moving forward.

There was a time when his normal reaction would have been to say, *I've got this*. Now, though, he wasn't sure what he had—and that was what scared him.

Before PTSD, nothing ever had. Now, almost everything did.

But this was the opportunity he needed. So it was time to put one foot forward and hope he could stay there for a while.

"When do you want me to start?"

Sloane Manning looked at the text messages on her phone, then at her phone messages. Still nothing. She'd been trying to call Carter for weeks. At least once a day. Sometimes twice. Not that there was much to say at this point. But she was concerned. Six years of her life had gone into that man—most of it waiting while he was in the military—and it wasn't easy to detach herself from the life she'd expected to have by now.

After her father had dismissed Carter from his job at the hospital he'd disappeared. Hadn't packed anything to speak of. Hadn't said goodbye or even left a note other than a vague text message. The only thing that had told her Carter was gone was that their apartment—*her* apartment—seemed so hollow and cold now. She hated being there. Hated being by herself there. Because it was *their* home, not hers.

Which was why she was moving back in with her dad when she got back from this two-week vacation. She'd waited long enough for Carter to make a move. But after three months it was clear he wasn't going to do that. In fact she didn't even know where he was. He'd been in Vegas for a while, but after that…

So here she was at the airport, ready to board a plane to one of the places she and Carter had always talked about. She was ready to give herself some good, hard physical licks in the canyons and the desert. Ready to start over on her own.

"Dr. Sloane Manning," the attendant at the desk called over the loudspeaker. "Last call for Dr. Sloane Manning."

Hearing her name startled her out of her thoughts, and almost in a panic she grabbed up her carry-on bag and ran toward the check-in before the loading gate shut.

"Sorry about that," she said to the attendant. "I was…"

What? Daydreaming about a romance gone bad? Everybody had one, didn't they? So why would the gate attendant care about hers?

"I was preoccupied."

The gate attendant made it clear that she didn't care, and that all she wanted was to get Sloane on the plane and start focusing on the next group of passengers, already filing in to catch the next flight.

So, Sloane hustled herself through, took her seat in the third row of the first-class section, leaned her head back against the headrest and hoped people would assume her to be asleep and leave her alone. The way Carter had done the last few months of their relationship. She in one bedroom, he in the other. Barely talking when they met in the hall. Barely even acknowledging each other's existence unless it was absolutely necessary.

With her eyes shut she could visualize everything. The apathy. The temper. The outrage. But most of all the pain. She could still feel it burrowing in, winding its corkscrew tentacles around every fiber of her being.

"Still no luck?" Gemma Hastings, Sloane's surgical assistant, had asked, when she'd informed her people early that morning that she'd be gone for a couple of weeks.

"It's done," she'd told her. "I've hung on too long and too hard. It's time to get myself sorted and start moving in a new direction."

What that direction was, she didn't know. But if she didn't move in some other direction soon, she was afraid she might never move at all. Her friends, even her dad, had been telling her this was what she needed to do. So, after three months she was finally taking their advice. She was taking some *me time* to readjust.

As for loving Carter—tossing that away wouldn't be as easy as stepping onto a plane and hiding out for a while. Still, what was the point in worrying about him when he didn't worry about himself? Or worry about them?

That was the worst of it. He'd given up on *them*. And quite easily. But here she was, still hanging on. Why? Maybe her feelings for Carter were some sort of remnant, left over from the days when she'd first fallen in love with him, when he had been kind and good, and the best surgeon she'd ever seen. Maybe her love was nothing more than an old habit she didn't know how to break.

Because she still loved him?

That was the question she didn't want to answer,

because the answer might scare her. Falling in love with one man, then watching him turn into someone else she didn't even recognize had been tough. Trying to stay in love with the man he'd turned into had been even tougher, because there had still been parts of the Carter she'd known left and she'd been able to see them struggling to get out.

But she'd also been able to see Carter struggling to keep them locked away.

She thought about the day they'd met. She'd already heard about him from her father.

"He's supposed to be the best of the best," Harlan Manning had said. "Good at everything he does and full of adventure—which he says keeps him from getting dull."

"Will he fit in here?" she'd asked her dad. "We're a conservative little surgery in most regards. Everybody knows everybody else. There's never any in-fighting, the way I saw it going on during my residency in Boston."

Generally everybody got along, did their jobs, and walked away contented. But from the description of Carter Holmes she'd had some qualms, because he'd seemed so—*out there*. He liked big sports—skydiving, mountain-climbing, motorcycling. And he liked the ladies.

That was only his personal reputation—which she totally forgot when she first laid eyes on him. Carter was tall, muscular. Deep, penetrating gray eyes. Dark brown hair, short-cut in a messy, sticking-out style which looked *so* good on him. Three days' growth of dark stubble which had made her go weak in the knees, imagining what it would feel like on her skin. And that smile of his...

OMG, it could knock a girl off her feet, it was so sexy.

He'd put all that masculinity to good use, too, asking the hospital owner's daughter out after only knowing her for five minutes.

Of course she'd said yes. What else could she have done? She'd been smitten at first sight, sexually attracted at second, and in love at third. Well, maybe not real love. But that had come about pretty quickly when, after their first evening together, Carter never went home. Not the next day either, or the day after that. In fact by the third day he had totally moved in to her tiny apartment, making himself right at home as if he'd always been there.

"For what it's worth, Sloane, Carter was crazy about you," her assistant had said. "Everybody could see that. So maybe if he gets himself straightened out..."

"*If,*" she'd responded. "Not going to hold my breath on that one."

But she was. Every minute of every hour of every day. And it was causing her to be distracted in her operating room. Distraction and heart surgery didn't mix, and if it continued, she'd either have to step down from her position voluntarily, or her father—in his position as chief—would remove her. He didn't play favorites when it came to patient care, and she was included in that. So, her distraction could conceivably cost her her job. Which was why she had to get away to sort it out. And maybe Forgeburn, Utah, wasn't the hub of the universe, but it *was* beautiful, according to Matt McClain, an old friend.

She'd met him through Carter, and liked him right off. He lived in Forgeburn now, so why not visit? Maybe Matt would have a different insight into Carter than she did.

So, her goal was to sort it out, get over it, then get back to a life where she was in control of herself again—her life as it had been before Carter's PTSD. She'd had goals then: becoming the head of cardiac surgery at Manning, having a family, a beautiful life. Then PTSD had happened and everything had changed.

"Thank you, Carter Holmes," she whispered as the pilot announced it was time to prepare for landing. "Thank you for nothing."

Matt's clinic was a few miles away. He'd made that perfectly clear. Which was fine, because it was time for Carter to see if his own two feet would hold him up again.

For that he needed space—and Forgeburn, Utah, had plenty of that. He also needed to be successful here, because getting back to his recovery program was contingent upon that. If he succeeded here, he moved forward in the program. If he failed, he moved back to square one and started all over. If he was lucky.

Being kicked out of the program was a setback Carter didn't want. What was more, if he got sent back to the beginning, did he have enough left in him to fight his way through it again? He didn't trust himself enough to believe he could.

Of course he did have a job in medicine again, a place to stay, and a small salary. Life wasn't great, but it was better, and apologizing to his best buddy was the first step in what he hoped would be many more steps in the right direction.

But not in Sloane's direction. That much he was sure of.

"This will be fine," he said to Dexter Doyle, the owner of what had to be the worst hotel within a hundred miles.

So here he was in his new home—one room with a double bed, a toilet, mini-fridge, microwave, desk and chair—all of it dated. It wasn't the best place he'd ever stayed, but not the worst either. Maybe it was more like a reflection of his life. All the right equipment, but all of it dated—almost to the point of no recognition. Well, *he* was the one who'd walked out on the best living situation he'd ever had, so he couldn't really complain.

"Is there a liquor store around here?" he asked, tossing his duffle bag on the bed, hoping bed bugs wouldn't scurry out.

"A couple miles up the road."

"And a television?" Carter asked, noticing the room didn't have one.

"Out for repair."

"I don't suppose you offer a wake-up call?"

He remembered the way Sloane had used to wake him up. Always with a smile, and a kiss, and a cup of coffee. Often a whole lot more. Her touch. Her red hair brushing across his face. The mintiness of her breath when she kissed him. Yes, those were the mornings he'd loved waking up.

Dexter pointed to the old digital clock next to the bed. "If you want to wake up, set the alarm."

"Well, then…" Carter said, sitting down on the bed to test it. As he'd suspected, lumpy and saggy. "Looks like I'm home." For a while, anyway."

But he was anxious to return to Tennessee, so he could work toward the next part of his life—whatever that turned out to be.

Upwards and onwards, he thought as he settled into his room. Things were looking up. Especially now that he wasn't around Sloane any longer. So, on the one hand he liked the feeling of freedom and the optimism that went with it. But on the other he missed his life with Sloane.

It was an ache that had left a hole that would never be filled. But for Sloane he had to endure it and follow the course. More than that, he had to get used to the ache—because she couldn't be part of him anymore. Not in a real sense. In an emotional sense. However, he'd never let her go. Not now. Not ever. Falling in love with her the way he had didn't leave room for anything or anyone else. Meaning his destiny was set. And it was going to be a lonely one.

For Sloane, though…he'd do anything.

Next morning, when Carter surveyed his new office, he was neither pleased nor displeased with it; he was mainly ambivalent. That was the way so many of his days seemed to go, unless he made a hard effort to fight through it.

This morning he hadn't started his fight yet. It would happen, though. Once he got himself involved he'd find his way through, instead of dwelling somewhere in the middle of it like he'd used to do.

He took another look at it his office. It was basic, but well-equipped. Spotlessly clean, with fresh paint. The white on every wall put him off a little, but color really didn't matter when the basic medical tools were at his disposal.

The truth was, it wasn't a bad little office, all things considered. Two exam rooms, a spacious storage closet, a reception area and an office. Matt would subsidize his rent at the hotel and the office for now, and then if Tennessee worked out for him, and he was good enough to come back here full time, he would take over the costs himself and buy out this part of Matt's practice.

If things didn't work that way... Well, he didn't know what came after that. As he'd been told, over and over, by his recovery counselor, *"Take it one day at a time, and strive to make that day the best day ever."*

In other words, he was not to mess up his mind with the future when getting through the current day was never guaranteed. It made sense—especially since he was given to projecting his future and that, so often, turned into a PTSD trigger.

Whenever it took him over he could almost feel the

impending flare-up course through his veins. His vision blurred, his hands shook, his head felt as if it was ready to explode. He was like a fire-breathing dragon, puffing up and getting ready for his next battle.

Unfortunately Carter's "next battle" had cost him dearly. His job, the love of his life… And now he was in Forgeburn, running a storefront clinic for seasonal tourists, and a handful of locals who lived closer to Carter's part of the practice than Matt's, keeping his fingers crossed that he'd survive this day and make it through till tomorrow.

On the door peg, in the room marked *Office*, hung a crisp new lab jacket. Carter smiled—maybe the first smile that had cracked his face in weeks or months.

At least he hadn't lost his license to practice. That was good, despite the fact he'd lost everything else. He liked being a doctor. No, he *loved* being a doctor. It was all he'd ever wanted from the time he'd been a kid.

When all his friends had been vacillating between fireman, policeman and whatever else all little boys wanted to be at some point in their lives, being a doctor had been it for him, because he had wanted to find a way to cure his brother James. Carter had promised James he would, when he was nine and James had been on his last days, dying from cystic fibrosis.

Two years younger than Carter, James had spent his whole life in and out of hospitals. He'd never been strong enough to walk more than a few steps, and he'd never breathed well enough to go outside and play— not even for a few minutes. For James, life had been all tests and procedures, and somewhere in Carter's nine-year-old mind he'd thought if he made a promise to save his brother and make him well it would happen. And it would give his entire family some hope to cling to.

But a week after his promise his dad had been sitting on the front step crying when Carter had arrived home from school. And after that, unlike his friends, who had gone back and forth on what they wanted to be, he never had. He'd been angry at the world for taking his brother. Angry at himself that he hadn't been able to do more. Angry at the doctors who'd always predicted a grave outcome for his brother.

He'd expected them to do better. Expected them to produce a miracle. Expected them to offer hope rather than rip it away. Which was why he'd become a doctor—a surgeon. Because he wanted to do the things that hadn't been done for his brother. Of course, the closer Carter had come to his goal, the more he'd realized that some outcomes would break his heart no matter what he did. That was part of the profession. But that hadn't discouraged him, because many more outcomes were good. And it was those outcomes he always dedicated to his brother—without fail.

But now—well, now he was a GP. And he was grateful for that. Maybe it was the only thing left in his life he had to be grateful for, since he'd destroyed everything else that mattered.

"It's nice," Carter said to the twenty-something girl who'd been following him from room to room: Marcie, his new receptionist.

Her father owned the building and had seized the opportunity to lower the rent if the medical practice employed her. Apparently, Marcie had never worked a day in her life and this was to be her first ever job. Matt had hired her since, legally, this was *his* practice.

"Daddy had it painted fresh," she said, her nose in her phone, scrolling, scrolling… Short skirt, long vest, tall boots, pinkish yellow hair… Not the professional image he'd hoped for. But a discount was a discount, and he'd have to make the best of his workforce virgin.

He actually chuckled. If his life weren't so pathetic this could be funny. It wasn't, though. Nobody could screw up so many things the way he had and call it funny. But, like he'd told Matt, he was a good doctor. That was the only sure thing he had to hang on to— his medical skills. Maybe—somehow—he wouldn't mess those up, too.

"So, how about we open up for business tomorrow morning?" he asked Marcie.

Her reply was a head nod as she continued to scroll.

Who was it that had said something about fastening up for a bumpy ride? Well, this was *his* bumpy ride, but he wasn't sure he was fastened up enough for it.

Time would tell, he supposed.

# CHAPTER TWO

So THIS WAS FORGEBURN. Sloane looked up and down the main drag, not sure whether she liked it or not. For sure, it was remote. And small. So small, in fact, that she could see both ends of town from her vantage point at the gas station in the middle.

It did have some appeal, she decided, as her gaze came to rest on a good-looking foothill that seemed as if it needed an experienced climber on it. It was red clay, not too steep, but steep enough that she knew her climbing skills—the skills Carter had taught her—would get her to the top. Something she would definitely do, since she was booked here in Forgeburn for the entire two weeks of her vacation.

Hiking the desert, climbing the rocks, dropping down into some of the canyons—these were all things she'd never done Before Carter, as she called it now. But they were things she loved doing now, along with scuba diving, parasailing, mountain biking, and so many other outdoor recreational activities.

She missed all those—missed doing them with Carter. Missed the way he'd congratulate her when she achieved something she'd never done before. First the congratulatory hug, then the congratulatory kiss, then the congratulatory run to the bedroom for the best congratulatory practice of all.

Yes, she missed all that. Missed the emotion and the elation. Missed the physical contact, even if it was a hug of condolence when she didn't achieve what she'd set out to do.

So... Forgeburn—she could see why Carter had talked about it so much. They'd planned on a visit—something longer than the two or three days off they usually got. And here she was, with all the time in the world. But alone.

She could have gone someplace else. Anyplace else. And maybe she should have. But here, with so much to remind her of what she no longer had, maybe she would start to remind herself that she no longer had Carter either.

Sighing, Sloane finished pumping gas into her car, then took one more look around before she headed down the road to Red Rock Canyon Resort—her home away from home for the next two weeks. Right now she felt—*nothing*. Carter had told her he'd felt that way much of the time and now she finally understood it herself. It was so empty. So lonely.

Good move coming here? Or bad move?

Either way, she was here, and there was plenty to do—or nothing, if that was what she chose. Her real choice, however, wouldn't happen, because that involved sleeping out under the stars somewhere, listening to the coyotes howl. Curling up with Carter in a single sleeping bag. Making love under the stars. And this evening promised a sky full of beautiful stars.

"Could you tell me if there are any evening hikes in the desert?" she asked the concierge as she checked in to the Red Rock Canyon Resort.

"We have one leaving in about an hour. It's five miles, and it leads into the desert to explore various constellations that are visible only because there's no city lighting getting in the way. But you must have your own hiking gear, as our rental facility is closed."

"Sounds perfect to me. If there's space, sign me up."

"We have other less strenuous options in the morning," said the concierge, Diego Sanchez. "Perhaps you'd rather wait, *señorita*?"

"No. I'd rather go tonight. And strenuous is good. Just what I need."

"Then I'll pass your name along to our tour guide. He'll contact you shortly about the equipment you need to bring. You *do* have equipment, don't you?"

Everything that Carter had ever bought her. She'd thought about throwing it all away and starting over, but for now it was all she had, and she hoped she would be able to use it without too many memories hiking along with her.

Even so, as she went to her room to get ready, memories were already creeping in—like how his temper had flared for no reason. When he'd panicked at an unexpected loud noise. And then there had been the nightmares, the flashbacks and triggers. And finally, a slow-growing lack of trust in *her*.

Before he'd gone into the Army he'd trusted her

implicitly. When he'd come home he'd seemed wary of her at first. Then eventually mistrusting. That had maybe been the worst of everything. Planning a life with someone who didn't trust her. That was when she'd started to wonder if she should, or could, go through with their marriage. Or simply put it on hold for a while.

After all, she'd already invested six years—what was another year or so on top of that?

Carter had answered that question by leaving before she'd had a chance to decide.

Up and down. That had been her life with Carter after he'd come home. That and her concern for his health, since he'd refused to see a nephrologist about his kidney condition. He'd needed to keep the remaining kidney healthy, but everything he'd done had seemed to contradict that.

Still, she'd stayed with him even when it had become clear that their feelings for each other were eroding, because she'd known who was underneath all that trauma—known the man he really was even though he hadn't anymore. And because she'd loved him, and some of that love had still been hanging on for dear life.

In the end, though, love hadn't been enough. And now here she was in Forgeburn, getting ready to look at the stars, hoping to find the one thing that would turn her in the direction that led her away from Carter once and for all. Because she sure wasn't headed toward him now.

After lacing up her hiking boots, then tucking

a few necessary supplies into the pockets of her cargo vest, Sloane looked at herself in the mirror. No wrinkles yet, which surprised her, with the way she worried. But there were bags under her eyes. Still cosmetically fixable, but there all the same. Yes, she definitely needed this vacation, she thought as she pulled her wild copper hair into a ponytail, then put a cap on her head.

"Ready," she said to herself as she headed toward the door. But was she really? If it was rest she needed, and time to think, why was she already filling her schedule with activities.

Because if she kept herself busy she wouldn't have to think. And sometimes thinking hurt too much.

"Are you a walk-in, or do you have an appointment?" the young girl at the desk asked Sloane, without looking up. The girl was buried in her phone.

"Walk-in. All I need are a few stitches for this cut on my leg."

One of the other night hikers had knocked her into the face of a rather jagged rock in his enthusiasm to get a better look at Venus and Mars, which were less than a degree apart. He been all excited that Jupiter was also nearby.

It had been a beautiful sight, with Venus by far being the brightest of the three. Of course when she'd managed to distinguish Venus from the rest of the planets her mind had drifted off to something far less astrological. In fact she had been contemplating Venus as the Roman goddess of love, sexuality, beauty, prosperity and fertility when the night hiker had clipped her and sent her into an undignified sprawl.

Now she needed stitches and antibiotics.

She could have gone to see Matt, but he would be such a reminder that she wasn't sure she was ready to face him. He and Carter had been so close once upon a time. Like brothers. But, like everything else with Carter, that friendship had died as well.

She would look Matt up. It was inevitable that she would see him at some point in her stay here. But not now—she wasn't ready. So as soon as morning had forced her to open her eyes, she'd asked about the nearest doctor. She had been told there was a tourist doctor nearby, and where she could find his office, and now here she was, seeking medical care.

The young girl leaned over the desk to appraise the cut, then settled back down into her chair.

"I'll put you on the list and he'll see you as soon as…" She shrugged. "When he's ready."

It was a plain office. Not much to look at. No outdated magazines to read. But it was freshly painted. She could still smell the remnants of new paint.

"How long have you been here?" she asked the girl.

She looked up from her phone and said, "We're new. Just opened."

"Is the doctor Matt McClain?" she asked, hoping it was not.

"Nope. He takes care of the cowboys. We're strictly here for the tourists, who get injured doing things like whatever it was *you* were doing that got you cut up."

"Do you need my name for your records?" Sloane asked.

"Doc will take care of that."

"Will he take care of my insurance papers as well?" This was an oddly run practice and she wondered what kind of doctor allowed it.

"Well, he won't let *me* do them, so I guess it's up to him."

Definitely odd. And if she'd needed something more than stitches she'd probably have gone looking for Matt. But she was here now and, since there'd been no other cars in the parking lot, it shouldn't be too long before she got called in.

She was right. Within another couple of minutes the receptionist gave her a wave to go on back, without so much as looking up from her phone.

So she took it upon herself to wander down the hall, find the exam room, then sit up on the exam table and wait. Another minute passed before she heard footsteps heading down the hall and her blood froze in her veins.

*No, it couldn't be.* She knew those footsteps. Knew them by heart.

Consequently, when the doctor pushed open the door, Sloane's head started to spin. "What are you doing here?" she asked, trying to hold back on her wobbly voice.

"Sloane? What are *you* doing here?" He closed the exam room door behind him but made no attempt to walk over to her.

"I asked you first," she said.

"I'm trying to start over. Matt gave me a job here. He needed help, I needed help…so it worked out. Now you."

"Vacation. I came here because—Well, I didn't know you were here. Last I heard you were in Vegas."

"Actually, Tennessee," he said. "Vegas before that."

"Now you're *here*? Seriously?"

"As serious as it gets. So, I'm assuming you want me to stitch up that cut on your leg?"

She'd almost forgotten about that, she was so flustered. "It happened last night. I was out stargazing and met up with the sharp end of a rock."

"Since when do you stargaze?" he asked, finally walking over to the exam table.

"Since last night."

"And what did you learn?"

"That Venus shines the brightest and it's best to stargaze on your own, or with a sure-footed friend."

"Meaning…?"

"Meaning I did the tourist thing and now I'm paying for it. So, why here, Carter? I'm assuming Matt gave you an opportunity, but you're clearly not working as a surgeon. More like what? A GP?"

"Exactly," he said, as he bent to assess the cut.

"But you've never done that kind of work."

"And *you've* never gone stargazing. So, I suppose we file it all under 'first time'." He looked up at her. "Everything has to start somewhere, doesn't it?" Then he ran his hand down the calf of her leg.

Sloane shivered to his touch the way she always had.

"Why are you touching me that way?" she asked. "We're over. You quit touching me that way months ago."

He took his hand off her leg, stood up and smiled.

"Actually, that was a perfectly good GP's assessment. I wanted to make sure your leg wasn't too warm, which might indicate an infection setting in."

"I'm a doctor. I know to disinfect it."

"And I'm a doctor, too. A doctor who's trying his hardest to be a *good* doctor."

"You always were good, Carter. Nobody ever questioned that. It was everything else that went with you…"

"My attitude?"

Sloane let out a deep sigh. She hadn't come on vacation to start this whole thing over again. She was trying to get away from it. Sort it out and put it behind her. But how could she do that when Carter was here?

"I've said all there is to say about your attitude. So how about the stitches?"

"I'd prefer to butterfly it. Less chance of scarring."

Butterfly stitches were not exactly stitches, but thin strips with an adhesive backing used to close small wounds.

"Oh, and when was the last time you had a tetanus shot?"

"Good on the butterfly stitches. Much better than needle and thread. And as for the tetanus shot…"

She shrugged her shoulders. She should know, but she didn't. Like most people, she didn't keep track of those sorts of things. Although she could have told him the exact date and time of the last gamma globulin shot *he* had taken.

It had happened because of a needle stick. One of his patients—a child—had got belligerent and whacked Carter a good one as he'd been trying to give the boy a shot to calm him down before an appendectomy. Carter had already administered a mild sedative when the boy had started flailing and caught Carter's hand. The one with the used hypodermic needle still in it.

The puncture hadn't been bad, or deep, but hospital policy had demanded a visit from the old gamma globulin needle to help give Carter a temporary boost in his immune system. Which had turned out to be a good thing since, as it had happened, the kid had been in the very early stages of chickenpox.

That had been one month and thirteen days before he'd shipped out to Afghanistan. So why did she remember that when she couldn't remember her own last tetanus?

"No clue," she told him, recalling the sexy way he'd dropped his pants so she could stick him in the butt with the needle. It had been slow, seductive, and it had definitely raised her libido a notch or two. In fact, had they not been in one of the hospital exam rooms, the way his pants had slid over his hips would have definitely led to something very unprofessional. And very good.

Even thinking about it caused heat to rush to her cheeks—and for a redhead that was a disaster, because it made her look like a beet.

"You OK?" he asked as he pulled the necessary supplies from a cabinet next to the exam table.

"Just tired. Which is why I came here."

"Well, that color you're wearing right now isn't your *I'm tired* color. Normally that's more pasty and white. In fact, as I recall, that color is your—"

"Just stop it, Carter! I didn't come here to rehash old times. I need some stitches and a tetanus shot. If you can't do that, I'll go find Matt and ask him to."

"He didn't tell you I was here? Because what are the chances that you'd simply bump into me in the middle of nowhere?"

He picked up a bottle of disinfectant and squirted some on her leg.

"When I saw you sitting on my table I assumed you were here to find me."

"Trust me, Carter. You're the last person I wanted or expected to find here. And, no, Matt didn't say a word."

Which made her wonder if Matt was trying to get them back together. Surprise meeting in a desert in the middle of nowhere? Maybe it was a coincidence. Or maybe not. Right now, she didn't care. She just wanted Carter to fix her leg so she could get out of there.

Carter hadn't expected to see Sloane in Forgeburn, of all places, and now that she was here he wasn't sure what to do about it. Stay away from her altogether? Allow a small amount of cordiality in? Just what was the etiquette here? What etiquette was involved in meeting up with the woman you'd loved for so long, then dumped?

He knew Sloane in every way one person could know another, so it wasn't as if they were strangers caught up in a chance meeting. Something like that would have been easier to deal with. They could have shared general chit chat, a string of pleasantries, talked about the weather—except, Sloane deserved more than the weather forecast.

The problem was, he didn't have more. Not for her, anyway. It was too difficult, too painful, and he didn't want to go on hurting her over and over.

"The wound is clean and, as cuts go, the edges are good. So I'm going to use about ten butterflies, then wrap it in gauze. If you're still here in a couple of days come back for a check. Or go to your own doctor when you get back home."

Which he hoped she would do—go home. Today. Right now.

"I'm here for two weeks," she said. "It's the first vacation I've had since... Well—that week you were on leave from the Army. You came home and we took a cruise down to Mexico. What was that? Four years ago?"

He knew exactly when it had been, but he didn't want memories of that week popping into his mind. It had been too nice, and they'd gotten so close. Closer than they'd been even after two years together. It was when he'd proposed to her. Well, it had been a pre-proposal—one of those *If I were to ask you, would you marry me?* sort of things.

It hadn't been until almost two years later that he'd done the real asking. And then it had been by satellite hook-up. It had been her birthday, and her friends and family had been having a party. He'd been left out, of course, being overseas. So when they'd talked later that night the question had simply popped right out of him, surprising him almost as much as it had her.

Marriage had always been his intention, though. Women like Sloane didn't come along every day, and he had been so head-over-heels crazy in love with her, almost at first sight, he hadn't been about to lose her. But he'd wanted to wait until he got home and do the proposal the right way, on a romantic weekend on the beach, or maybe up in wine country.

Somehow he'd seen it happening at dawn, not dusk. They'd be strolling hand in hand, wherever they were, and when they stopped for a break he would pull an engagement ring box from his pocket. Or they would be having brunch, sipping mimosas, and he would discreetly slide the ring box across the table.

That had been the other Carter Holmes, though. The one who'd replaced him didn't have a romantic bone in his body. Even reminding himself of the things he'd thought before made his hands shake.

"I'm going to give you a prescription for an antibiotic. There's a pharmacy about ten miles down the road. You can fill it there. If I remember correctly, you were allergic to—"

Damn, why did he have to remember so many things about her? He'd been trying not to since he'd left, and on good days he sometimes succeeded. Now, though, everything was coming back. More than he wanted. More than he could deal with.

"Penicillin," Sloane said, sliding off the exam table

then bending down to straighten out her pants. "So, how much do I owe you for today?" she asked as she straightened up and looked him directly in the eye.

"Really, Sloane? Do you think I'd charge you for this?"

"To be honest, I don't know *what* you'd do. I didn't expect you to leave me without an explanation, but you did. I didn't expect you not to return my calls and texts for three months, but you did. I didn't even expect you to join the Army, but you did. So, tell me… How am I supposed to anticipate your next move, Carter? How am I supposed to know what you will and will not do?"

"I know I didn't do things the way I should have, but…"

But what? What was his excuse? He'd been doing it for her? She wouldn't believe that, even though it was the truth.

"But what's done is done, and I can't go back and change things."

"No, you can't. Neither of us can." She headed for the exam room door, then stopped and turned back to face him. "Look, us being here at the same time is a coincidence. But could we find some time when we could get together and talk? I have questions, Carter. And I deserve answers."

"Let me figure out my schedule, then I'll get back to you. Do you still have the same cell number?"

"*I'm* not the one who changed, Carter. You are. Yes, it's still the same. I didn't want to change it in case you actually did try to call or text me."

During his few hazy weeks in Vegas the last thing he had wanted to do was return her calls and have her figure out that he was even deeper into the pit than he'd been before he'd left. His drinking had been worse. He'd been taking those pills. And gambling... All the things that had distracted him from what was real.

Then in Tennessee cell phones had been confiscated and handed back only for emergencies and once-a-week contact with family or a loved one. Since he'd had no family then, or even a loved one, there'd never been any reason to ask for his cell phone back for that one allotted hour.

"I wasn't exactly in a position to reach out to anybody. It was rude, and I'm sorry, but that's who I was then."

"And not now?" she asked him before she left his office.

"It's complicated, Sloane."

And he couldn't make promises, or even lead her in the direction of thinking that he might be getting better because he didn't know if he was. Time would tell, he supposed. Time and new surroundings. But how could he tell her that? How could he tell her that *she* was part of the past he was running from?

"Life is complicated, Carter," she said. "For everybody in some way."

He sounded so—not bitter, more like apathetic. As if he'd given up or given himself over to his battle.

"So you've given up?"

"It's called hitting rock bottom." He took a couple steps toward her, then stopped, as if a barrier had been lobbed into his path. "And my choice is to not drag anybody else down with me."

"You owe me an explanation, Carter."

"For what? For losing one kidney and a spleen to shrapnel? Damaging my other kidney? For PTSD after too much gunfire, too much death, too many people to save that I couldn't? Is that what you want to hear? Because if it is I've said it all before and look where it's gotten me."

She wanted to see some emotion—some of the old Carter trying to fight back. But what she saw in his face was—*nothing*. His eyes were blank. His expression resigned.

This wasn't the Carter she'd used to know. Used to love. Not at all. This was a different man. One she didn't understand. Couldn't explain. One who seemed to be calculating every facial expression and every word. She'd been through so much with him, but this—it broke off another piece of her heart.

"You still drinking?" she asked him, not sure why she was even bothering.

He shook his head. "Gave up the pills, too. Momentary interruptions in my process are only that—momentary. Then it all comes back. So, what are you really doing here? Come to save me from myself?"

"I'm on vacation, like I told you."

But she wondered if subconsciously she'd chosen Forgeburn not so much expecting to find him here but to be closer to a part of his life when his life had been good. He and Matt had made so many plans about biking, hiking and climbing over the years, and it was something Carter had talked about so often. Getting back to his roots, he'd say, even though he wasn't from the area. Maybe the sentiment had appealed to him, or maybe it had simply been the need to step out of his problems for a while.

Whatever it was, could she have actually come here expecting to find answers? Or even expecting to find Carter himself?

"You'd talked about the area so often—maybe I thought I could find some kind of closure here. You took that from me, you know."

"I know I did," he said.

His voice was soft now. The animosity was gone, replaced by a sadness he couldn't conceal. At least not from the woman who'd loved him for so long.

"It was never my intention to hurt people—most of all you. But that's how it turned out, and in the end who cares? Who really gives a good damn?"

"I do—did," she said, fighting back tears.

She'd promised herself she wouldn't cry. That no matter what Carter said or did she wouldn't let him reduce her to that again. But here she was, fighting it because her heart was breaking yet one more time. For her—and for Carter.

"I cared."

"You should have never waited for me, Sloane. You could have had better. We both knew that."

For an instant his expression changed. Did she see regret? Or a sadness deeper than anything she'd ever seen from him before? It was there and gone so quickly she didn't know, but in that instant she'd seen Carter. The real Carter. He was still there, which did give her hope. Not for their relationship. That was over, and she had to reconcile herself to that. But she did hold out some hope for Carter—something she hadn't done in a long, long time.

"Maybe that's what you thought," she said, "but it's not what I thought."

Standing on tiptoes, she brushed a light kiss to his cheek, then backed away.

"What I knew was that I still loved you, but you didn't still love me. That's a difficult adjustment to make after so many years. I wish I could have done better at it. But I suppose that's a moot point, isn't it? Since you made the final decision about *us* without me."

Sloane didn't know whether to laugh or cry. Sitting in her rental car in the parking lot, she was too unsteady to go anywhere yet. Maybe the kiss had been a mistake—maybe it had been the last thing he wanted from her—but it had told her something she wasn't prepared to know. She still loved him. Maybe not in the breathless way she'd loved him at first, but in a more deep-down sense. It was something more profound—something she didn't understand and wasn't ready to think about.

Carter was a handsome man and, while she'd rarely let a man turn her head, she'd always reacted to him. He'd taken off some weight since she'd last seen him, and it looked good. Was he working out again? Because for the first time since he'd been injured he looked toned.

But he'd always been a head-turner, hadn't he? Sometimes he'd shown up for work in tight leather pants, which had given all the ladies quite a show before he gave himself over to his day and changed into scrubs.

She'd loved that side of him because he'd known what he was doing—had had fun with it. He'd loved having people looking at him, speculating about who he really was—a bad boy or simply a narcissist. In truth, he had been neither. Carter Holmes had simply been a man who'd enjoyed life. He'd liked to play around with it to see what turned up. And he'd taught her to enjoy it along with him. To be spontaneous. To let go occasionally and live in the moment.

That hadn't been her when they'd first met. After her mother died she'd been raised by a loving but very serious father who'd overwhelmed her with his serious world. Yet Carter had made her life so—*good*. So much fun to anticipate.

Those days were so far in the past, though, she almost wondered if they'd happened at all. Nothing seemed real anymore. It hadn't for such a long time. Even now—being here and discovering Carter was here as well—was an altered reality, and the pieces of it hadn't come together in her mind yet.

"I didn't want to stir the pot," Matt said to her an hour later, when she went to his surgery and challenged him about not telling her that Carter was in Forgeburn.

"So you just let me bump into him accidentally?" She shook her head, angry because of so many things.

"There was no guarantee you *would* bump into him."

"Yeah, right. This is *Forgeburn*, Matt. It's only a ten-minute drive from one end of the town to the other. How could I *not* bump into him?"

Matt looked out into his waiting room. Today it was overflowing with patients.

"Look, Sloane… When you called me and told me you might come here for a few days Carter and I hadn't made any specific plans yet. And, honestly, neither of you told me how bad it was between you. Carter said something to the effect that you were having problems, but I didn't know until after he was here that they were permanent problems. By then you were already on your way. So don't blame me for what you and Carter have or don't have going on. I'm only the bystander who's watching the world cave in around two of my friends."

Sloane did understand his position, but that didn't make things better. Nothing did right now, so she decided to head back to her hotel, shut herself in her room, and decide whether she should stay or go.

In so many ways she wanted to stay—maybe simply to find some closure. That was her due, and she hadn't had it—not with the way Carter had left her. But leaving wasn't such a bad idea either. This time *she'd* be the one to walk away. There would be a certain satisfaction in that.

But acting that way wasn't who Sloane was. She'd loved that man for too long, and because of everything he had been through she had no desire to hurt him. If—and that was a great big *if*—he still cared enough to be hurt.

Sloane didn't know if that was even possible. Or if what she might do would hurt *her* even more than before. It was a lot to think about. But she wasn't in the mood to think, or to do anything that related to Carter.

Except, despite her best efforts, Sloane still couldn't get him off her mind, and she was suddenly afraid that she might slip back to where she had been three months ago, when he'd left her. Not that she'd come very far from that position up until now. Still, she didn't want to backslide.

But with Carter so close to her now was there any kind of chance she could really move forward? Or even move on? She hoped so. But there was no confidence backing that hope. None whatsoever.

# CHAPTER THREE

CARTER EMPTIED THE bottle of cheap whiskey he'd just bought down the drain, then placed the empty bottle on the stand next to his bed and stared at it. Cheap booze, expensive booze—it was all there, waiting for him to take that first drink. No one would know if he did. No one would care, either. But the bottle reminded him of where he was trying to go. And, that's what he still needed so much of the time. A reminder of where he'd been and how bad it was. A reminder of all the things he'd lost, that he couldn't get back. But it was also there to show him the way out if there was a way to get out.

This was *his* hell to pay, though. *His* test to achieve. To conquer. So the damned bottle would sit there and taunt him for as long as he needed to be taunted. If that was forever, so be it. But because of The Recovery Project there had been times when he'd actually felt optimistic. Not overly so, but just enough to get him through the steps they required.

But there were still occasions when Carter didn't think there was a way out, and felt that he was simply biding time until something even more drastic than PTSD invaded his life.

Much of the time his ambivalence defeated him. Or at least set him back a step or two. But always, no matter where he went, when he set that bottle out Carter did so with hope. And, yes, there *was* a tiny thread of it left in him when he cared to look for it. Which he didn't too often. Especially not where Sloane was concerned.

Tonight Carter was restless, in part because of his new life and in part because Sloane was here. Consequently, he paced the dirty hotel room like a caged tiger—back and forth. An hour of it, non-stop, hoping to tire himself out.

But when he stopped he was only physically tired, not emotionally. The thoughts in his brain wouldn't turn off. Thoughts of the two of them, what they'd had, what they'd planned. The big things—talking about having a family, buying a house. The little things—sleeping in late on Sunday mornings, taking walks, bubble baths for two.

"Why?" he whispered, finally sitting down on the edge of the bed, dropping his head into his hands. *"Why?"*

What his cognitive therapy counselor had told him was that there was no answer to *why?* Of course Carter already knew that, because it was the same question so many of his patients asked him. *Why did I get cancer? Why did my daughter die?*

*"Instead of asking yourself why it happened, ask*

*yourself how you're going to get through it."* That was what the counselor had said.

So how was he going to get through this with Sloane? Minute by minute, hour by hour, day by day? Could he simply ask her to leave and let her know that being anywhere near her scared him more than the bullets had in Afghanistan?

Of course there were no answers popping into his mind. He hadn't expected them to. In fact the only thing in his mind was Sloane. Which meant he needed something to cradle him through the emptiness that was beginning to set in. So it was time to take a ride. That took concentration, and that was what he needed right now. To be concentrating on something other than what wasn't meant to be.

The air was still warm enough outside, even though it was nearing mid-November. And something about being in a place without confines appealed to him. So Carter slipped into his leather jacket, grabbed his helmet and his medical bag, and headed for his motorcycle.

But his phone rang before he reached his motorcycle, and a minute later he was on his way to Red Rock Canyon Resort, where there was an outbreak of food poisoning. Fourteen people down so far.

It actually gave him a little adrenalin rush, having something that would keep him busy coming up. And it made him feel *useful*—which hadn't happened to him in a long, long time.

"Latest count is twenty-one, Doc," reported Paul Jacob, the night manager. He was a nervous, twitchy man, pale and very thin. Tonight, he was so twitchy Carter wondered if he should offer him a sedative.

"What have you been doing with them so far?

"We've been telling them to stay in their rooms, because we don't know if it's contagious, but some of them won't. They keep coming down to the desk, asking for things."

Paul dabbed sweat beads from his brow.

"I've got my night staff out right now, trying to get people back to their rooms so we can keep everything organized, but word is spreading about an illness sweeping through the resort, so I'm afraid some people aren't being so cooperative. A few have even left."

"Well, if it's food poisoning it's probably not contagious, so I'm not too worried about people leaving. And you think it's something from the buffet?" Carter asked.

He didn't often work with sick people since he was—*had been*—a surgeon. He hadn't since his rotation through internal medicine back in med school, so this aspect of medicine was fairly new to him. Food poisoning… There were so many types. He'd spent ten minutes in the parking lot before coming in, reacquainting himself with what he might expect—thank heavens for phones that could browse the internet.

"I've had my staff asking around and there seems to be the one food that's common to all of the people who have complaints. Eclairs. Not sure if that's any help, but—"

"With cream filling?" Carter asked, as an idea began to formulate in his head.

"Yes," Paul said. "Made fresh today. All our pastries are made fresh, with fresh ingredients, so I don't see how—"

"Sneezing, coughing…improper handwashing after sneezing or coughing. Or simply from the skin. That's how it spreads."

If Carter was guessing right, and he was pretty sure he was. "So, the most common symptoms you've seen are vomiting, nausea and stomach cramps?"

Paul nodded.

"And it started shortly after dinner?"

Once again Paul nodded. "You know what it is?"

Carter nodded as well, and half smiled at what was to be his diagnosis. Staphylococcus food poisoning was the fastest-acting food poisoning of all. It could start as soon as thirty minutes after eating contaminated food. Also, the symptoms fitted what Paul had seen.

This type of food poisoning was not often dangerous, unless you were high-risk because of age or another illness. So Carter was keeping his fingers crossed that he was correct.

This kind of food poisoning usually worked its way out on its own in twenty-four hours. His only duty as a doctor would be to address the side issues— especially dehydration. No drugs, and no real treatment unless dehydration became severe.

"Do you have the room numbers and names of everyone who's reported ill?"

"I do—but there may be more who haven't called for a doctor."

"Is there any way for you to check with all your guests to make sure they're OK and see if they need medical attention?"

Carter was worried that someone who was considered high-risk might have collapsed and not be able to report to the front desk.

"Maybe ask everybody to report their status, and if there are any guests who don't have your staff go to check them."

This was a large resort. He'd read in his file that it had four hundred and fifty rooms.

"How many guests do you have registered right now?"

Paul did a quick computer check.

"Close to six hundred. And there are always those who sneak in an extra person or two without registering them, because they think they have to pay extra. Which they don't. One fee accommodates the room's posted capacity and all buffet meals."

He handed a computer printout to Carter.

"These are the names and room numbers of all the guests who've complained so far."

Carter's mind boggled at the number. There were—conservatively—six hundred people in this hotel who might have eaten the eclairs, and yet he could only treat those he knew to be sick. Twenty-one seemed like an unusually low number. Much too low, he decided as he looked over the list of names. There would be more. Many more.

Now his excitement was beginning to change to worry. For he could only treat the symptoms. Tomorrow he'd send samples to the lab and hope for a speedy diagnosis, then deal with that accordingly if something else turned up.

"I need a doctor," a youngish man said, stumbling up to the desk and then practically falling over it. "Bad cramps."

He was pale, quite obviously in distress, and too sick to care that his shoes didn't match and his shirt wasn't buttoned correctly.

"Looks like this is where I start," Carter said, taking hold of the man's arm. "I'm a doctor. How about we go back to your room and I'll have a look at you there?"

Poor guy, Carter thought as he led the man, who said his name was Jeff, to the elevator bank. As illnesses went, this one wasn't serious. But right now Jeff wouldn't believe that.

"So, how many of those eclairs did you eat?" he asked, as he led Jeff onto the elevator.

"A couple." The man moaned. "They were good."

Which meant Carter had his night cut out for him.

A lot of people were sick here. Sloane had heard about it when she'd gone down for a late dinner and the dining room had been closed, with a posted note that food service was suspended until further notice.

They'd left a list of local diners and a pizza delivery service on the door, but Sloane hadn't been in the mood to go out. And she wasn't a huge fan of pizza.

So she'd grabbed a bag of pretzels from the vending machine, then returned to her room. It didn't matter much to her anyway. Food wasn't her thing. As often as not, since Carter had left, she'd forget to eat a meal and need to be reminded to eat something.

In her defense, it was difficult eating when you didn't have an appetite—which was the case now. But there had been a time when she'd loved to cook for Carter on the days when their schedules had worked out together. Loved the way he'd always created the ambiance, too. Candlelight, wine from one of the local wineries they'd visited—a hobby they'd shared. Dim light. Soft music—Ella Fitzgerald, Frank Sinatra, Nat King Cole... All this, even when the only thing she might have fixed was a simple pasta salad.

He'd been a romantic. Something he'd kept to himself until their fourth or fifth date, when they'd gone to the beach for an evening picnic. Harbor sounds and moonglow over the water...

She knew she'd fallen a little in love with him before that night, but when he'd asked her to dance in the sand with him—that was when he'd won her whole heart. That was the dream that haunted her so often now.

Too many memories, Sloane thought, as she ate the pretzels and then decided to return to the vending machines for a bottle of water, in case what was infecting the guests was waterborne. She didn't want to be sick here. Actually, she didn't know *what* she wanted, other than water, so she slipped back into her shoes and headed to the hall.

Halfway to the elevator, she stopped and watched

a familiar figure heading her direction. Practically running.

"You OK?" she asked, noting how frazzled Carter looked.

"Two hours…twenty-six patients."

"With what?"

Carter looked—*animated*. It was the way he'd used to look before a challenging surgery. It was a look she'd liked on him then—and now.

"Some kind of staph bug, I'm guessing. Nothing I can do except tell them they'll be better tomorrow and let them know that if they're not to have the hotel get in touch with me. Also make sure they're not dehydrating."

"No serious consequences?" Sloane asked, taking care not to get too close to him.

Getting close might signal that she had personal intentions of some sort, which she didn't. Why start anything between them if she didn't have to?

"Not yet. Just a lot of people with ruined vacation plans. But I found out there's someone down the hall—Type One diabetes—who's sick. I might have to do some different management. Especially if her blood sugar drops."

"Can I help?" Sloane asked.

"Um…yes. Please," Carter replied, looking stunned by her offer. "If you don't mind?"

They'd never really worked together. Yes, they'd been in the same hospital, often on the same shifts. But never together as a team. And even though she hadn't brought a medical bag on this trip—hadn't expected to do anything medical—Sloane followed Carter to the room, not sure what to make of this.

"Just tell me what you want me to do when we get in there," she said, as Carter raised his fist to knock.

He actually chuckled as a little girl opened the door to him. "I'd tell you if I knew, but since I haven't treated very many sick people—"

"And you think *I* have?"

"Well, there's nothing like having two eminently qualified surgeons show up to tell you that your illness will run its course in a few hours." He looked down at the girl, who hadn't yet unfastened the door chain. "We're doctors," he said to her. "Did you call the front desk because your mom is sick?"

The girl nodded her head, but still didn't unfasten the chain. "I think my mom's really bad this time," she said. "She ate an éclair, and she's not allowed sugar."

"Could we come in and have a look at her?"

The little girl, who couldn't have been more than ten, looked terrified. "She told me not to open the door to strangers."

"Would you like to look at my medical bag? It will prove I'm a doctor." Carter held it out for her to see, then opened it and let her have a look inside.

Reluctantly the child undid the chain, then stepped away from the door. "My mom's in the bathroom. She's throwing up."

Sloane beat Carter to the bathroom, opened the door and found—

"Call an ambulance!" she shouted out to Carter, who was still busy trying to make the child feel at ease.

By the time he had his phone out Sloane was already on her knees at the woman's side, assessing her pulse.

"Weak, erratic…" She looked at the child, who was now standing behind Carter. "What's your mom's name?" she asked.

"Jeannie," the girl said.

"Jeannie, can you hear me?" Sloane called. Then she looked to Carter. "Can you toss me a blood pressure cuff?" she asked, as he plugged one ear to better hear what she hoped were arrangements for an ambulance.

He nodded, and bent down to his medical bag, which was on the floor at his feet now. He found the digital wrist cuff, then handed it to her. "Ambulance is about an hour out. Maybe a little longer."

*"Seriously?"* Sloane sputtered, patting Jeannie's cheeks to raise a response. But the woman didn't respond.

"That's the way it is around here. There aren't enough services for the size of the area. According to Matt, it's too spread out. Getting help takes too long."

"Is there any other way to get her to the hospital?" Sloane asked.

"There's a guy who runs a charter helicopter service who will stand in for medical transport when it's needed," Carter said, and he dialed the number he'd stored in his phone earlier while at the same time pulling a blood sugar monitor out of his bag and handing it over to Sloane.

So far he seemed—*good*, she thought. Better than he'd seemed for his last several weeks at the hospital. And while Sloane didn't have time to assess the reasons why, she did acknowledge to herself that this was a little bit of the old Carter showing through. Always collected. Always efficient. Always in charge.

"Jeannie," she said, "if you can hear me, you're going to feel a little pinprick on your finger. I've got to take your blood sugar."

Which was what she did. She drew a drop of blood, let it soak into the test strip, then inserted the strip into the meter. Five seconds later…

"Seven hundred fifty," she whispered, bending down to smell the woman's breath. It smelled like nail polish—a typical smell in ketoacidosis indicating that Jeannie's insulin was too low and her blood sugar too high.

"The helicopter can be here for transportation in fifteen minutes," Carter said, stepping back into the confined space. "Then it will take about forty minutes to get to the largest hospital in the area, or about fifteen to get to the Whipple Creek Clinic."

"She needs to go to hospital," Sloane said without hesitation. "She's got ketoacidosis. Her blood sugar's at seven-fifty."

All which meant there was the possibility of kidney damage or stroke—translating this into a life-threatening situation, especially since Jeannie was comatose.

"Does your mother eat other things she's not supposed to?" Sloane asked the little girl. "And sometimes get very sleepy and sleep for a long time?

"Her name's Molly," Carter said. "Molly McKinley. She's ten and she's in fifth grade. She makes all As, except in math, which she hates, and she makes Bs in that."

"How do you know all that?" Sloane asked, totally surprised by how much he'd interacted with the child when she hadn't been watching. It was the way he'd used to be. Always interacting, always instilling trust. He was so much the old Carter right now she had a hard time remembering him as the Carter he'd turned into.

Carter simply smiled and shrugged. "Guess I just have a way with kids."

Yes, that was the old Carter—*her* Carter. His real smile. His sense of humor. But, as much as she wanted to hope for something more, she couldn't let herself. She'd lost hope months ago, and where Carter was concerned she'd been fighting a daily battle not to let any of it back in. Hope hurt. And she'd already hurt enough. Cried too many tears.

"Anyway, back to your mom," she said, her attention returning to Molly. "How often does she eat things she's not supposed to?"

"Once a day. She treats herself at night because she doesn't eat anything bad during the day."

So Jeannie was a ritual offender in her diabetic diet. Meaning if she made it through the day without blowing it she'd blow it at night. Also meaning her diabetes was probably never stable.

"How often does she eat bad things other than her nighttime treat?"

"Not as much as she used to. Sometimes two or three times a week."

Here was a brittle diabetic, with food poisoning, comatose from diabetic complications, who, in some way, went off her diet at least once a day. This was serious.

"I think we should get an IV into her," Carter said, pulling himself away from Molly. "I have an idea the food poisoning has only exacerbated an already bad situation. My guess is she was already dehydrated due to her condition, and the food poisoning just stepped it up."

"Do you have something in your medical bag? Because I didn't see…"

"Not in my medical bag. But I have a locked hard bag on my bike that's got a set-up."

His last several words were said on his way out through the door. Which left Sloane there with nothing to do but monitor Jeannie's vital signs. And think about Carter.

Sighing, she looked over at Molly, who was still standing there, wide-eyed. Not sure whether to cry. Not sure what to do. Just like *she'd* been after Carter had left her.

"Come here," she said, patting the spot on the floor next to Jeannie. "Why don't you sit and hold your mom's hand for a little while? I'm sure that's exactly what she'd like right now."

Just as what Sloane would like was her own hand in Carter's—as she'd wanted it for weeks after he'd gone.

# CHAPTER FOUR

"Is she stable?" asked Cruz Montoya as he helped Carter lift Jeannie onto a stretcher.

Cruz owned the helicopter service that hosted tourist rides and doubled as medical transport when it was necessary. Cruz himself was a former Army medic—one who had evacuated patients, who had pulled out dying soldiers under the worst and most dangerous of circumstances.

"No. Her vitals aren't stable and her blood sugar's not responding to insulin yet. There are no signs she's anywhere near coming out of her coma."

"So what about her?" Cruz asked, nodding sideways toward Molly, who'd stepped as far back from the activity as she could. "Is someone going to take care of her?"

"Her grandmother will be here to get her tomorrow, and in the meantime one of the other guests has agreed to watch her. She has three children of her own, and management vouches for her. It's the best we could do under the circumstances."

"Well, if that doesn't work out my mother's here,

and I'm sure she'd be glad to look after her for as long as needed."

"I'll keep that in mind," Carter said, looking over at Sloane, who was busy sorting out the oxygen tubing, IV tubing and heart monitor, getting everything ready for transport.

"Can you do this, Carter?" she asked. "The helicopter, I mean?"

It was the same question he'd been asking himself. *Could* he go up in a helicopter? Or even tolerate its noise?

"I guess we're going to find out, aren't we?" he said.

"You don't like choppers?" Cruz asked him.

"And a lot of other things. I took a bad hit in Afghanistan—lots of damage…"

Cruz nodded as if he understood. "Well, I'll try to go easy on you. I had a few quirks when I came back. Glad one of them wasn't flying or else I'd be in real trouble."

"Well, let's hope flying isn't one of mine." Carter grabbed the foot-end of the old-time military stretcher and placed his bag between his patient's feet. "Just letting you know I don't always know what sets me off."

"Are you on a program?" Cruz asked.

"One down in Tennessee. The Recovery Project."

"Where you work with bears?" Cruz asked. "I've heard they have a lot of success. Hope you're one of them."

"You and me, both," Carter said as he helped Cruz

load his patient on the helicopter, then climbed in beside her.

He really wanted some diazepam, or something else to calm him down. His pulse was racing faster than he'd ever felt it race. But this was his emergency run, and he wasn't going botch it by either backing out or taking a sedative that at best would make him drowsy and at worst put him to sleep.

"So, how long did you say this trip is going to take?"

"Forty," Cruz said, checking to make sure his passengers were fastened in securely.

"I can do forty," Carter said, hoping that if he sounded confident he would *be* confident.

"That's forty there and forty back. You up to that?"

Carter gulped. Forty minutes seemed like an awfully long time, but eighty...

*Face your fears, Holmes.*

How many times had he heard those words over the course of the program. Well, if ever there was a fear to face...


"The Recovery Project," Sloane whispered as she searched for it on the internet.

She'd overheard Carter's conversation with the helicopter pilot, and even though he had chosen not to tell her he was in a program, she was curious about it.

Something about bears, the pilot had said. And, sure enough, the project put PTSD patients with rescued baby bears. They took total care of them. Fed them, gentled them, got them ready to turn them loose back into the mountains if their condition warranted it.

It seemed like a good program. Granted, it was an alternative type of treatment, but from what she was reading it incorporated all kinds of PTSD treatment and was especially good at dealing with *acute distress disorder*, which was the type of PTSD Carter was diagnosed with. According to the program's description, it offered factors that office-based therapy and therapy groups could not. One of the primary goals was to allow those with PTSD a safe place to feel and address emotions through the human-animal bond.

Carter and a bunch of bear cubs? The thought of it brought a smile to her face. As improbable as it seemed, Sloane hoped it worked. But why hadn't Carter mentioned that to her? Why couldn't he have trusted her enough to tell her what he was doing? It was a huge step forward for him, and she was proud he was taking it on his own. But she was discouraged that he hadn't included her.

*Was it still a trust issue?* Had she betrayed his trust in a way she didn't understand?

Even the thought of that caused Sloane's stomach to churn.

Carter hesitated, seeing Sloane sitting in the hotel lobby, waiting for him.

The trip to the hospital and back hadn't been awful. Nothing had triggered him or really got to him at all. Which was a step in the right direction, because so many of his battle casualties had been transported to the hospital by helicopters. Hearing them circle overhead had become a sound he dreaded.

But not tonight. He'd barely noticed, as he'd been focused on his patient, not on himself. Like The Recovery Program had its PTSD victims focus on the bear cubs. A calculated misdirection, he guessed. One that seemed to work. One he hoped would work for him.

Tonight proved that it just might.

"No problems?" Sloane asked, taking the initiative and approaching Carter.

"Everything's fine. I got the patient checked in to Emergency, grabbed a cup of coffee and came right back."

"And the noise of the helicopter didn't—?"

He shook his head. "I'm good. And I appreciate your help."

"I saw four other patients for you while you were gone."

Carter's eyes softened. "Do you realize that stabilizing Jeannie was the first time we've ever worked together? We were a good team."

Too good. And he hoped that wasn't giving Sloane ideas.

"Anyway, the manager called me on the way in, so I've got another patient to see. Then I think I'm going to hang around here the rest of the night, just in case."

"Does Matt know about the program?" Sloane asked him.

"Yes."

"So it's just me who doesn't know your plans?" she asked.

"We're not together, Sloane. What makes you think I'd want to drag you back into my mess?"

"It's a worthy program, Carter. But I was the one who always searched for the right fit for you, so don't you think I would have been interested in knowing that you're in a program now?"

"I don't know *what* you'd be interested in knowing, Sloane." Carter hated doing this, but she was getting too close again, and in the end that would only hurt her. "And, since we're not together anymore, do you really think I have to tell you everything I do?"

"You never had to do that, Carter. I never asked. I never demanded. When you did tell me, it was because that was what you wanted to do. Not because I was forcing you into it."

Her pain threw him back to all the times before, when they'd had this or similar arguments. It had always triggered him. Any friction with Sloane had triggered him because she'd had him so high on a pedestal he'd always been afraid he'd fall off and disappoint her.

"I know you never tried to force me. But the expectations—"

"Mine or yours?" she asked.

"Both. They were too much. I couldn't stand up to them—even when you were telling me you knew I could do it. Sometimes I could, but sometimes I couldn't, and I didn't know how to deal with that—especially when something was triggering me."

Namely, *her*. Knowing how disappointed she would be if he failed had been a trigger. Knowing how much he was hurting her had been a trigger. Also coming to terms with the fact that he couldn't take care of Sloane the way he needed to had been a trigger. And all the triggers had added up to one big failure, and that had been the biggest trigger of all—failing Sloane.

"Have you ever just tried to work through one of those moments? I know when you were back at the hospital you didn't turn away from anything. But the longer you stayed there, the more you seemed to doubt yourself. Was it something I did, Carter? Or something I didn't do? Because if that's the case—"

He cut her off with the wave of his hand. "Look, would you care to go to the lounge for a drink? Maybe sit down and sort through some things."

She raised her eyebrows. "The lounge? Is that still the way you fix everything? With alcohol?"

"Wine for you…a nice Chablis. And fizzy water with lime for me. Sometimes it's not easy, but it's one demon on a long list I *can* control."

"That's great! You know what they say about little steps and how they turn into big ones. You always were disciplined when you set your mind to it. So, what about the—well—you know. You were smoking a lot of—pot. Taking a lot of pills. Oh, and I'll take a fizzy water as well. Going night hiking in a while and I want to be clear-headed."

"Good thinking on the water. And as for the pot and pills—three months off that, too. I'm working it out as well."

"Excellent, Carter. Especially since you're taking these steps on your own. A lot of people don't have that kind of determination. And I'm also happy to hear The Recovery Project is working for you. It should give you hope for much more progress. I'm really hopeful, too. Because maybe, somewhere down the line, we can be friends again. I know the rest of it's over, but I always did value your friendship."

"I'm keeping my fingers crossed for a lot of things, Sloane."

But for them? He wasn't ready to go that far. He'd done too much damage. He'd hurt her too much. And he didn't trust himself enough yet to think he could, or even deserved to have Sloane back in his life.

Carter looked up at the chandelier in the lobby. A thousand crystals glittered overhead, looking like little bits of shattered mirrors, reflecting everything around it. That was how he felt. Shattered. And with so many things reflecting him.

"I may not have all the answers, and God knows there are a lot of things I can't control, but there are some things I can. And what I need to do is to get through this program and see what happens after that."

"Like becoming a full-fledged bear rescuer?"

He chuckled. "Possibly. Being a GP wasn't what I had in mind when I went to medical school, but here I am—so who knows?"

"If that's what you want, Carter, you should go after it. Whatever makes you happy. Because I think the happier you are, the better your PTSD will get."

Carter could almost envision the two of them, living in a mountain cabin, running their own rescue. Maybe even developing a PTSD program to go with it. The lifestyle would be different from anything he'd ever thought about, but it would be good. Only with Sloane, though. And since there *was* no Sloane in his life now that dream disappeared almost at the same time it appeared.

"I still like being a doctor," he said. "But at least with a bear you don't get someone who purposely destroys their health by going against their doctor's order the way Jeannie does."

They went to the lounge, ordered fizzy water, then talked for a while longer. It was mostly about friends and incidental things. Nothing heavy, nothing about his illness. Nothing about what they had or what they'd lost. Oh, did you know Mrs. Levy's poodle had puppies? By the way, there's a new bakery down on Mulberry Street. They have great pastries. It wasn't as easy as he would have liked, but it wasn't nearly as awkward as he'd expected it to be. Surprisingly, the time passed quickly, maybe too quickly, and all too soon Sloane was scooting toward the edge of her seat.

"Look, I know you're back on duty now, but I do have a couple patients I promised to check in on before my hike. So if you don't mind...?"

"Not at all. Besides, I've got a couple to see myself, then I'm going to try and get back to my room for a quick shower and a nap before I have to come back here to do some rechecks. So, when did you get interested in night hiking? I remember we used to talk about it, but you were never as keen as I was."

"Since I got here. It's amazing how the desert literally springs to life at night. The stars, the animals, the feeling that you're the only one in the universe…"

Sloane smiled.

"It's something new for me, discovering things on my own. Usually you were the one doing the discovering and I was the one who tagged along. But this is different. It's mine. And it's really exciting because they've put me in a small advanced group. Anyway, since I'll be out, why don't you use my room here and save yourself the trouble of going home and then returning."

She fished the key card from her pocket and handed it to him.

"I'll just let the day clerk know where you'll be— unless you want to do that yourself?"

He drew in a deep breath and let it out slowly, as the mere brush of her hand on his sent tingles up his spine.

"Are you sure you want me there? Because it seems like I would be taking advantage, in case you did want to return for any reason."

As he handed her back the card, Carter pulled his hand away from hers a little more slowly than would be strictly called for. But, even in that little touch, so many memories had sprung up—good memories— he was reluctant to break the contact because in that moment, they were the way they used to be. Nothing had changed them, nothing had separated them. But that was only a fantasy, and as he broke the sensation that was trying to overtake him, the memories vanished, and they returned to being the same Sloane and Carter they were now.

"I might go rifling through your things."

She laughed.

"I have the same old things I had when we were together. I haven't been in the mood to buy myself anything new, so feel free to rifle."

He studied her for a moment. She was so beautiful, yet he could see the worry in her eyes. He'd put it there, even after all the times he'd told her not to worry, that he could take care of himself. Which, he couldn't, and that was painfully obvious. Then there was that cycle, the more obvious he became, the more she worried. Round and round, like a carousel he couldn't get off. Until the day he did.

"I'm not sure we should be doing this," he said.

"Doing what?"

"Trying so hard. Like you said, we need to take baby steps leading to bigger ones. I don't want to go back to the place where you tried to take care of me and I resisted just about everything you did."

He couldn't return to those awful months where she had tried so hard to help him that he had felt trapped. He knew it was because she cared, but what he knew and what he felt were two different things.

"It was smothering, Sloane. Not that you meant to do that, but I was so resistant that any attempt to help me seemed like I was being smothered. And it wasn't just you. It was all those counselors early on. They didn't have the right things to offer me. Not then. But what my counselor told me was that it was just me, not being ready to admit all the things I'd eventually have to admit. One being that you weren't really smothering me; I was smothering myself in pity and all kinds of other emotions I couldn't yet face."

"I never meant to do that, Carter, and I'm sorry that's what it felt like to you. Why didn't you say something?"

"Because I wasn't saying much of anything. How could I, when I didn't even know who I was anymore? Sometimes it just seemed easier to go along and hope I didn't mess things up too badly."

"And I was left imagining all sorts of things since you wouldn't tell me, then trying to put all the pieces of your jigsaw puzzle together. But you were getting farther and farther away from me, and I was trying everything I could think of to help you. Even though nothing was working."

"Why did you stay, Sloane? Why weren't you the one to leave?"

"Because every now and then I'd catch a glimpse of you, and that gave me hope. I loved you, Carter. I didn't want to give up because I thought you needed me. Or because I wanted you to need me. But I was wrong about that, too, wasn't I?"

"Maybe you were, at least toward the end. I'm sorry about that, but because I didn't know who I was anymore, there was no way you could have known. And maybe I was angry with you for that. Maybe I expected, or assumed, you, of all people, should know who I was," he said, feeling like a louse.

"The truth is, I don't know what was motivating

me at that point. Frustration. Anger. Fear. Maybe some self-loathing. Could be I was trying to prove I was still me, even when I knew I wasn't. The worst part was hearing myself saying something hurtful to you, and not being able to control it. But, I couldn't stop myself. Because you were always there, you turned into my target."

"I knew it was. And often the only thing that kept me sane through it all was knowing that the Carter I fell in love with wouldn't have done that. It was all I had to hold on to."

She was right. The real Carter *wouldn't* have done that to her. But the real Carter hadn't come home from Afghanistan and he wouldn't. In a sense he had died there, and the Carter who had taken his place wasn't the man Sloane had fallen in love with.

"Anyway, about your room…"

"The offer's still open and you don't have to read anything into it. I was only trying to make the next few hours a little easier on you. Take it or leave it."

"Sorry I overreacted," he said. "And I do appreciate the offer, but I need to stop by my office to see a few late-night patients after I'm done here, then after that I think I'll just go back to my room."

He looked longingly at the key card, now in Sloane's hand, and wished he could take it, with or without strings. But, that's not where he was, or even anywhere close to where he should be. She was too tempting, even with such an innocent gesture, and he had to be careful not to give in. Not to persuade himself that just this one time…

Carter slid out of the booth after Sloane but followed her out of the lounge rather than walking with her.

"I still don't get a lot of things right," he said, once they were in the lobby.

She smiled half-heartedly, then nodded.

"No big deal. This isn't easy and neither of us is winning any awards for getting it right. But I really am excited by your progress, Carter. No matter what else happens between us, I want you to succeed probably as much as you do. I always have."

"Trust me. A checkmark in the win tally of my life is a lot of incentive. I don't have too many of those on there yet, but I'm not giving up."

He reached over and took hold of her hand, and squeezed it, "Promise."

"I'll hold you to it," she said, squeezing back.

"I hope you do."

And he meant it. Even if they couldn't be who they used to be, maybe they could have something else. He hoped so, because not having Sloane in his life left him with a great big hole in his heart.

His whole objective at one in the morning had used to be drinking enough to pass out. That had been his normal in the past. Now he didn't *have* a normal. He took it as it came—whatever it was—and struggled through the best way he could.

In a few minutes the struggle would be with Sloane. He wanted to be near her so badly, even though he knew he shouldn't. But his impulses sometimes still took control, and Sloane was an impulse that he couldn't cure easily.

"So, how were your patients?" Carter asked a little while later, as she passed in the hall.

"Everything's fine. Everybody recovering quite nicely. I'll get my patient notes to you later, if that's OK?"

"No need to rush. My receptionist doesn't transcribe, and it takes me forever to get everything recorded, so I'm really not in a hurry."

Sloane laughed. "She really didn't impress me as a good fit for a medical practice."

"But she comes with the office," Carter said. "One of those buy-one-get-one offers. And I may not be here much longer than two months anyway, so I can cope with her."

"Two months?"

"Then on to my bears. It's the second part of the program. We get all the teaching during the first part, and start on the path to recovery. Then they give you a short reprieve, to see if you're responding well enough to the program or lagging behind so much you have to repeat the first part of your therapy. They want to make sure you're ready for each step you're supposed to accomplish so they can recognize and respond to issues they don't know about. A lot of people with PTSD cover up certain aspects of it, and the counselors at The Recovery Project expect that and prepare for it."

"And they're watching you right now?"

"Not directly. This is my time to see if I can work through what I learned in the first part of the program. But I do call my counselors twice a day. If they think I'm having problems they can't work through long distance, or if I think I'm having problems, they'll call me back to Tennessee to see what I need. It's a tight program. A lot of it's based on faith in yourself, but most of it's based on trust."

"Sounds like you're really sold on it."

"I am, because I'm hoping I can come back here and practise when I'm through it. Maybe buy my part of the practice from Matt. Somewhere in the future see what I can set up here to help other people with PTSD problems. Forgeburn has a lot of potential, with its wide-open spaces. It's a great place to get away and discover yourself, and if it works out for me here, it should work for others."

"And Matt's OK with you leaving in a few weeks?"

"He's great about it. In fact, he's excited for me He's going to do some kind of co-operative exchange with the Whipple Creek Clinic to make sure he's covered. I mean it, this is the place I want to start over, Sloane. It's not what I had before, but it's what I need now. Something simpler and scaled back. A chance to breath. And, heal."

"I guess I expected you to come back to Manning Hospital if you returned to medicine. But this sounds good, Carter. It sounds as though you've made some excellent plans for your future, and I'm excited for you."

"Thank you," he said simply. "It's going to take

a while, but I've got all the time in the world so, as we've been saying, baby steps…"

"Do you think you'll ever return to surgery?" she asked.

"Not in the immediate future. I think the stress of it is part of what triggers me, and my counselors are telling me I must keep my stress levels down. So, it's not in my plans right now, and I have no idea about the future."

"You know Daddy will always take you back don't you? If you get through your program and decide you want to go back."

Carter knew she meant well. She always had, and he deeply appreciated it. But going back to where he had been? That wasn't going to happen because his life was about moving forward now.

"Tell him thank you for me and that if I want to be a surgeon again, I've got a long way to go to get there. Right now, it's just not my aim, but Forgeburn is. So, I hope he's not holding my position open hoping that, by some miracle, I'll come walking through the hospital door one day, cured and ready to take up surgery again. Because, nothing's going to cure me, Sloane. I can be helped and taught to take better control of myself and my life. But I'm fighting a lifelong sentence, and I can't predict any outcomes for myself. That's one thing I've learned in surgery. Work with where you are today and don't plan too diligently for the future because you're in transition and things will change."

"You've come a long way in three months, Carter.

I hope we can maintain some kind of relationship, so I can see where you're going because I'm really happy about your progress. I only wish I'd found better help for you months ago, so you could have been on your way sooner, and I'm sorry I didn't. But it's all good now, and I'm confident it's going to work for you, especially seeing how far you've come."

He hoped she meant that. But right now, she seemed so lost, he wasn't sure. And it was his fault. Every ounce of sadness and doubt he saw in Sloane was what he'd put there. For that, he was truly sorry. And that, above all else, was why he'd left.

It broke his heart seeing the results of his handiwork, and for Sloane to put any part of that behind her, he had to leave. Had to give her a fresh start. It had never been because he didn't love her. He did when he'd rode away. And still did, now.

But could he ever really love her the way he had? Totally, completely. Especially knowing what his love had cost her? Would it be better to hang back, or pull away altogether? And could she ever love him the way she had, especially after she'd stepped into the role of caregiver of sorts?

The answers weren't clear. And, they weren't easy, not for either of them. Their love had changed, and nothing was going to be the same. But, could it work differently?

"It hasn't been easy, but I'm optimistic the outcome will be better than what I have going for me now."

"That's all I ever wanted for you," Sloane said. "And I suppose I thought I was helping you."

"You were—by being there. I needed you there, Sloane. Supporting me, but not trying to cure me. That's my battle, and the only way I can win it is if I figure out the strategies by myself."

They stepped outside to the veranda and sat on a stone wall overlooking a meticulously-sculpted desert garden with pink-blooming prickly pear cacti, scarlet hedgehog cacti and Joshua trees. The colors, even in the dim lights on the pergola next to them, were breathtakingly vibrant, and his gaze fixed on another couple, walking along the edge of the garden, holding hands, so absorbed in each other there was nothing else in their world. He and Sloane had been that way once, but now, in the dimming of the day, they sat separated by too much distance, physically and emotionally, and he didn't know how to repair it.

"I'm here, Sloane, because I was worried about slipping back into old patterns that exacerbated my PTSD. The way you worried made my anxiety worse because I didn't like seeing you suffer. And I didn't want you worrying about me all the time. Watching. Waiting. Trying to anticipate what I might do next, when that's something that can't be anticipated. It wouldn't have worked for us. In fact, in the long run, I think it would have destroyed both of us. And, you didn't deserve what my illness was doing to you. I couldn't watch that, and there were so many times seeing how you suffered caused my anxiety to increase because there was nothing I could do to help you."

"Did I ever complain, Carter? Did I ever say anything that led you to believe that I didn't want to help you through this?"

"You didn't have to say anything," he countered. "I knew you, and I could see how I was affecting you. I could see how nervous you were becoming, see the distractions you were experiencing at work because of me. I was putting you at risk, Sloane. In your personal life and worse, in your job as a surgeon. Most of all, I could see it in your eyes, the way you looked at me, the way you struggled to be patient when I knew you wanted to scream or kick something."

He reached over and took hold of her hand, then scooted just a little closer.

"In the state I was in, I couldn't stay there and let it keep happening over and over, so I left. And I'm so sorry that's what I had to do, but my life was closing in on me. I knew I was getting to my now-or-never point."

"But, the way you left…"

"It was bad form, and I regret it. But I debated a clean break versus something long and drawn out. And if it had come to long and drawn out, I don't think I could have left you. Not if you cried, or held on to me, or simply asked. At that time, Sloane, I wasn't strong enough to do anything other than what I did. So, I suppose I chose what most would consider the coward's way out, but it's what I thought was best for both of us."

"It wasn't best for me, Carter. You did what you thought was best for you, and you didn't even tell me what was happening, or how you were feeling. We might have been able to work out some of the problems differently than we did but you didn't give us a chance, and after so many years..."

Now there were tears in her eyes. He was making her cry again, like the many times she'd hidden herself away from him and cried. He'd heard her. And now, he saw her. But he wasn't sure he was ready to face the way he hated what he always seemed to do to her.

"Look, I—I um—"

To hell with what he needed. Sloane's needs came first. They always had because that's the way he'd always wanted it. Sloane before him. At least prior to his PTSD. Then he'd done selfish things. A few at first, like missing a meal when he knew she'd cooked for him or staying out later than he'd told her he would, which he knew it would cause her to worry. Eventually, it turned into the bigger things—staying out all night, the addictions that were getting closer to being out of control. That's when he'd shoved Sloane behind him. That's when he actually believed he owed it to himself to come first in everything. His way, or no way.

But now... Carter moved closer to Sloane and pulled her into his arms as she cried. Quiet sobs on his shoulder. And he held her, stroked her hair, rocked her gently.

"I wasn't able to work out anything by the time I finally left," he told her. "But, it was me, not you. Never you, Sloane, and I should have told you that much, tried to make you understand. By the time I left though, I'd already lost me. At least the good parts of me who knew what I was leaving behind. The rest of me—it didn't really matter."

She sniffled but didn't pull away from him.

"You always mattered, Carter. The good, the bad—sure, I was struggling, but there was never a moment you didn't matter. Until I received your text message. Then I was left wondering what I was doing, and why I wasn't the one leaving you. I had cause, you didn't. But I couldn't walk away, and it wasn't even because I loved you. And I did. It was because I thought I could help. I truly believed my feelings for you would be part of your cure. I was wrong, though. Wasn't I?"

He loved her so much he'd had to walk away. She'd loved him so much she'd had to stay.

"I honestly don't know if you were wrong, or not."

She finally pushed away from him, the wiped the remaining tears with the back of her hand, then sniffed.

"It shouldn't have been such a mess. But it was too complicated, and overwhelming, going from a life that made sense to one that didn't. And we did make sense, Carter. Even now, with all you've been through, and with the way our feelings have changed, you know we made sense."

"Once upon a time," he said, with a wistful sigh.

"Once upon a time without the happily-ever-after ending. Shouldn't stories like ours have a happy ending?"

"I used to think so, but after what I saw when I

was in the Army, and after what I went through—too many people never get their happily-ever-after ending."

He stared at her face for a moment. A bit red, a bit blotchy. But so beautiful he ached from the memories of when that face radiated happiness and joy. Then, but not now.

"Look, it's getting late and I've got a couple of late-nighters coming to the office, so I need to get going. If we need to talk some more…"

"Not now," she said, looking up at him. "Like I said earlier, I'm signed up for that night hike and it's about time for me to go. So, I don't want to talk anymore right now, Carter, because I've got to figure out where all of this is going."

She stood up, too, then took three steps forward and placed a soft kiss on Carter's cheek—an old habit she didn't want to break. And she didn't care if she should, because it was the only reminder from their past that transcended their problems and, for that instant, carried them back to when their life together good.

"Once upon a time," she whispered, then walked away.

Carter watched her until she joined up with her group of hikers on the other side of the desert garden. No matter what it took, he wasn't going to hurt her again, even if he had to run to a place where he could lose himself forever, if that's what Sloane needed. Putting her first again—it's what he had to do even though the outcome would not be what he wanted. But when you loved someone they way he loved Sloane…

# CHAPTER FIVE

CARTER LOOKED LIKE HELL. After a long night, followed by a long day, he felt like it, too. Four more re-checks at the hotel and an unexpectedly long queue of patients waiting at his office until halfway through the night, and he was officially exhausted. And grungy. And filled with a fast flurry of thoughts that simply wouldn't go away. All that, plus his back hurt. Maybe he'd pulled a muscle? Or bumped into something that, by morning, would be a nice purple bruise. Whatever the reason, he just wanted to take his aches and pains and go to sleep. Except, when he tried, sleep rejected him. Caused him to pace the room, then take a couple of acetaminophen for his back, hoping a little bit of over-the-counter relief would finally let him put his head down on the pillow and close his eyes.

Acetaminophen. Such a mild relief for a man who'd been addicted to morphine when he was in the hospital, and anything he could get when he was out. But, it was all he allowed himself, even though a few of his back twinges were beginning to kick him a little harder than he cared for. Which meant it was time to force himself into some kind of relaxation to allow the spasms to subside. Physician, heal thyself. Yeah, right. There were just too many things to heal so he was just taking them one by one rather than overwhelming himself.

Of course, as spasms went, what he was having now wasn't severe. Not like when he'd been injured, anyway. He'd had a stage five nephrology injury, the worst of the worst. It had been a shattered kidney, excruciatingly torn from its pedicle—basically what had attached his kidney to him. So, he'd had to lose one kidney. And have some surgical repair to the other. Not as excruciating, but painful all the same. Then had come the nephrologist's pep talk. A lot of people lived a normal, productive life with only one.

Yeah, right. Normal and productive.

All that, and he'd hardly even noticed they'd removed his spleen. Sure, he'd removed dozens of spleens and sure, he'd been the one giving the pep talks. It's nice to have a spleen, but not necessary. Then the "normal and productive life" malarkey.

What goes around comes around, Carter supposed, as he looked at himself in the mirror and frowned. He needed sleep. A shower to try and ward off the building anxiety, then at least four hours of hibernation before he started all over again. Also, he couldn't afford any more thoughts about Sloane—they weren't conducive to shutting his eyes and hoping visions of sugarplums were strong enough to fight their way in.

But that wasn't happening. Not in the shower. Not in his bed. Not in the rickety, revolting chair next to the bed—the one he'd thrown a sheet over, so he didn't have to touch the chair's fabric. The more he fought it, the more his anxiety crept in. If he went to sleep now, he could still get in four hours…three hours…two hours.

What would have happened, he wondered, if he had taken Sloane up on her offer of her room? Or maybe he had subconsciously hoped she'd come back? Or had he simply liked the idea that he was sleeping in her bed, with his head on her pillow?

If that was the case, his diagnosis would have been he was still in love with her. And not in the "fond friend" kind of way, but in every sense of the word. Not that he didn't already know that.

"Well?" Carter asked the mirror as he started to pace again, knowing if he went to sleep right now, he'd only get one hour "Are you, or aren't you?"

He didn't want to do so much as even think the answer because, if he did, he might have to do something about it.

"What? Try to win her back?"

That question came with another scary answer. Sloane still loved him. There was no denying that. And if Carter fell into that, took a sidestep away from his promise not to involve her again, he'd be back at the beginning.

Love didn't change everything in his case. In fact, it made things worse. Thank God, some reason had latched on to him because while yes, he did want to win her back, he knew he couldn't do it. He wasn't ready. And Sloane wasn't over what he'd done to her before.

Then, there was the fundamental issue of how she triggered him because he hated what he was doing. He was traveling down a crooked path, and love was hard to sort when PTSD was hanging on for that journey.

"And there you have your answer," Carter said, then backed away, grabbed up his shirt, put it on and headed for the door. Maybe he'd have an early breakfast, or simply take a walk. Either way, it was better than what he was going through in his room—his isolated, cockroach-ridden little room.

Who was it that said something about how, if you loved something, you should set it free? He didn't remember the entirety of the quotation, but he did understand the drift of it. Since he loved Sloane, and he wasn't good for her, it was time to let go.

"Damn," Carter said, heading to his motorcycle.

Why did it always have to be so difficult? Why did his feelings for her make him ache so badly?

Because what he wanted, and what he got to have, were two entirely separate things. That's why.

Shuffle your thoughts, Carter warned himself. It was a tip he'd picked up from his counselor on what to do when he knew he was getting too close to his anxiety limit. Think of something else. Redirect his attention.

Which is what he did now. He pulled out his phone and looked at his calendar for the day. Six patients scheduled in the office this morning, and two outside. Not bad, he thought. The only problem was, he had two hours before anybody in Forgeburn stirred. Which meant he had time to kill, and empty time was his worst enemy.

As often as not, when he wasn't occupied, the whole overthinking process would start, then something he didn't want to think would squeeze its way in and eventually take over.

Sighing, he was feeling his lack-of-sleep hangover. Thankfully, his back spasms had let up, which was a good thing, otherwise he wouldn't have been able to climb on his bike and head over to the Red Rock Inn for a morning coffee and a cloak-and-dagger glimpse of Sloane. But, by the time he got there, and found a seat at the counter in the hotel's all-night diner, it was too late. Sloane had beaten him there, she was right by the entrance where she couldn't miss him. And, she didn't.

"You up early, or haven't you gone to bed?" she asked him, heading to the counter to order a latte rather than taking a seat next to him in the blue and brown-striped banquette that ran the length of the tiny diner.

"A little of both, I suppose. If you don't sleep all night, then it only serves to reason that you're getting up early."

Sloane was too bright-eyed from her overnight expedition. Too animated.

"Did you have a good time?" he asked her, even though the look on her face told him she'd loved every minute of it. Why did he have to know her so well?

"There were three of us, plus the guide, and we

got into some really nice areas. We heard coyotes. We didn't get close enough to disturb them, but we could see the glow of their eyes. The air and the ground temperature were cool, which was nice, since we covered nearly ten miles. And there were so many different little night creatures out there: mammals, birds, insects that hide during the day. Oh, and the reptiles—there were so many of them scattered around, looking for a rock that still maintained some daytime heat. When they got warm enough they went off in search of a meal… It was absolutely breathtaking how much goes on in the more remote areas at night. I'm hoping I got some good photos, because we encountered an enormous variety of nocturnal life—like snakes, skunks, scorpions, kangaroo rats, jack rabbits, owls, and even a bobcat."

"You weren't in any danger, were you?" Carter asked.

Even though she'd been with other people, he worried because he knew what Sloane was like. She got excited, and ignored everything but what she was focused on. Like the time he'd taught her how to mountain bike. She'd taken three detours into the dirt because she had been so distracted by how she pedaled, she'd forgotten to watch where she pedaled. Eventually, it always came together, but in the new undertakings in her life, Sloane's excitement too often overshadowed her abilities. So, yes, he worried. He always worried about her. He couldn't help himself.

"No. Our guide gave us some basic rules to follow and told us if we didn't do exactly what he said we'd have to go back to the resort." Sloane paused for breath, then continued, the flush of excitement still rosy on her cheeks. "I wish you could have been there, Carter. You would have loved it."

"Maybe next time," he said, even though he knew there wouldn't be a next time.

"You look…terrible," Sloane said, in her usual morning-perky voice.

She had always been a morning person. He'd been the one who'd thought the only reason to have a morning was to sleep through it.

"You don't like the new look?" Carter said, looking down to check that he'd put on fresh clothes after his shower, since he'd been too groggy to really notice. Luckily he was good. Or at least his clothes were.

"What I don't like is the way *you* look, and it has nothing to do with your clothes."

"Being tired will do that to you."

He watched her pick up her to-go latte, then walk over to his table. She was hesitant, like she wasn't sure if she wanted to be involved with him this early or would rather put it off until later. Or, never.

"Which is why I'm going into my office early, hoping I can grab some sleep before I start seeing patients."

"Later, I'd like to show you something."

He raised a weary, yet very wicked eyebrow.

"Really?"

Sloane laughed.

"Not *that*. But earlier, up on Flat Top—it's a rock formation rock formation we came through a little while ago—there was a herd of desert bighorn sheep emerging, but we didn't have time to stop and take pictures so I thought if you had some free time maybe we could go up there together. The hike's not very impressive considering where we used to go, but the view... I can see why you like Forgeburn. If I weren't so city I might move here just for the view"

She held up her camera, then asked. "Want to come with me?"

"Right after lunch?" he asked, surprised, yet pleased, she'd asked him. "Unless there's an emergency, my afternoon is free."

Her smile was so big and bright he couldn't turn her down. Never had been able to, when she looked at him that way.

"So how far is this Flat Top?"

"Just a couple of miles. The hiking trail is a little advanced, for most of the people here, but the guide said there were a couple of rough ones in the area, so I'm hoping to see what they're about. Maybe you'd like to hike along with me for that, as well."

Hiking was one of the many things they'd been good at. Hiking someplace out of the way, finding a secluded spot, making love in the open air. That had been very good, as well.

"Just let me know when you want to go, and if I'm free..."

He shrugged. This was a dangerous idea. Too many reminders. Too much of their past inching back in. But before his illness, he'd never been able to say 'no' to Sloane and, apparently, that was also inching back in, as well.

* * *

Carter seemed rested, but restless. Sloane could tell from the way he lagged back. And sure, asking him to come with her probably wasn't the best idea she'd ever had. But she'd remembered the way they used to get so excited when they discovered something new in their journeys, and before she knew it, the invitation had slipped out. So here they were, looking for sheep, and Carter had barely spoken a word since they'd left the hotel. Getting some sleep might have improved his physical condition, but his mind wasn't here.

"You OK?" she finally asked, after they had hiked almost a mile in silence.

"Just weighing some options. Nothing to worry about."

"Anything you want to tell me?" she asked, as they stopped for a few minutes to have some water and a regroup.

"Not really. I was thinking ahead to what life is going to be like living here."

"And…?"

"And I think it's going to be good. I'm not sure I'm meant to live in the city anymore. It's too—confining."

"Is that your PTSD talking, or you?"

"A little of both, I suppose. My PTSD put me in the position to find something new, and I like what I've found. Sometimes isolation is good."

"But do you want to stay this isolated for the rest of your life?"

"What I want for the rest of my life is to be able to count on myself, and if I can do that here, in the desert, this is where I want to be."

For a city girl, Sloane had been surprised how much she had enjoyed the desert, too. It was something she could get used to, but so far Carter had made no mention of her staying here. She had listened to him very closely, hoping to hear something that would encourage her, but every time he had got near something that sounded like the possibility of hope for them, he had backed away from it. Maybe that was for the best, though, as she was changing, just like he was, and maybe the person she'd turn into wouldn't be the woman who had once loved him to distraction. She hoped that wasn't the case, but she couldn't count it out.

"It's a good place, and if it's what you need, I'm happy for you."

But not for herself as, now, Sloane was facing the same dilemma he was. Where was she supposed to be, and was it with, or without Carter?

As they approached the narrowing of the trail she spotted a little Gila monster, out sunning itself on a rock. It was watching them warily, probably not wanting to give up its place in the sun. She didn't blame the creature. The sun here was glorious. And the air so clean, and the sky so blue. Normally, she didn't notice these things, but now that she had, she wondered if it had something to do with what could be emerging as a desire to stay here with Carter? Not that he'd asked her, and not that she expected him to.

But still, is that what she wanted? Was her subconscious directing her in a way her consciousness was still resisting?

"They're venomous," Carter said. "Beautiful though."

"But not deadly."

"It's a hell of a bite if it gets you. It kind of chews its way into your skin then hangs on for dear life. Leaves you with a neurotoxin that's going to hurt. The bite area's going to be afflicted with edema and you're going to get weak because your blood pressure will drop critically. Just saying…"

"It's a hell of a bite if you let it bite you. But it's such a slow mover you'd have to be an idiot not to get out of its path."

Sloane pointed her camera at the creature, who'd yet to move, and shot several photos. Then she stomped on the ground and laughed as the lazy lizard finally decided to waddle away.

"See how it runs," she said, looking back at Carter, who was stretched out on a large rock, sunning himself much the way the Gila monster had been. He was breathing a little too hard, she thought. But maybe he still wasn't in the best of shape.

She snapped some photos of him, then returned to the path.

"You can stay there if you want. But that rattler sneaking up behind you might have some different ideas about what it wants to do with your rock."

That was all it took for Carter to jump up, then spin around to look for the snake.

"There's no rattlesnake here," he said.

"But there could have been."

They'd always played little jokes on each other. It had been part of the dynamic between them she'd loved. And, while she hadn't meant to do it, it had come naturally. Sloane didn't regret it, though, because just for that moment it was nice getting that little piece of them back.

"And you, Sloane Manning, are a wicked woman."

Carter caught up to her just as the trail narrowed to barely allow one person through and grabbed hold of her. He spun her around to face him. Then smiled.

"Stand back, woman, while I take the lead."

"For fifty feet," Sloane said, pointing ahead to a big red rock that definitely had a flat, tabletop appearance. "That's our destination."

"And no sheep in sight," Carter said, squeezing past her.

For that instant, when their bodies pressed together, Sloane held her breath. It felt so good, having him that close. His body squeezed tight to hers. So many memories came flooding back, of all the times when a simple movement like that had started something more.

"Oh, there will be sheep," she said, practically forcing the words out of her mouth. His effect on her was so strong she was almost dizzy with it.

Carter paused briefly, still pressed to her, and studied her face the way he'd done so many times before. He'd claimed it was because he could read her. Maybe he could. Or maybe he wanted to. Whatever the case, she couldn't look him in the eye. He might see things he wasn't meant to. Things she'd put away, or was trying to put away. Things that still hung on. He didn't need to know any of that. Didn't have that right any more.

So Sloane looked off to the side, taking great care not to make direct contact lest his siren effect would lure her in. She was already a wreck and she didn't need to deal with any more of that. Even though she still loved him.

But it was a dangerous love now, because it hurt so much.

"Lead on," she said finally, squirming away from him.

"We were good, like you said before," Carter said before he turned back to the trail. "I'm sorry I destroyed it."

"We both destroyed it," Sloane said. "You by pushing me away, and me by not recognizing when I needed to step away and let you lick your own wounds."

She fell into line behind Carter but kept her eyes on the red dirt trail.

"Neither of us got it right."

He stopped and spun to face her so abruptly she bumped into him.

"You have no blame in this, Sloane. I did what I did because I couldn't control myself. Not my actions, not my thoughts. That's where it started, and anything that came after was simply a reaction."

"I loved you so much, Carter…" Sloane said, and tears started slipping down her cheeks.

Carter brushed them back with his thumb and gently pulled her into his chest.

"I know you did," he said, so quietly it was barely more than a whisper. "And you were all I thought about while I was in Afghanistan. All I wanted was to come home to you. But I never came home."

Sloane sniffled, then looked up at Carter. His eyes were so distant. He was staring at—nothing. It was such a sad sight she almost couldn't bear to look at him.

"Why did you go?" she asked him. "Your career was set. You were getting some amazing offers from hospitals all over the country. Then one day you came home and simply said you'd joined the Army. But you wouldn't tell me why, except to say it was something you had to do—your patriotic duty. Why did you have to do it, Carter? I have a right to know, since you came back so broken. It was an honorable thing to do, and I was proud of you. But the cost was so high and I never really understood why you broke us apart to do it."

Carter took Sloane's hand and pulled her away from the narrow path to an area that opened up into a wide expanse of red rocks and desert plants, then motioned for her to sit down on a rock next to him.

"I never told you because—because I wasn't sure you'd understand."

He took hold of her hand and kissed her open palm, the way he'd always done.

"And you're right. You do have the right to know. It was an obligation I had to fulfill for someone I loved deeply."

"Another woman?" she asked.

There had been other women in Carter's past. She knew that and it didn't bother her, because he'd always been honest about it. But another woman who had the kind of influence it would take to persuade him into joining the Army? And at a time when their first anniversary of being together was coming up?

"Who was she?"

"He. Who was *he*? And *he* was my brother. You remember me telling you about James?"

"He died young didn't he? Cystic fibrosis?"

Carter had never really said much about James and she had always sensed that the loss was still painful, even after all these years. So, she'd never asked him much. At least nothing she'd thought would bring up sad memories for him.

"James was two years younger than me and he was sick. As you know the CF was very progressive with him, and we always knew he wouldn't be with us for very long. But it never stopped us from including him in all our family activities. He was such a—a vital force. Always happy. Always the one to cheer us up when we were down or worried about him."

Carter sniffed, then wiped away the tears forming in his eyes.

"One of the things he always talked about was growing up and joining the Army. My dad was a career Army man, and James wanted to be just like him. Of course we knew that wouldn't happen, but it meant so much to him—especially when Dad would let him wear one of his uniform hats. Anyway, I made a promise to James that I'd become a doctor when I grew up, and then I'd find or invent something to cure him, so he could go in the Army. He believed me. But he was only seven, and most seven-year-old boys look up to their older brothers. The thing was, I truly believed I could save him. But I couldn't. In my nine-year-old mind after he died, I felt like I'd broken my promise, and I lived with that for years."

"So you joined the Army for James?" she asked.

"It was all he ever talked about so, yes, I joined the Army for my brother. I couldn't have lived with myself if I hadn't."

"What a beautiful thing to do," Sloane said. "I wish I'd known."

"How do you tell someone you're going to war as a means of atoning for something you promised when you were little more than a baby?"

Carter sniffed again.

"My parents were both gone by the time I enlisted, and I suppose the reason I didn't tell anybody why was because my parents' way of coping was to not talk about James, which became my way. We were all so damaged by his death and even though I was young, I think the denials we adopted are what got us through. For me, the denials also helped me cope with my guilt, and while I know it's not the best way to deal with the loss of someone you love so much, I just did what my parents did, and every day it seemed to get easier, and much farther away."

He paused for a moment and looked away.

"I should have told you all that, and I'm sorry I

didn't, but I've never talked about James with anybody but you."

Sloane did understand and felt truly sorry for his loss. She felt even worse for his family's need to ignore the loss by not talking more about James. It could have brought them together in a way they'd missed. It could have made them stronger, or closer. That's what had happened when her mother died. She and her dad had kept Mum included as part of them because she was, in every way. And while the loss had been great, it had always been comforting to know her mother through her father's eyes. It had made her dad and her stronger and closer.

"You're lucky to have had him, even if it wasn't for long. I think he would have been proud of you."

"I hope so," he said, taking one more swat at his tears. "Anyway, if you want to catch a sheep, there's one standing in the middle of the path looking at us. I think he might attack, judging from the way he's got his head lowered, and how he's snorting in the dirt. Do they always paw the ground like that when they attack?"

Sloane stood up quickly, but there was nothing ahead. Not a bighorn sheep, not even a tiny little lizard.

"Got ya back for the rattlesnake," Carter said, laughing, and then took hold of her hand and pulled her along the trail.

Yes, *this* was the way they used to be, and Sloane was glad to be back there, if only for a little while.

But could it last? On some level, could they get together again? Or would separate ways be their best course?

# CHAPTER SIX

THE HIKE OUT to find the bighorn sheep with Sloane had been fun, Carter reflected as he got on with his afternoon surgery. Much in the way things had used to be between them. Spontaneous. Connecting with each other the way they'd used to connect.

The one thing Carter regretted was that they had only had a couple of hours, as he'd been called back to attend a patient with a sprained wrist. But at least they'd found a small herd of sheep, and Sloane had gotten her pictures. He'd enjoyed seeing her happy, even though her happiness didn't offset the problem that she was such a huge reminder of so many things in his life that had gone bad. He wasn't blaming her for anything. But simply seeing her…

"Mrs. O'Brien?" he asked the older woman who opened her hotel door to the length of its chain and peeked out. She was staying at Cliff Edge, a charming hotel just a few miles away from Red Rock. It accommodated the less active vacationer, which he guessed would be Mrs. O'Brien since he had distinctly heard the clack of an aluminum walker coming from inside her room.

"Are you the doctor? she asked.

"I certainly am. My name's Carter. Carter Holmes."

"Well, Carter Holmes. It's about time you got here. I called over an hour ago."

There was no point in telling her he'd been out hiking and had to practically run the two miles to get back as quickly as he had. Or that he was halfway to being dehydrated, and his back was starting to bother him again, not to mention some very out-of-condition legs that were cramping. When people needed a doctor, they needed a doctor, and nothing else mattered. In a way, he liked the unplanned nature of that. In his surgical practice, nothing had been unplanned. Here, almost everything was, and Carter was finding the challenge of not knowing what he'd be doing in an hour invigorating.

"Sorry to keep you waiting. Next time I'll try to be a little more prompt. Anyway, tell me about your wrist. What happened?"

"I hurt it getting in the shower."

"How long ago?"

"Last night, about this time."

And she'd waited twenty-four hours to call him, which had ruined the evening plans he'd hoped to have with Sloane. Such was the life of a GP, he supposed. And, something he was going to have to get used to.

"Well, why don't you go sit in the chair next to the bed, then I'll take a look."

"Could it be broken, do you think?"

It wasn't likely, considering the way she was using it.

"I should know in a few minutes, after I listen to your heart and lungs, and take your blood pressure."

"All that for a broken wrist?"

"Just being cautious."

Carter watched her walk to the other side of the room and take her seat. She was remarkably sprightly for someone on a walker, and he wondered if she really needed it. But, that was a decision for her real doctor, not him.

"I don't have to get undressed?" Mrs O'Brien asked.

"Nope. But if you could let me listen for a minute…"

Which she did. And for someone her age, which he guessed to be near eighty, she seemed in great shape.

"Everything's normal," he said, taking a gentle hold of the wrist she held out to him. There was no bruising, no swelling, no outcry of pain when he ranged it. "

"Your wrist seems fine to me," he said, finally. "So, when does it hurt."

"It doesn't, but like you said, I'm just being cautious."

And lonely, he guessed. Like him, she was probably all alone in the world, and simply craving a little attention, if even from a stranger. Carter understood that. These last months had been lonely for him, as well.

"I think as a precaution, I'll put an elastic bandage

on your wrist, then check back with you every day for a while, to make sure it's getting better."

It hadn't been a necessary medical call, and the bandage wasn't necessary, either. But a few minutes of time might work wonders for her. It had for Carter, when he finally found The Recovery Project.

"Will I be restricted from any activities?" she asked.

"Just rock climbing and canyon hiking," he teased. Instantly, her fixed scowl turned into a pleasant smile. "And no motorcycles."

"I gave those up when I was seventy," Mrs O'Brien said. "My husband and I used to travel cross country on our bikes. The best trip ever was from Seattle, up the coastal highway to Alaska. It was so beautiful, we stayed there a couple of years."

What she'd done in her life wasn't too unlike the plans he and Sloane had made. In a way, he envied Mrs. O'Brien. She had lived a great life despite her hardships.

"Is that why you're here?" he asked. "Was this someplace you and your husband lived?"

"No, we didn't live here. But we sure did climb every rock and explored every canyon you could find. I wish I was still up to some of it."

"Well, give that wrist a couple of days and maybe we can take a short hike together. I'll see if there are any easy trails around here you could manage."

Mrs. O'Brien beamed from ear to ear. "I'd like that," she said.

And this was the real reason Carter was making

this house call—to doctor in a way that was different than he ever had. Or had ever even imagined. It would give him a chance to be personable with his patients, something he'd never done much of before, but Sloane had done all the time. Of course, she would see that as progress. But only if he told her, which he wasn't going to do as he had made the decision he had to start separating from Sloane again. If he didn't start now, he might never get around to it. He had to do it, though. A baby step. The first of many which were all destined to be difficult if every one of them led away from Sloane. But in order to save her, that had to be his course, painful or not.

"I'd say he's good to go." Carter smiled at the couple in front of him.

Mr. and Mrs. Mallory were on holiday with their son, Kevin, who had cystic fibrosis. Clearly not wanting him to miss out on anything, they'd come to ask Carter's opinion on whether Kevin could go on a donkey ride through the canyon. And, while Kevin didn't remind Carter of James, he brought memories of his brother flooding back, holding on strong.

"You'll have to use caution, of course, and take along the proper equipment, but I'd say Kevin is certainly strong enough to take a donkey ride down into the canyon."

Something his own brother would have loved doing.

"Can you go with us, Doctor?" Judy Mallory asked.

She was nervous. It showed. And Carter understood that better than most. There'd been too many times when he'd gone off to do something with James—something James hadn't always been up to. Playing at the playground. Taking long hikes—long in a child's vision. Going to a friend's house to play video games.

He'd never truly seen his brother as disabled. Of course he'd been so young back then. But his parents had always been cautious, and Carter had always seen that as them depriving James of a real life.

As a child, it had never occurred to him that their restrictions were protective. But here was a boy, not much older than James when he'd died, and his parents wanted him to experience life. They wanted him to be involved in everything he was able to—including a donkey ride down into one of the canyons.

Carter would go along to ease the Mallorys' peace of mind for James' sake. For his brother who'd been restricted from everything.

'What time would you be leaving?" Carter asked.

"We're not sure which day the hotel will arrange it for yet, but it will be late in the day, when it's a little cooler. We're making special arrangements for it to work into Kevin's schedule. You know—between breathing treatments, chest physiotherapy…"

"Well, I've got my hiking boots sitting by the door in my hotel room, just waiting to go. So, let me know when you're going after you find out and I'll be ready. Barring medical emergencies, of course."

He tousled Kevin's curly hair. The boy wasn't frail the way James had been, and he certainly wasn't plagued by a typical CF cough. As of now his lungs were clear—a condition he'd check again just before their hike. And if ever a smile spoke a thousand words, Kevin's did.

"So, this is what you want to do?" Carter asked the boy as he packed up his medical bag.

"That's why we came here," Kevin said.

"Well, make sure you get plenty of rest, and keep up with your treatments. And if you're doing as well as you're doing right now, whenever the hotel sets the schedule, we're going to have an adventure."

That was what James had always called their excursions—adventures. Because, for him, anything outside their home was an adventure. It did ache, though, knowing how much James would have enjoyed the adventure Kevin was about to have.

Carter nodded to the Mallory family as he exited the room.

Downstairs, in the lobby, he dropped down onto one of the several plush sofas in the sitting area, trying to steady his breathing. He hadn't really exerted himself, and nothing about this felt like the anxiety. This wasn't a panic attack. It had nothing to do with PTSD and everything to do with how crazy bad he still missed his brother. It had been over twenty-six years now, and the pain of it was still acute.

"You OK?" Sloane whispered, sitting down next to him and taking hold of his hand.

"Yes, as far as my PTSD is concerned and no, because I just came from seeing a young boy with CF. It brought back some memories," Carter said, not sure why she was there, but glad she was. "I didn't expect to see you."

"I was just coming back from the spa. I decided to indulge myself a little bit. They have a nice facility here. Maybe you should think about indulging yourself from time to time because you look a little tired. A nice freshen-up might do the trick."

"Have you ever known me to be the spa type?" he asked, giving her a weak smile. "The massages you gave me were everything I ever needed, but to have a stranger do it?"

He faked a shudder.

"All I'm saying is, you need to take better care of yourself. Something seems off."

"I'm just struggling with the pace here. Being on call twenty-four seven has got my system out of whack, but eventually I'll adjust."

"When was the last time you ate, Carter?" she asked in all seriousness.

"Are you trying to diagnosis something?" he snapped. "Because I don't need you doctoring me."

"I'm not trying to doctor you, Carter. I'm just trying to be your friend."

He gave her a curious look for a moment, then stood.

"Then if you're a friend who's concerned about my eating habits, ask me to dinner."

"Really?"

"Everybody's got to eat sometime, I suppose."

"Meaning you haven't been?"

"Meaning I'm waiting for my invitation."

And, to be honest, he couldn't remember his last meal. He hadn't been particularly hungry these past few days—probably due to a combination of new job, new life and Sloane—and if his belly wasn't prompting him to fill it up, he didn't think about food. At least, he hadn't for a day or so.

"Well then, you pick the place and I'll pick up the tab. How does that sound?"

"It sounds like you just made yourself a dinner date."

What if he was getting a little too cozy with Sloane? They did have history. And they both knew that the end of her stay, she'd be leaving while he'd be staying. So, where was the harm in spending a little time together? At the end of it all, Sloane would have the closure she needed, and deserved, and he would simply feel better that he'd done it the proper way this time.

"If you don't mind going to a roadhouse?"

"As in?"

"Lots of noise, probably some dancing, food coming in second to the atmosphere."

It wasn't her kind of place, but it was impersonal, and that's what they both needed. What they didn't need was something intimate like they'd always been drawn to in the past.

"Works for me," she said.

"How about I pick you up around seven?"

"On your bike?"

"Only wheels I've got."

Which meant sitting so close together he'd practically be in between her legs, while her arms were wrapped around his waist. Pleasant thought, but precarious.

"I'll stop by Matt's and grab a helmet for you."

"Then I'll be waiting," she said, pushing herself off the sofa.

Before she walked away, she took a long, hard look at him.

"Are you sure you're good with this? Because I didn't come here to take up all your time, and it seems that's what I'm doing. Especially considering that, well—we're not getting back together."

Carter stood up as well.

"But we can still be friends, can't we?"

Famous last words of most break ups. Words that never came true. Would that be the case with them? Would they say their goodbyes this time, make their promises to remain friends, yet never quite get around to it? Carter hoped not, but he wasn't optimistic. He and Sloane had different lives now. His was just starting while she was well-established in hers, and he didn't see any situation where they could simply meet in the middle and truly be friends. There was too much water under that very old, very shaky bridge now. And, Sloane needed to be away from him.

"Ah, yes. This is where they make the promise then never fulfill it. Is that who we are now, Carter? Two people going through the right motions but who realize those motions aren't going in the same direction anymore?"

"I hope not, but…maybe."

"Well, at least we're being honest. That's progress, I suppose." Sloane pulled out her phone and glanced at the time. "Look, it's getting late and I still need to return a call to one of my surgical patients back home. Then check in with my dad to let him know I haven't dropped off the face of the earth. How about I meet you in the parking lot at six-thirty?"

"Sounds good," he said, just as his phone started to ring.

It turned out to be Mrs. O'Brien who was worried that he'd wrapped her wrist too tightly, and could he stop by to look at it? After he agreed, and hung up, he smiled at Sloane.

"This is really awkward, isn't it?"

"A little bit," she agreed, then walked over and brushed a kiss to his cheek. "See you later."

Later was going to be so, so tough. But facing up to what he'd been was part of his recovery. And if anybody knew what he'd been, it was Sloane. Yet, she still wanted to go out to dinner with him. It wasn't enough to make him optimistic, but it also didn't leave him discouraged as so many of their attempts to be together in the past year had. So, this was good. Yes, very, very good. In fact, it was good enough that if he were a whistling man, he'd leave this hotel, whistling.

Carter lagged back a few steps as they headed toward the motorcycle. She knew why he did that. He liked watching her walk—she'd known that from the first time she'd met him. They'd been walking down the hospital hall and he'd hung back just a step or two, got himself so wrapped up in what he was watching he totally forgot what they'd been talking about. She'd known what was happening. Had felt flattered then, as she still did now.

"Enjoying the view?" she asked.

"Always have," he said. "That part of me hasn't changed."

Sloane stopped and spun around to face him. Smiling.

"I meant the desert. It's vibrant this evening, with all its rusts and golds."

"So did I," he said, trying to act innocent.

"I'll bet you did." Sloane picked up her pace across the parking lot until she reached Carter's motorcycle. "Well, here we are."

"Make sure when you get on the bike your helmet is strapped properly, and your face shield is down."

"Like I didn't always do that?"

"Like you didn't always do it properly."

He checked the way she'd put the helmet on, then ran his fingers between the chin strap and her quivering flash, causing her to suck in a deep breath.

"Too tight?" he asked.

Sloane shook her head, because right now she knew her words would come out shaking as hard as her hands were. It had been a long, long time since "the Carter effect," as she'd once called it, had been so strong. Way back, during the early days, she'd always quivered when he touched her. But that had worn off after he'd returned home from Afghanistan, and so often his touch had seemed rough and impersonal.

But now—this was the old Carter, and her responses where the same as she'd always had with him.

"No, it's good," Sloane finally managed. "Just not sure I like having all this weight on my head."

It was a lie, of course. But he didn't need to know what was really happening to her. Not when he was checking her helmet, not when he was helping her onto the back of his bike, and not when she was practically wrapping herself around him.

All of it caused her to quiver, but that was her secret to keep. Time was, though, when she'd have told him what his touch did to her, when all their plans would be tossed aside and the remainder of the day or night would bring her more than simple quivers.

"It's OK if I lean into you?" Sloane asked him as he engaged the motor and started pushing them forward with his feet.

"Lean, squeeze, grasp—whatever makes you feel safe."

All of it, she thought. It all made her feel not only safe, but incredibly aroused, and as he geared up his motorcycle for the fifteen-mile ride she only hoped it would be a fast fifteen miles. Because those old feelings were coming at her with a vengeance now, and she needed physical distance between them.

Except nothing on the back of his bike gave her that distance, and as they roared off into the sunset she was mentally kicking herself. So far, being around Carter had been almost easy. Nothing about this even came close to *easy*. In fact, in so many ways, being this close to him was one of the toughest things she'd done in a long, long time.

The roadhouse was busy, and people were standing shoulder-to-shoulder in some areas. Mainly near the bar. Carter's first inclination was to squeeze in with them and order a couple of beers, but he caught himself before he took that first step, surprised and yet glad he'd actually remembered he didn't drink.

Sometimes it eluded him, and he came so close. Tonight, though, maybe his self-induced prohibition was to prove himself to Sloane. He wanted to because there was still a wariness about her. It was like she wanted to trust him again, but couldn't quite make it all the way there.

"There's a booth in the back," he shouted over the noise of the crowd. "How about you go get it while I go order us—what? You don't like pizza."

"Why don't you order yourself a pizza and get me some kind of salad?"

"Ranch dressing?" he asked.

"Some things *do* change. I'm liking balsamic vinaigrette now. Or something similar."

He gave her an appreciative nod before he headed to the bar to place his order. Sure, he could have waited for a server to come to the booth, but the noise level in here was too much, and being with Sloane was almost as bad.

But he could deal with it. At least, he hoped he could because he wanted Sloane to see how far he'd come. Noises could be a trigger, though, so he was keeping his fingers crossed. Very nervous fingers at the moment...

"Iced tea always goes with a salad," he said, setting the glass down in front of Sloane and deliberately climbing into the other side of the booth, as far away from her as he could get.

It wasn't that he didn't like sitting next to her, because he did. He loved it. But not right now, when the noise level was poking at him.

"You remembered," she said, smiling.

"It's what you always ordered," Carter said, setting a plate of lemons in front of her, as well as several packets of sweeteners.

"I remember all your habits," he said, clenching his fists under the table as the noise seemed to keep getting louder and louder. "Left shoe first, then right. A brand new toothbrush every other week. Ice cream every Sunday—strawberry. Never covering your feet under the blankets when you came to bed. Parking in the spot farthest from the hospital and walking the rest of the way, even in the rain."

He relaxed as the fond memories started to take over.

"You're a creature of habit, Sloane. Iced tea goes with salads, beer with pizza, wine with pasta. Did you know you do that—specify your drink according to your food, and never, ever change what goes with what?"

"No," she admitted. "And I didn't know you always watched me so closely. I mean, maybe I can understand why you liked watching me walk away, but my toothbrush habit?"

"Same brand and color of toothbrush every time. And yes, I did watch you closely because it was fun getting to know all the aspects of you."

And she had been glorious to watch as well, especially in those intimate moments when they had come together to dance, or make love, or simply lie on a blanket and gaze at the stars.

"Toothbrush and all my other habits aside, could we move to a quieter booth in the back room? I'm having trouble hearing you."

Was she really having trouble hearing? Or, was she noticing his building anxiety and trying to get him away from the cause of it without being too obvious? Because, if that was the case, it was a kind gesture, and it reminded him of all the times she'd tried to help him, but he'd taken it the wrong way. There were so many things he'd gotten wrong. Things that had caused him to lash out at her when she didn't deserve it. He hadn't seen it then, and he was only just beginning to see it now.

"If we move, will you dance with me?" he asked, then held out a hand to help her out of the booth.

"I'd love to," she said, "as long as it's a slow dance."

They walked hand in hand to the back room but instead of heading to the farthest booth, they fell naturally into the sway of the gentle saxophone playing a solo tune, from the dimly-lit stage, that was meant to seduce. It was a constraining sound, yet a lonely one that told him to hold her tight, to not let go. To dance like it was the last dance of his life. And maybe it was, because without Sloane in his arms, there was no reason to dance.

"You OK?" Sloane whispered into his ear.

"Trying to be," he said, as his hands slid naturally to that familiar spot on her lower back, the place he'd always held her when she raised her arms to twine around his neck.

But she wasn't doing that tonight. Her arms were properly placed on his shoulders in a loose grip, and it made him sad that they'd lost this particular intimacy. And all he could think was that he simply didn't want to be here. Not like this. Not when the memories were too strong, too painful. "Look, could we change our order to a takeaway and get out of here?"

"You don't want to dance?" she asked him. "Because we can sit it out, if that's what you'd rather do."

"I um—I just need to leave."

And now, the anxiety was overtaking him again and he knew this time it wasn't going away. Too many memories, too much noise...

"Remember that night we went dancing in the sand?" she asked him.

He stepped away from her. Broke the contact hoping to break the pattern of his attacks. But it wasn't working. Everything was fighting him. Worst of all, he was fighting himself, and losing.

"Sand fleas," he said, attempting to lighten up the moment. But, even to his ears it came out sounding grumpy.

"What?"

"I remember we got pretty chewed up by sand

fleas. You were screaming for me to get them off you, when I was trying to get them off me."

He really just wanted to end this—the conversation, the night. Go back to his room, try to sleep and start again in the morning. But the perplexed look on Sloane's face—he'd put that same expression there before, then walked away. This time he needed to stay and fix it.

"I, um—I'm on the verge of an attack, Sloane," he said.

"That's the first time you've ever told me it was coming on. So, you tell me. What do we do?"

And that was the first time she'd ever asked him to tell her how to help. It was something he should probably discuss with his counselor, but to Carter it seemed like he and Sloane had just taken a big step—together.

"Try to change my focus."

"From what to what?" she asked, taking a step closer to him, then starting to reach out to touch him, but stopping herself before she did.

The soothing music of the saxophone stopped, and, in its place, a loud, piercing guitar took over, with offbeat drums thumping in the background. It was hideous to his ears. It sounded like gunfire—like hell had opened up and released a band of screaming banshees.

"From this place too anyplace else."

He looked around for the green, neon exit sign as his breaths started coming faster. Tried remembering that time in Napa where they'd gone up in a hot air balloon and spent the afternoon floating over vineyards. Miles and miles of grapes. A beautiful sight. Carter closed his eyes to picture them, he and Sloane above the clouds and the vines so tiny below them. Floating…drifting…watching Sloane loving the ride. Refocus, Carter. He told himself. Other thoughts. Nicer thoughts.

But the wail of the obnoxious guitar took all that away from him, and his hands started shaking.

"Let's get out of here," she said, taking his hand.

He heard her words, but they were distorting now. They were coming from Sloane, but they were so far away, and he couldn't get to her.

She gave his hand a squeeze and started pulling toward the door.

"Let's go outside, then try to sort this."

He looked at her, not sure whether to pull away and run in the opposite direction to spare her yet another one of his breakdowns or let her help him. He'd never allowed that before, but…

Someone on the dance floor bumped him from behind and Carter drew in a sharp breath, then spun around to confront his attacker. But Sloane stopped him. Physically put herself between the oblivious man who was so wound up with his lady he probably didn't even know there was another person in the room.

"Carter," Sloane said, gently placing both hands on his chest and pushing him back. "Let's go sort this. Now. It's your crisis. You have to guide me through it."

This was a different Sloane altogether. She'd never reacted to his attacks this way before. In the past, she'd always been too sympathetic, too bending. But not this time.

"Sure," he said, following her as they made their way off the crowded dance floor and headed straight for the rear exit.

Once they were out, Carter fell to the ground, and simply lay there, looking up at the stars, still gasping, still struggling to fight his way through this. Then, when Sloane joined him there on the ground, she simply sat with him in the shadow of a smelly trash bin and held his hand. For now, that's all he wanted.

# CHAPTER SEVEN

OPENING THE HOTEL room door, her mind still on Carter all these hours later, Sloane headed directly into the hall and nearly tripped over him. He was sitting on the floor outside her door, eyes closed but not asleep.

"Since I dropped you off at your hotel, I assumed you'd still be there, sound asleep," she said.

Or pacing the floor for hours, which was something he'd used to do. Last night, however, when she'd suggested they call her hotel to send a car, and then subsequently dropped him off at his room, he'd been quiet. Subdued. She hadn't expected that. Hadn't expected him to acquiesce so easily. But he had. He'd simply kissed her on the cheek and walked away from the hotel as if he *hadn't* just been on the verge of what had looked as if it might be a major meltdown.

So...was this program Carter was on working for him? Getting counseling...training bears. Sloane hadn't been sure about it when he'd told her, but she was seeing something different now. Something more like the man she'd used to know. And while it excited her, it also scared her. because she wondered how long this effect would last before he'd revert. Or *would* he revert?

Maybe. Maybe not. For Carter's sake, she hoped he wouldn't.

"Been there long?" she asked, and her heartbeat went a little crazy, the way it always did the first instant she saw him.

"A couple of hours."

"Without knocking?"

"Didn't want to disturb you." He picked up a bag from the floor and handed it to her. "Apple, banana, salad, cookies—"

"I don't eat cookies," Sloane interrupted.

"I do," he said, finally standing. "I'm sorry about what happened tonight. Normally I can feel these things coming on, and I use the grounding techniques I've learned when I don't feel like I can simply walk away. Or in some cases run away."

"What grounding techniques?" she asked, holding out her hand to him to help him off the floor.

"Sound—turning on loud music, but not like what we were hearing last night. Classical works for me, especially a rousing Beethoven symphony. Normally his seventh does the trick. I know it by heart and I hum along, which gets me away from my anxiety."

He smiled.

"Especially if I conduct it."

"You've learned to conduct?"

Carter laughed.

"Hell, no. But swinging my arms around pretending that's what I'm doing takes me to a different place, which is where I need to be."

"If you want, I could teach you to conduct."

Sloane had an undergrad degree in music and for a while had thought about becoming a professional. But the lure of healing changed all that.

"Or I could just do it my way," he said, not intending to sound contentious. "Because I like the freedom of doing it my way. It's cathartic and energizing, and it works."

"I didn't mean to—"

There she was, trying to take over when he clearly needed to guide his own journey. To help Carter, she was going to have to be more aware of her own actions.

"That's OK."

"You know this isn't easy for me," she said.

Walking away from him in less than two weeks wasn't going to be easy, either. But he wasn't offering her any hope for a future together, and she was trying hard not to get her hopes up.

" "Me either," he said. "Which is why if the music doesn't work—and sometimes it doesn't—there are various smells that will snap me back. A lot of people are triggered by smell, and for me peppermint oil works, so I always carry a vial of it."

From his pocket he produced a small silver vial, usually used for carrying nitroglycerin pills, and held it out to her.

Sloane took it, uncapped it, and immediately smelled the scent. It was amazing watching him take charge of his PTSD episodes. She hadn't seen this before and she was so—proud. Yes, proud of him.

"I'm so glad it's working for you."

"Most of the time it does. Sometimes, though…" Carter lowered his voice as a group of tourists walked by them. "Sometimes it doesn't, and the problem is I don't know when it will or won't work. Sometimes the PTSD wins no matter what I do."

"And last night?"

"A little bit of win, and a little bit of being defeated."

"Does that happen often?" Sloane asked. Because from what she had seen, he'd been able to control his attack much more than he hadn't been able to control.

"More than I'd like it to. But overall my number of episodes has decreased. If I feel something coming on, half the time I can—I don't call it control so much as divert or distract it. That was a huge emphasis in the first part of my program—taking charge of yourself when it's trying to take over. It's not easy, and sometimes it's so damn difficult it drops you to your knees then causes you to curl up in a ball and cry. But when you succeed—it's a feeling I can't describe."

The thought of Carter curled into a ball broke her heart, and she was the one who wanted to cry. But the focus here was him, and she had to remember that. To turn this into anything about her could defeat him.

"And when you don't succeed?"

It used to be he'd take it out on her. Screaming. Throwing things. She'd put away all her breakables months ago.

"It's a toss-up. Sometimes if I fight myself hard

enough I can change the direction of my episode. Or lessen the blow of it. Sometimes, though, it's easier to simply go someplace else. Get away from people. Even hide, if I have to. But my counselor will be helping me make some changes with all that when I get back to the program."

It sounded good, and Sloane felt encouraged for him. Especially as he was beginning to take responsibility for his actions whenever he could. The old Carter had been so full of blame. It had been directed at anyone who happened to be near him when he broke down.

Yet last night—none of that had happened. The episode had occurred, but he'd beaten it.

"So, why are you here, Carter?" she finally asked. "Sitting on the floor outside my hotel door?"

"Not really sure why. I keep an empty booze bottle next to my bed as a reminder of where I've been, and something about that bottle scared me when I got to my room. If it had been full… Anyway, I called my counselor, as we're supposed to do when we feel ourselves slipping and told her how I wanted to go to the bar and drink. One of the things she told me to do was go take a walk to clear my head. Which is why I ended up here."

"How often are you tempted to drink?" she asked him.

"Every time I have a meltdown. Which is why we're required to call one of our counselors. It becomes a major step in the prevention of something we're not supposed to do. In my case, drink. If we don't, and we do give in, then we start back at the beginning of the program, if they even allow us back in."

"Isn't that kind of harsh?"

"PTSD is harsh. You couldn't expect the treatment to be any less harsh. So, I keep the bottle nearby as a remind of what I've lost and what I stand to gain."

"Good for you, Carter," she said, stepping back and motioning him into her room. "So, it's four miles, Carter. You walked four miles to get here? Because you thought I would do—what?"

"I'm not expecting anything from you, Sloane. I just wanted you to see that I can control myself sometimes. That I don't always get pulled under."

"I did see that in the roadhouse, how you went from just on the verge to well, something almost calm. Or, accepting."

"Not accepting. That's giving in. Too many people do that because it's easy. I did that when I left you because fighting the demon is so hard and sometimes it's less painful to simply let it take you over."

"And all those months when I kept telling you to fight…"

"I was fighting you. Because you, in a lot of ways, were the demon—the one who was always there, being my conscience when I didn't have one. The one who was always reminding me that once upon a time I had been a good enough person to win someone like you, but all that had changed. I wasn't good anymore. Didn't deserve anything or anyone."

"You should have told me," Sloane said as the door

closed behind her and she realized just how small her room was with both of them in there.

While she, herself, wasn't given to panic attacks, she could sympathize with Carter with one aspect of his—claustrophobia. She was certainly feeling it right now. Cramped space. Not enough air. His scent was the same—the aftershave she'd given him years ago, that he'd never quit using. And so much of the man she'd used to love was showing through right now.

"There was nothing to tell, because I didn't know. A lot of the time, I'm figuring it out as I go."

"And all this new self-awareness—do you trust it?"

Sloane wanted to. But she wasn't quite ready for that. Not yet. It wasn't as if she wanted to make him prove himself. It was just that she'd tried so hard and been so hurt. Now she was just plain afraid to hope, to trust, to give herself over to something that might or might not happen. It was too much to deal with—especially since she'd thought she was at a place in her life where she could take a step or two forward. That was until she saw Carter again. Now, she was confused. And, conflicted. There were too many emotions, too many memories running through her to deal with. Especially not here, alone in a hotel room with Carter.

"Sometimes I almost do." He sighed heavily. "But I don't let myself get too heavily invested in it because what if I fail again? I've already hit the bottom once, and if I do it again I won't bounce back. Not that I'm bouncing now. But at least I can see the changes I need to make, and I understand what I've got to cope with for the rest of my life better than I used to."

He walked up to Sloane and stopped just short of pulling her into his arms. But he did reach out and brush his fingers over her cheek.

"I'm sorry for what I did to us, Sloane. I could see it happening—see what I was doing to you—but I couldn't stop it. You were the only one who was really there, and even though I knew that I couldn't control myself. You were an easy target because you loved me."

Sloane reached up to Carter's face and took hold of his hand. The feel of him was so good. She'd missed it—missed the simple things. The touching, the looks they'd exchange that said so much, the smiles. But she couldn't let herself fall into the trap of believing in him again. He'd hurt her so badly, so often. And believing in him—that was *her* demon to fight. Because every ounce of her wanted to. But every ounce of her knew that loving Carter made her too vulnerable.

"I did love you. Maybe I even still do, in some ways. But you hurt me so badly, and while I know it wasn't your fault I can't do that again. Can't go back to that place or to who we were. That doesn't exist anymore."

"It wasn't my intention to hurt you," Carter said, stepping away from her. "And it was never my intention to see that look of confusion, or maybe even apprehension, that was on your face a couple minutes ago, when you found yourself alone in the same hotel room as me."

He crossed over to the far wall and sat down on the arm of an easy chair.

"Remember that first time we went away together for a weekend? Palm Beach?"

Sloane did, but she didn't want to.

"The room was so tiny we had to crawl over the bed to get from one side to the other."

But it hadn't mattered, because even though they'd practically been on the beach, they hadn't left the room except to eat. It had been a horrible place to stay, but her memories were nothing but good.

"That was back when we were young and naïve."

It seemed like so long ago, and so much had happened since then.

"Whatever happened to those two people?" he asked, twisting on the chair, trying to favor his lower back, obviously looking for a more comfortable position. "They were a pretty good couple, weren't they?"

"The best," she whispered, promising herself she wouldn't cry. "Young love like that is always the best."

So many hopes, so many dreams. Now look at them. Barely able to look at each other, let alone speak. This wasn't the way her dream was supposed to have turned out. She'd had it since she was a little girl—to find her one true love, settle down together, live happily-ever-after.

There was nothing happy in the way she lived now. There was no one true love.

"Well, we were good at it."

She nodded.

"Very good at it."

Sloane leaned back against the window and stared at him for a moment and her breath caught. This was Carter she was talking to now—not some difficult manifestation of him. If only she could hold on to that—to him—and not let him get away.

"Carter, when you left me…did you hate me? I never knew. You said I was one of your demons, and I actually do understand that. But did you—or maybe *do* you—hate me? You were so distant for so long, and everything I tried to do—it always just made you angry. I did try," Sloane said as the tears finally came. "It wasn't easy standing back, watching you self-destruct, but it got to the point where there wasn't anything else I could do. I'd tried everything, and the harder I tried the more you resisted me—I'm beginning to realize why, which makes me wonder if you hated me."

"I didn't hate you," he said, taking several steps in her direction, then stopping. "Not then—not now. But I couldn't live with you. Not anymore."

"Why?" she asked.

"Maybe because I couldn't live with myself. There were always too many reminders of someone I was never going to be again. Everywhere I looked."

Sloane swiped away a tear as he crossed the room and pulled her into his arms. It felt good being there. But it didn't feel like she belonged. There was nothing natural here. Nothing from before.

Still, Carter's arms were strong, and right now she needed strong arms. Needed someone to lean on—

someone who understood why, in this moment, she wasn't the same person she'd been either.

Resting her head against his chest, she listened to the steady, strong beat of his heart and recalled when that heart had been weakened by his injuries, and his chart had listed him as "critical." He'd always reached for her when he was awake, and she had always been there for him to hold, believing he'd needed her strength for recovery.

That was what she'd wanted to do, anyway. To lend her strength, her support, everything she was, to help make him whole. But that had never happened, because Carter had never healed.

"What else could I have done, Carter?" Sloane asked, her head still on his chest.

They stood in silence for a moment, she still in his embrace, he still holding her tightly against him. No kisses, no caresses. Simply memories of this same embrace, so many times over the years. She'd come to count on it, to love it, to respond to it in a way she knew she would never respond to the embrace of another man. It was still a proper embrace, one meant for support, but the line was hers to draw. Or step across.

"It was never you," he whispered, tilting her face up to his. "I tried, Sloane. God knows, I tried. But I couldn't make it work. Every time I looked at you— every time we were together…"

Sloane reached up, put her fingers over his lips to silence him. This wasn't what she'd had in mind when she'd thought of closure, but maybe she'd been wrong about that all along. Maybe she'd been too analytical about him, too much his nurse and not his lover.

She reached for him, placing her shaking hand on the back of his neck, lifting her lips to his. "This is what's left," she whispered. "Only this."

It was a bittersweet reminder of why she was there. But she wanted this. Wanted a different memory of their parting. And there was no shame in her for what she wanted, as she'd expected there might be. This man had been a large part of her life for so long—she deserved to have what she wanted.

They kissed—first lightly, but then their desperation grew quickly. His tongue was in her mouth, searching places it had searched a thousand times before, and her hips were tilting so naturally to his, her back arching to the touch of his hand as it always had done.

Her body was sending a message, and she could feel his answer, even though words were not spoken. They didn't have to be. His eyes said yes. But there was some doubt in them. In his, probably in hers, too.

His tongue sought hers again, and this time he ran his hands through her wild red hair, separating the strands with his fingers. She loved the way he did that—so delicately, yet so provocatively. It always caused her flesh to quiver, always caused her breath to shorten. He pulled her even closer to him, until nothing separated them but fabric. It was as if he wanted to fold her inside him, keep her safe the way he'd always kept her safe.

Pushing away from him just slightly, Sloane

pressed the palm of her hand against his chest and pushed him backwards onto the bed. Then she tumbled down on top of him, interlocking their hands above his head. At first she nibbled his chin, then moved lower, to his throat, where she pressed light kisses.

Removing one of her hands from his, she raised herself up just slightly and ran her fingertips over his face. He'd used to be clean-shaven. His face was as smooth as a baby's bottom, she'd always teased him. But she liked the feel of his stubble. It was a new look for him—slightly rough, definitely sexier than anything she'd ever seen on him.

"You feel so good," she finally whispered.

"Is this what you want, Sloane?" he asked. "Because we either stop right here, or..."

It was what *he* wanted—what he'd always wanted. Only with Sloane.

There'd been other women these past few months—women he'd met along the way. They'd wanted him—he'd wanted them. But somehow something had always stopped him, made the moment go bad or go away.

It was Sloane, he realized, now that he had her back in his arms again, and her lush curves and her soft skin were everything he remembered. No one was Sloane. No one could be Sloane. Not ever.

Which was why this between them now was *not* a good idea. One time, maybe two times, and then she'd be out of his life—but this time forever. That was the only way it could end. He'd walk away again, only this time he'd set her free before he did.

His last memories of them together like this were so bad. He'd been selfish, his words hateful. Which was what he needed to remember. The look on her face then—there'd been so much pain, so much confusion. The way she was looking at him now was a different look—more knowing, more mature. But it was still Sloane. And he had no right to her.

Still, when he felt her slide over in bed he didn't stop her. Nor did he stop her when she unfastened his jeans, then eased them along with his briefs down over his hips.

Carter sighed again when she raised up slightly and removed his pants all the way. Her exploration took her places only Sloane knew.

He shut his eyes, thinking about how unbelievably good this felt, physically and emotionally, and when Sloane gave a throaty moan then slid her mouth from his chest, then on down.

"Look at me," she said finally, disengaging from him for a moment and urging him into bed.

He did, and he saw that her eyes were fully open, locked on his eyes. Searching for something? he thought. Probably something he didn't have.

"What?" he asked.

"Just look," she said, positioning herself face to face with him again. They were so close they were breathing the same air. "So I can look at you."

That was when Carter knew what this was about. It was about taking all the ugliness he'd brought down on them and turning it into something good and beautiful, so she could walk away from him for the last time. It was what Sloane needed.

"You've always been so beautiful," he said as he reached across and began to ease her shirt up over her head. She helped with her bra, and they both worked together to remove all the clothes that stood between them.

But they didn't hurry. They lingered over caresses and kisses, each remembering what the other liked, each trying to give pleasure. It was a fragile experience, slow and familiar, yet eventually developing into something with a new, different urgency—like the one they'd known at the beginning, which had eventually slipped away into a more intimate proficiency over time.

He took his time, nuzzling against her, knowing he would not be here again. He was nibbling and kissing his way up to her earlobe, where she'd always been ticklish, and understanding he would never again hear her whispered laugh again his cheek. He could feel her thigh muscles harden as he slid his hand down her belly, occasionally stopping to kiss the trace he was making. She quivered when he did that—when he kissed her belly, her hip, moved around to her bottom. He was taking much the same trail she had when she'd kissed him, only without the scars.

"Ooh…" Sloane whispered as he rolled her onto her back and slipped inside her.

This was the way it had been—the way it should have always been. And as he began to find his rhythm he heard a strangled sob. Not from pain, but from heartbreak. He was willing to stop, to pull himself away, but Sloane was not, and she took up his rhythm—a slow snapshot. A memory yet to be made.

After several hard thrusts against him, urging him on with her, there was nothing he could do but give himself over to the exquisite tightness, the heat, the increasing intensity. But first, before he let the rise and fall of impending climax sweep him under, he reached down and stroked her cheek, then her hair.

"I never meant to hurt you," he said.

"I know."

Maybe she did. He hoped so, because Sloane was the only woman he'd ever loved. And that was the closure he wanted her to have—that knowledge.

"Please, Carter," she whispered.

And that was all it took. He could no longer hold back, even though the idea of not continuing was tinged with regret. But as she forced her hips into him, and he pounded harder and harder to meet her urgency, all thoughts of anything but this moment disappeared.

"You feel so good," he whispered, his voice coming in gasps between thrusts. Then came that maddening clutch on him she always took and held, the heat, the voices in his head urging him on…

Suddenly there was only now. And he wanted it all. Hard, fast. No thoughts about anything before and after.

"Sloane!" he cried out as the moment came to its brink.

But she said nothing in return. Nor did she shout out, pant or moan.

Sloane responded to her need with his own until she was exhausted, curling herself against his chest the way she always did afterwards. But this time he felt the moisture of her tears on his arms. So, he held on to her tighter, like it was the last night of the world.

In many ways, it was.

# CHAPTER EIGHT

THE DAY STARTED off like any other. Or at least like any other day Sloane had had in the past six or seven months. She woke up alone, with no idea where Carter was, and really no expectation of finding him.

He'd showered, she discovered, and taken his medical bag, so maybe that meant he'd gone off to work. She hoped so because, despite her big mistake last night—and it truly was a huge one—all she wanted this morning was to know that what they'd done hadn't shaken Carter to the very core and set him off in some new direction with his PTSD.

After a quick shower, Sloane pulled on her clothes and walked over to the window, parted the curtains and looked out. What she expected to find she wasn't sure. Certainly not Carter, lounging poolside the way some of the early birds were already doing. despite a little November chill in the air. In fact, unless someone here at the Red Rock was ill, she didn't expect to find him at all.

But that was her habit—always scanning a crowd, looking for him. She'd been doing that since he'd left her, never quite sure what she'd do if she did happen to see him.

A knock on her hotel room door startled her, and she spun around to stare at it for a moment before she crossed the room to open it. She didn't really expect to find Carter standing in the hall either, wanting to come back in, although a tiny part of her did want that. Which meant that tiny part of her was disappointed when the person in the hall turned out to be one of the hotel staff, carrying a tray with food.

"I didn't order that," she said, not yet stepping back to allow him entrance.

"It's from the house doctor. He stopped by the kitchen a couple hours ago and left the order." He pulled back the linen covering on the tray to reveal a bowl of fresh fruit, yogurt and toast. Her favorite breakfast, actually.

"Could you put it on the table next to the bed, please?" she asked, feeling a little embarrassed by the rumpled condition of her bedding.

"Yes, ma'am," he said, sliding in past her, leaving the tray and hurrying out.

In Sloane's mind he'd made note of the state of the bed and was on his way to tell all his co-workers what he'd discovered. In reality she was sure he saw morning-after beds all the time and probably didn't even pay attention to them.

A morning-after bed. Her and Carter's morning-after bed.

"What did I do?" Sloane moaned as she slid into her shoes, deciding to forego the breakfast in favor of going to find Carter, so she could tell him that last night had been a one and only.

She texted him on her way out the door, asking him if they could talk. Surprisingly, he texted back immediately, telling her he was with a patient at another hotel, then had two more appointments before he went to his office. What he offered her was some time after work, although he didn't know when that would be. Oddly enough, he ended his text with, Hands off this time, Soane. I can't go through that again.

The message hurt in so many ways—because that was basically what he'd said months ago, when he'd moved out of their bedroom. Still, it was the message she would have texted him if he hadn't beaten her to it. Because, like Carter, she couldn't go through it again either.

She'd missed that part of their life as she'd missed so many other parts and getting involved the way they had last night didn't fix things. Didn't even come close to helping either.

They were adults, though, repeating a doomed past, and that was all it was. A moment of weakness destined to fail. She laughed bitterly. A moment that had never failed to be good. Now, wasn't *that* just ironic? The one place where they could come together perfectly turned out to be the one place they had no business being.

Well, that wasn't the cheeriest of thoughts, but it was the one she took with her when she left the hotel, not sure what she was going to do with her day—especially since this wasn't the vacation she'd planned.

Or wanted. But maybe, deep down, it was. Maybe she'd planned to find a little bit of Carter here, or even Carter himself, and she'd been fooling herself all the time.

Why, after all, would she have even thought of a place like Forgeburn, let alone come here? Because Carter had mentioned it so often?

A text message interrupted her thoughts.

Permissions from the Department of National Resources just came through. Going down into the canyon with Kevin Mallory and family early this evening. Easy hike. Want to come?

Suddenly her prospects for the day looked much brighter.

Sure. When?

Probably around five. I'll let you know more after I check the weather then make sure he's good to go.

Maybe a morning lounging by the pool wasn't a bad idea at all. She had her electronic reader with her, and a queue of romance novels and mysteries she'd been promising herself she'd read. So, a quick change into a pair of gray jersey pants and a pink t-shirt, and her morning was set.

Sure, she would have been better off, and smarter in the long run, if she'd gone out with one of the tour guides. But when had she ever done the smart thing when it came to Carter? Which meant this was merely history repeating itself. Carter called and she ran, with her heart pounding a little harder. And that meant she wasn't over him. Oh, she'd probably already known that somewhere in her muddled thinking. But to admit it?

It was going to turn into a problem, no doubt. Just like last night, while it had been wonderful, was a problem. Because if he wanted a repeat of it she wasn't sure she could say no.

One *come hither* crook of his finger and she'd *gone thither* all over the place. For hours. Some of the time she'd even taken the lead.

It was still a good five hours before he would get the plans underway to take Kevin down into the canyon, which meant free time. He'd thought about asking Sloane if she wanted to have lunch with him. At least that had been his full intention. But when he'd been called to the Sunrise Canyon Hotel and told his ride would meet him at the Red Rock, there wasn't much else he could do but go. Work was his primary goal here, and as much as he wanted to give Sloane her opportunity to say what he was sure she'd want to say, it hadn't worked out. Not yet. And, maybe a large part of that was his fault, because he didn't want to hear it.

Sure, they were over. They had to be over. But the reality of it wasn't easy because he didn't want to hurt her more than he already had.

"So, how far along is your wife?" Carter asked the man who was driving him in his truck. Like so many people out here, he lived in an isolated area, but Hugh Lewiston had managed to get his wife, Shelly, to the Sunrise Canyon Hotel, which was about ten miles closer to Carter than the Lewiston ranch was.

"She's right on her due date now. It's our first," Hugh said, beaming.

"Has she been seeing a doctor?"

Hugh shook his head. "Once in the early part of her pregnancy. He said she was healthy, so we didn't see any point in spending money for something we already knew."

Carter leaned his head against the back of the truck seat and closed his eyes. "No tests or anything?"

He'd delivered babies in Afghanistan—the babies of civilian women—but always in a hospital. They'd known to come in, known there was medical help for them there. But Shelly Lewiston? This made him nervous.

"How old is Shelly?" he asked, looking over at Hugh and guessing him to be in his mid-forties. Which meant, if Shelly was close to that age, she might be more prone to problems with delivery and also with the baby.

"Just turned forty-two."

"Has she been sick much during her pregnancy?"

"Not once," Hugh said. "In fact she was working the ranch with me up until yesterday. That's when she got a backache and decided it was time to go put her feet up. She wasn't having labor pains, though. Not until this morning."

"And how far apart are they?"

Probably a couple of minutes. I really didn't stay long enough to count much. I thought it was better to call you, then come get you, since the road out there is a little tricky and I didn't want you getting lost."

Carter gritted his teeth as the truck hit a rut, then looked down at his hands…white knuckles balled into fists. But this wasn't PTSD. It was simply a surgeon going into an unknown situation, preparing to do God only knew what.

Suddenly, for the first time since he'd climbed in next to Hugh, he was actually able to relax. And he wanted to call Sloane and tell her. But he didn't. What was the point?

"Well, I'm glad you did. Home births aren't always easy. Or in this case a hotel birth."

"You don't think there are going to be any problems, do you?" Hugh asked as they turned into the parking lot of the Sunrise Canyon Hotel.

There was quite a crowd gathered. Probably two dozen people were standing in the parking lot, making what seemed like a tunnel of people for Carter to pass through to get inside. And when he did he knew why they were out there. Shelly was sprawled out on one of the lobby couches, moaning, while at least six women stood around her, ready to help deliver the baby.

"OK," he said, making his way through the crowd, sounding as confident and in charge as he ever had in his life. "How far apart are her contractions?" he asked of anyone who'd answer.

"Continual," one of the women said.

"Anyone here medical?" he asked as he set his bag down on the floor and immediately took Shelly's pulse. She was too involved in another moan to notice him. "Nurse, doctor, midwife, medic?"

When no one answered a wave of nausea washed through him, but he fought it down and positioned himself to examine Shelly.

"Just relax," he said to her, and he took a look.

Sure enough, the baby was crowning. In fact it was fighting its way out like a football player fighting to get through the line. "You're going to be a mother in just a minute here."

That caused Shelly to look up. "Are you the doctor who was an Army surgeon?" she managed to force out.

"I was," he said, as he snapped on a pair of gloves and went to work. "But I traded all that for this."

"Why?" she asked, as her breathing started turning into more of a panting.

"PTSD. Thought Forgeburn was a good place to work through some of it."

"Sorry to hear that," she said, then raised herself up as a hard contraction hit. "Hope the military is taking care of you."

She addressed it with such a lack of shock or pity it surprised him. One of the things he'd learned in his program was that admitting the problem was the first step. Admit it to yourself, then to other. In other words, it was nothing to be ashamed of, so why bother trying to hide it?

"I'm in a great program." He smiled and, surprisingly, it wasn't forced. This was the first time he'd just come out and admitted it to someone who wasn't either in his program or close to him, like Sloane and Matt. It felt good. Almost like a weight had been lifted from his shoulder. No doubt all of Forgeburn would learn of his condition by the end of the day, but that didn't matter. He was going to be doctor to some of them, and they had the right to know.

"So, are you ready to become a mother because..." He turned the baby's head just slightly. "Next time you feel the urge, give me a big push."

The woman seated behind Shelly prepared to sit her up, and when the next contraction came, in only a few seconds, all the ladies standing around watching yelled, "Push!"

Which was exactly what Shelly did as Hugh staggered over to a chair on the other side of the room and then collapsed into it.

"One more push and—" He glanced over to make sure Hugh was OK, then literally caught the baby as it slid out. "Somebody—in my bag I've got a handheld suction..." He looked at Shelly, who was stretched out flat on the sofa, trying to see her baby. "As soon as I get him cleaned up and examined you can hold your little boy."

"A boy?" Hugh called from across the room as the bystanders who'd stayed in the hall during the blessed event started to cheer.

"A boy..." Shelly whispered, watching Carter clamp the cord, cut it, then put Ilotycin in the baby's eyes to prevent conjunctivitis after the birth.

One of the woman stepped forward to wipe the

baby down, then wrapped him in a soft blanket that had come from another hotel guest. During this, Carter checked Shelly to make sure there was no excessive bleeding and that the placenta had been safely delivered.

"Want to hold your son?" he asked, taking the baby from the woman who was holding the newborn. "Because I think he's waiting for you."

Carter lowered the baby into Shelly's arms, then stepped back as Hugh made his way over to take his first look. Then wobbled on his feet again.

Carter who was on his way up caught Hugh, who was on his way down, and lowered him to the ground, where he knelt beside his wife, then reached out to stroke his crying son's hand.

"He's got a set of lungs on him, doesn't he?"

"Good, strong cry," Carter said, backing away from the scene as he saw Cruz Montoya stroll into the room.

"Somebody call for me?"

"I did," Carter said. "It was an easy birth, but because of the mother's age I'd like to get her to a hospital, or even the clinic over in Whipple Creek—just to have some routine tests run and maybe watch her for a day."

"You're flying with me?" Cruz asked.

"Yep," he said, giving no thought to how nervous he'd been last time he'd flown. One hurdle down and stomped into the ground, Carter thought, as he and Cruz helped mother and child into the old green canvas, war-variety stretcher Cruz brought with him.

And that's just what he did, with no qualms. He helped carry the stretcher out, then climbed into the helicopter without so much as a rolling stomach or a bead of sweat.

"I heard you made your PTSD public," Cruz said, as he fastened in for the flight.

Carter chuckled. News really did travel fast in Forgeburn.

"They say it went perfectly, and then Dr. Holmes and Cruz took them over to Whipple Creek Clinic for the night."

"They flew?" Sloane asked the server who'd brought her a fruit juice smoothie.

It was warm for November, and after an hour of lounging she'd finally given in and changed into her swimsuit. The sun on her exposed skin felt good, even though overall she was rather pale. That came from staying inside, working too much. She rarely had leisurely days like this, when she could simply sit and bask.

"I heard the crowd cheered him on as he climbed into the helicopter."

"Why would they do that?" Sloane asked the young man.

"Because they all knew how hard it was for him to do that."

"Then they all know—?"

"The whole PTSD thing? Sure. He talked about it when he was delivering the baby. But it's no big deal.

Everybody's got their problems. The doc's aren't any better or worse than anybody else's."

Maybe that was true. At least, in Forgeburn. But Forgeburn wasn't a typical sampling of the real world and, someday, Carter would have to face that without his cheering squad. This was a start, though—and an opportunity to prove himself to the people who needed him. And she was encouraged because he was finding a life here. Maybe not the one she'd expected of him. But a life, nonetheless. He deserved that.

"Any news on how they're doing?"

She wasn't concerned so much about mother and baby because in Carter's hands they would be fine. But she was concerned about Carter.

"Only that the doctor is back in his office and Cruz is taking a small tour group out for some sightseeing."

Should she casually wander over to Carter's office? Maybe to congratulate him on the delivery? Or to simply see how he was doing? She wanted to. But she also wanted him to come tell her. She had always included him on the big events, and now she wanted him to do the same for her. So, she took a sip of her smoothie, then continued reading her book. It had been a big morning for Carter, and she was glad he'd managed every bit of it on his own. That's what he needed to help him regain all his confidence—independence. It was a double-edged sword, however. For Carter, it was good. But for her...

# CHAPTER NINE

CARTER HADN'T SEEN Sloane since the evening before, even though they'd texted a little. But that was fine, because after delivering Shelly and Hugh's baby he'd come back and got busy in the clinic with the usual things. Scrapes and abrasions, broken bones, a couple of open head gashes—nothing serious.

In fact his tiny waiting room had been full of people talking about what they were calling "the miracle birth," even though there had been no miracle involved. Now everyone was gone, and Sloane was on his mind again.

"Look, I'm going to step out for a little while. Call me if someone comes in."

It wasn't as if he needed to see her—especially since she was going out with him and the Mallory family later. But he wanted to see her, and there was a wide difference between wanting and needing. At least that was what he was telling himself as he got on his motorcycle—thoughtfully returned by the road-house owner—and headed down the road.

What was he hoping for? He didn't know. But he

was hoping for something, and hope was something he hadn't had in a long, long time.

For sure, today had been a lazy one. Between sleeping late, then lounging, followed by an hour in the spa and another hour having a facial, Sloane was about as pampered as she cared to be—because being pampered meant empty thoughts, which meant an open door to thinking about Carter.

She hoped Carter was still up to it, physically, because he had had a challenging physical day, and she worried that he looked so tired every time she'd seen him since coming to Forgeburn. It was probably nothing, she decided. He was simply trying to re-adjust to his new life. Still, she worried. It was too ingrained in her to stop.

"You look tired," Carter said, stepping up behind her as she sat in the café sipping a smoothie.

"Funny. I was just thinking the same thing about you."

"Getting used to the pace, little by level. I worked harder in surgery, standing on my feet for hours, but the whole re-learning process here is taking it out of me. Mind if I sit down."

Sloane nodded, then even offered him a sip of her smoothie—another one of those ingrained things. She always shared with Carter, as he did with her. In fact, some of their better moments involved feeding each other, teasing a meatball to her lips, teasing a bite of bread to his lips. Yes, they'd shared food, and so many other things, so the smoothie offer came naturally. So did his acceptance of it.

"Are you ready for Kevin's big adventure?" she asked. "I saw him on my way in. He's so excited."

"I'm glad we could do this for him. Every little boy deserves a big adventure." Carter reached across, took her cup, and helped himself to another sip.

"So does every big boy," Carter said, sliding the smoothie back to her, then taking hold of her hand when she reached for it. "I'm glad you're going, Sloane. And not just as a doctor, but as the person I've loved having adventures with."

It fit so well there that she was almost taken in by him. Did he want a repeat of what had happened last time he'd come to her hotel room? Did he expect them to get back together?

"What are you doing, Carter?" she asked. "Are you here to see Kevin, or is something else going on?" She pulled back her hand. "Maybe another patient?"

"Just hanging around," he said. "It's still an hour before we go on that hike, and since I had nothing else to do…" He shrugged.

"You had nothing else to do so you thought you'd come to the hotel and do me in your spare time?"

"One time, and see how you are? No hidden motives here, Sloane. I was just hoping to see you."

Sloane laughed.

"Have I always been so…suspicious?"

"I think it's something I probably put there. Another thing to regret, I suppose."

"If you want to spend the rest of your life regretting that's up to you. Personally, I don't, which is one of the reason I came here—to confront my own issues."

"Issues I caused?"

"Some, maybe. But also issues I allowed you to cause."

"I never meant to do that."

"But it's so easy to lash out at the one closest to us, isn't it? I know you never meant to hurt me, and I'm not holding it against you that you did. And that, Carter, is probably the biggest issue I've resolved since I've been here and witnessed how hard you're trying to overcome your own issues. I know that it probably sounds more sentimental than you like, but I'm proud of you."

"Actually, sometimes it's good to hear that. Especially from the people you respect. Or, in your case, respect the most."

Respect, not love. That was another of his issues, being hurt every time she was forced to come to terms with what Carter wanted from his life, and it was painfully obvious it wasn't her. In time, she would get over it. Or at least, be able to put it away in a place she didn't revisit. But until then, that little twinge of sadness still overtook her from time to time. "Well, the next thing you should hear is that it's time to get started with Kevin's trek into the wilderness. So, have you got all the medical supplies we might need packed?"

"I do. And I've probably overpacked, trying to think of every scenario that could happen."

"He's going to be fine, Carter. His own pulmonary specialist cleared him, you cleared him, and there's really nothing to hold him back. Kevin and his family know the risks—all we have to do is make sure none of those risky situations happen." She reached over and took hold of his hand and said, very tenderly, "This isn't your brother. His condition isn't like your brother's was, and nor are his prevailing health issues. I know it's hard to separate the two, but you have to keep yourself focused on Kevin's needs and not your guilt over James."

"I used to take him on little adventures. He was never able to walk—always too weak. And his wheelchair…it was so specialized it cost a fortune. My parents were always warning me I'd better not damage it, because they'd reached their insurance limit for durable medical equipment and didn't have the money to buy him anything else. So one day—I was probably eight, making James six—I marched down to the hospital and told the receptionist I needed another wheelchair for my brother. That I wanted to fix one up so I could take him places outside the house.

"She just looked at me and said, 'Young man, we're not in the business of giving away medical equipment here. You'll have to talk to your insurance provider.' Well, it about broke my heart. because I had so many big plans for James. You can imagine how crestfallen I was when I left there. But before I got back through the doors an older man signaled me over and asked what I needed the chair for. I told him about James, and how I wanted him to experience things other kids did. As it turned out, he did the wheelchair repairs for the hospital, and in his shop he had dozens of chairs. People would donate them, and he'd hang on to them until he met a worthy cause."

"You were a worthy cause?"

"Not me. James. Mr. Penrod had a small-sized chair that was perfect. He put some heavy-duty tires on it, and a couple other gadgets that would hold James upright—he never really had the musculature to sit up very long on his own. When it was done, Mr. Penrod dropped it off in his truck and from then on James didn't get left out. Wherever I went with my friends, James went, too.

"Sure, he had to be on oxygen, but Mr. Penrod had built a cylinder-holder on the chair. And, sure, James had to be strapped in a certain way—with cross-body straps. But all my friends learned how to do that, and James was never excluded unless he was tired or not feeling well. And he was such fun. Nobody ever looked at him as that little brother who always tagged along, or that kid with the disability who slowed them down. That was the best part. James was included, and everybody *wanted* to include him. They didn't do it because they had to."

A glistening smile lit Carter's eyes as tears ran down Sloane's cheeks. "I would have liked to meet him," she said, sniffling.

"He would have loved you. At least I'd like to imagine the adult James would have. Anyway… I'm going to go check the temperature, then make final arrangements with Cruz to spot us overhead."

"Do you need me to go with you?" she asked, hoping he would say yes, but expecting him to turn her down.

"Not need so much as want." He stood, then held out a hand to her.

When she stood, he pulled her into him, and for a moment they were so close, staring into each other's eyes, it was like time was standing still. She expected what? A kiss? An embrace? But none of that happened, and she could see the change come over him. Going from desire to caution. So, she was the one who backed away. And she was the one who broke the spell that had almost come over them.

"On second thought, I think I'll run up to my room and change my…socks."

But, before she turned away, she did brush a light kiss to his lips. Not from habit this time, but from affection. Maybe they couldn't share true intimacy again, but she wasn't going to change her nature just to avoid her feelings. She loved Carter and she wasn't against showing it.

"You do know you're about to give a little boy the dream of his heart. It's all good, Carter." With that, she ran her thumb delicately over his lips, then sighed. "All good."

By the time they were ready to start their hike down Little Swallow Canyon, at least two dozen people had gathered in the lobby to see them off. People here cared. Some of these were staying at the hotel, but others lived in Forgeburn. He recognized them and was grateful for their support.

"Anything else you need?" Matt McClain asked. He was one of the well-wishers, but because he was also owner of the medical practice, he'd supplied a good many of the medical things they were going to take.

"Nerves of steel," Carter responded, his voice so quiet and concentrated, Matt could barely hear him. He held out his hands to Matt, to show how hard he was shaking.

"You're in your element doing this," Matt reassured him. "Live in the moment and have a great time."

Yes. Live in the moment. That's something he was doing a lot of these days. "I've spent the better part of the late afternoon walking up and down Dry River, trying to put together every scenario that could happen. So, I'm ready to have some fun with this. Thanks."

Matt slapped him on the back. "Well, you've got Sloane, two rangers and Kevin's parents on the ground. And Cruz has eyes in the sky, along with his dad and sister. So, you're pretty well covered. Oh, and the rangers have closed that part of the trail until you get back. They don't want people following along, or taking pictures. This is an important time for the Mallory family, and I don't want it ruined by well-intentioned people who'll simply get in the way. I hope you don't mind my interference but I knew which strings to pull to get it all set up."

"I appreciate it," Carter said, staring outside as

one of the rangers brought the little trail donkey up to the door.

It had special gear rigged for Kevin—mostly to hold him on the seat and keep him upright. It was quite like the chair Mr. Penrod had rigged for James, and when Carter realized that his hands stopped shaking. This trek was nothing more than what he'd done with his brother, and back then he'd never let the thought of dire consequences get in the way."

"They're on their way," Sloane said, stepping up to Carter and slipping her hand around his waist. "Right now they're trying to calm Kevin down, because if he gets much more excited than he already is—well, his breathing…"

"Don't want to see that happen," Carter said. He turned to face her. "I know we've got a lot muddy water under our bridge—or shall I say *my* bridge—and you have no idea how much I hate that. But I want to tell you that one of my counselors at The Recovery Project has talked to me about facing my fears head-on. He said if I can't do that I'll never fully come to terms with my life, such as it is."

"I wish I knew more about what your life turned into after you left me, Carter. I do want to understand, because the man who's about to do this amazing thing for a little boy is part of the Carter I remember, and not the one who got on his motorcycle and never looked back."

"I looked back, Sloane. More than you'll ever know. All I am now is the Carter who's straddling a couple different lives. The first part of the program has taught me to see that very clearly. I'm neither one person or another. Eventually I'll know, or maybe I won't. For me, right now, it's getting by day to day. I can't set any goals other than moving along in my program, and I can't allow myself to have hopes and dreams because that puts too much pressure on me. That's my bottom line, Sloane. And it's not a very pretty one—at least, not yet. But if you truly want to get to know me, that's who I am…an aftermath, I suppose you could say. Anyway, here comes Kevin and his family, so I think it's time to get on that trail."

"Carter—one last thing before we go… The progress is there. Maybe you can't see it yet, or it's not the kind of progress you expected. You always have been a bigger-than-life kind of guy. But I see how hard you're working, and while the changes might not be earth-shattering I can see them. I do wish I could have been the one to help you along, but that's just me needing to be involved. *All about me, not you.* You've made an excellent choice with The Recovery Project and I'm so glad it's helping you. That's all I ever wanted."

Without a thought, care or concern, Carter pulled Sloane into his arms and kissed her. It wasn't a passionate kiss that would lead to more. But it was a familiar kiss. The one he'd always given her when she'd needed reassurance. The one she'd always given him when he'd needed comforting. And this kiss lasted a good long while, until Carter pulled back and whispered, "I think we're being watched."

Sloane opened her eyes, looked around her, and

sure enough they were surrounded by people. In fact the rapt attention of the crowd was so single-focused she actually expected the people to break into applause. Bu, all they got were some oohs and ahs, which were quite enough for her and, judging from the scarlet stain creeping up Carter's neck, enough for him, as well.

"So—let's do it," she said, stepping away from Carter and heading to the door, where, outside, the cutest little gray and tan donkey stood waiting.

"He's the gentlest one we have," the handler said to Sloane. "Sometimes we take him over to the children's hospital in Piperidge for the kiddies there to ride. A couple of them have problems similar to Kevin's, and Henry—my donkey—loves the attention. Don't you, boy?" he asked as he patted the donkey's rump.

"He looks perfect for Kevin." Sloane turned just in time to see Kevin's parents wheel him out through the door. "And, judging from the look on Kevin's face I'd say he thinks so too."

"OK," Carter said, stepping up to Kevin. "We've gone over how this is going to work. I'll put you up from the left side, with some help from a ranger, while your dad fastens you in from the right. Try not to move until we get you situated—and that includes getting a helmet on you."

"Do I have to wear it?" Kevin asked. "It looks heavy."

"It has communication gear in it. You can talk to me anytime and I'll hear what you're saying. Just like I can talk to you anytime. So if you feel funny, get scared, need a drink of water, want me to hook you up to your oxygen—*anything*—tell me. Is that a deal?" he asked the boy.

"Deal," Kevin said, sticking out his hand to shake on it. "As long as you take lots of pictures."

Carter looked around, and saw that everyone there, except for Kevin himself, had either a phone or a camera ready to shoot. And as they got the boy hoisted up on Henry's back at least two dozen photos were clicked off.

He wished he'd done that with James—captured some of those memories—because in time memories faded, or took on different shades and shapes.

"Well, then..."

Carter hoisted his pack over his back. It was heavier that the pack he usually carried, and he knew that Sloane's pack was equally heavy. But it was a momentous day in a young life, and none of that mattered. Kevin was about to have the adventure of his life.

"Let's hit the trail."

He put on his own communication helmet, and they were on their way.

The trail head wasn't too far, but they took it slow and easy, to allow Kevin to get the feel for riding Henry. And, just as Carter had expected, the jubilant crowd of onlookers followed them for the first little way.

By the time they reached the trail head most of them had dropped away—probably to get themselves ready to welcome Kevin back, which would be in about an hour.

The rangers led the donkey, followed by Kevin's

parents, who flanked Henry's sides. Then, bringing up the rear, were Carter and Sloane. They were keeping themselves a fair distance back, because their desire here was to make this outing as normal as they were able to. Dragging two doctors along wasn't normal, so they stayed back, taking pictures of the vegetation, and the little lizards that would dart out of the rocks, get scared and dart right back in, and the lazy hawks circling overhead, looking for a tasty tidbit to sustain them through the rest of the day.

Even though it was heading into the evening, the sky was still so blue it was breathtaking. Every now and then they would head the rotors of Cruz's helicopter in the distance, but he never got close enough to be intrusive. For being the Los Angeles boy that he was, Carter was beginning to find some sense of purpose here in Forgeburn, and it had a lot more to do with an ideal than looking at it as his last chance. Here, he was needed. He was useful. And, he was wanted. Being in Forgeburn gave him a whole unique perspective on how to solve his problems. Or, at least, how to approach them. And this is where he wanted to be. No vacillating on the decision. He was good here. Felt good. Even felt some optimism for the first time since he'd been injured. His program had a two-month level two that he could be facing any time, then after that, a third level. Overall, he was into it for another six months, and after that—

"You're looking serious," Sloane said. "Anything you care to talk about?"

Carter glanced at her, then smiled. "Want to pose

for me? That rock up ahead would be a good spot, if you don't mind climbing up on it."

"Since when have I ever backed away from a little old rock?"

She hurried to get out in front, then scaled the boulder with all the skill of a professional.

"So, how do you want me?" she called down to him. "In a victory position, hands on my hips, surveying my vast domain? Or something a little more provocative? Maybe stretching out on the rock, being interactive with it?"

"Whatever feels natural," he called out as he approached her.

"Then this…"

She simply stood there, hands clasped in front of her, a big smile on her face. She left her cap on, left her ponytail as it was, and waved to the Mallorys who, while only a hundred feet ahead, seemed as if they were in another universe, and this universe was only for Carter and her.

"Snap away."

"Already did," he said, laughing. "I have a fully documented photo file of your journey up the rock, up to and including finding your perfect position."

Sloane's response to that was to pull out her phone and snap a few photos of Carter. He photographed well. Much better than her. Always had.

"So, can I come back down now?"

"If we want to stay caught up to Kevin."

She looked at the boy, then back at Carter. "He's leaning a little too hard to the right to suit me. I think we need to take a break—get him straightened in his saddle, take his vitals, maybe make sure he's been drinking."

She scaled down the rock, then pulled a bottle of cold water from her ice pack.

"Just precautionary," she said, handing the water to Carter, who ran on ahead and stopped Kevin for a few minutes.

"He's a little bit warm," Carter said as Sloane caught up. "Lungs are good. Pulse is steady. I say we keep going once he's had some water and a protein snack I brought just to bolster him if he needed it."

To be honest, he didn't know if they did a damn thing to help. But James had always taken one along, and he'd truly believed they raised his stamina. So with Kevin it only stood to reason that if they did help it was a good thing he'd brought a few bars along. And if they didn't help maybe the placebo effect would work.

Either way, the break was necessary, because his back was starting to ache again, and Kevin did need a little down time. So, they rested for fifteen minutes, then started again, but this time with Carter walking next to Kevin, steadying himself on the donkey's rump, and pointing out various rock formations, little animals that darted away, and all the other things associated with the desert.

"I saw a common side-blotched lizard a while ago," Kevin said. "It was standing up on a rock, watching us. Didn't even move when we went by."

"Maybe he was too afraid to move," Carter said. The way *he'd* been so often this past year.

"Or maybe he just liked watching. Some people do, you know."

"You're not a watcher, are you Kevin? Because standing off to the side and watching what other people want you to see isn't much fun—especially if you have a list of things you want to do."

"I do have a list. Next thing on it's the Statue of Liberty."

Carter admired this kid, and he admired the parents who were fighting hard to give him the very essence of life that sustained him. In so many ways he was braver than Carter was. But not braver than James. His brother had written up his own wish list. Unfortunately, their parents had only allowed small wishes and dreams, while James had wanted to conquer the world.

"Would you believe I've never seen that? I've been to New York City, but only long enough to change planes and get to my next destination. I've always thought I would go back, but so far it hasn't happened."

"You should go, Doc Carter. Going to see it is better than just sitting around thinking about it. Right, Dad?" Kevin addressed his father, who was walking on the other side of the donkey.

"We do our best to give Kevin the world. It's not always easy, but we manage. And as far as the Statue of Liberty goes…maybe in the spring?"

Kevin drew in a breath that sounded a little wheezy. Nothing to get alarmed over in the world of a child with CF, but still…

Carter motioned Sloane forward with her medical

supplies, pointed to his own chest and mouthed the word *wheezing*. Immediately she dropped back, sat her bag on the ground and shuffled through the supplies for an inhaler. She also pulled out her stethoscope, then stood and rejoined the party.

"Can we stop for a minute?" she called to the rangers, who responded immediately. "Kevin, I need to have a listen to your chest while Doc Carter takes your blood pressure. You OK with that?"

The child nodded—but he was anything but OK with what was happening, as could be seen by the scowl on his face when the rangers lifted him from the donkey.

After taking Kevin's blood pressure and finding it lower than he liked, Carter stepped around to talk to Kevin's parents. "I'm not going to tell you that something serous is going on, because he's only showing mild symptoms of respiratory discomfort. But I'm also not going to tell you that he's good to keep going—because I don't know yet."

"He told us he wants to fight through this," Kevin's father reiterated.

"But if he's on the verge of having problems…"

Kevin's mom took a good, hard look at her son. "It's not worth it. He's had his donkey ride, and it was the ride of his life. But I don't want it to be the ride that costs him his life."

Carter recalled the last time he'd taken James on an adventure. He really hadn't been feeling very good, but he'd wanted it so badly. He'd had friends at the park, who were going to meet him there, so Carter had taken him. After that, James had gone to bed for the rest of his life—which had been a grand total of seven days.

That was when he'd made that promise to fix his little brother, and that was also when his seven-year-old brother—with more profound wisdom than a child that age should ever have had—had taken his hand and said, *"That's OK, Carter. Sometimes things don't get fixed."*

And damn. Here he was with Kevin now. He was older and wiser, and yet still very much the nine-year-old who took all the blame on his young shoulders.

"You OK?" Sloane whispered, coming to stand next to Carter.

He shook his head. "My brother once told me some things don't get fixed."

"But this isn't your brother. It's Kevin, and he's fighting to get through this donkey ride."

"And the decision is up to me. Break his heart or take the risk."

Sloane laid her hand on the small of his back and began a circular rub. It felt good. Too good. Too distracting. Because right now the only thing he wanted was to get lost in her touch. Pretend that nothing else existed.

Except it did.

"Would you loosen his clothes, give him the inhaler, then get some oxygen in him?"

"Then the decision's made?"

Carter nodded. "For Plan A. But I do have a plan B, so keep your fingers crossed."

"It's the right thing," she said. "Kevin may not see it now, but next spring, when he goes to see the Statue of Liberty, he'll remember the doctor in Forgeburn who made the hard choice that gave him another shot at his list."

Sloane walked forward to inform the rangers, while Carter had a quick talk with Kevin's parents. Naturally they were disappointed, but they understood that a little caution exercised now was for the best.

"Well, Kevin," Carter said, stepping to the side of the big flat boulder where the rangers had lain the boy. He was drinking water, and sweating too much. "As much as I'd like to take you out of here on Henry, it's not safe. You're running a little bit of a temperature and your lungs are wheezy. You're also looking a little too tired. So, while I hate to do this, I've got to get you out of here quicker than Henry can."

Kevin didn't say a word. Instead he turned his head and didn't acknowledge Carter at all.

"But I do have another plan that may be more fun than this."

Kevin still didn't acknowledge him, and that was understandable. He was breaking the kid's heart the way his brother's heart had been broken so many times.

"Ever flown in a helicopter?"

"No," said Kevin, sniffling back tears of frustration.

"I have, and it's pretty neat. But what's even neater is the way you're going to get *into* that helicopter." He looked up and saw Cruz coming into position. "Can you see the helicopter up there?"

"Uh-huh…"

"Well, it can't land. There's no place safe around here."

This was beginning to pique Kevin's interest. "If it can't land, and I can't go up there to get on, how am I going to get to it."

"Easy. Cruz is going to drop a basket out the door. It's been well-secured inside, so it won't fall or do anything crazy. Once it reaches the ground we'll get you in it, and you'll be pulled up through mid-air, until Cruz's father and sister can pull you inside."

"You mean I'll be suspended in that basket for a little while?"

"That's exactly what I mean. And I'll go along beside you, just to make sure you don't get scared."

"Scared? Heck! I never knew I wanted to do this until now, but you *have* to let me do it, Doc Carter. It'll be like I'm flying all by myself."

Kevin's face took on a slight glow of excitement, but his eyes told the real story. Another adventure—another way to live outside his disability.

"Well, then, let me signal Cruz to drop the basket for you and the harness for me and we'll get this party started."

He looked over at Kevin's parents, who both seemed mortified.

"It's all good," he reassured them. "Kevin gets a new adventure, and once he's in the chopper we'll simply fly him to the nearest hospital."

Not Whipple Creek. While it served as a fine first aid station, and did take care of minor problems, Kevin's condition warranted more. Especially now, before anything major occurred.

Within a minute the orange stretcher basket was floating through the sky, being watched over by the very capable Cruz family.

"Which hospital?" Cruz asked.

By now Sloane was in charge of the radio, as Carter and the rangers got Kevin into position in the basket. "Whatever you think is best."

"Then it's north, to Salt Lake City. I'll radio through to let them know what we're bringing in. Is he OK?" Cruz asked.

"Kevin? I think he's having the time of his life."

"I meant Carter. How's *he* doing?"

Sloane glanced over at him, watched the way he was strapping himself into the harness like it was an everyday thing.

"He's doing great, Cruz," she said. "Better than I've seen him do in a long, long time."

"It's Forgeburn. I tell you. There's something curative here. Good for the weary soul."

"Maybe it is," she said, and walked over to Carter. "Hospital's being taken care of and Cruz is ready to ride."

"Hear that, Kevin? We're getting ready to fly."

"Um…can I have a drink of water first? My throat seems like it's beginning to close."

Carter and Sloane exchanged worried glances, but it was Carter who came to the rescue. "It's nerves. Once you get off the ground and relax you'll feel better."

He handed Sloane the water bottle while he did a double-check on both the basket and his own harness. Then he looked up, waved to Cruz, and in the blink of an eye both Carter and Kevin were lifted off the ground. Carter's harness kept a little lower than Kevin, to prevent tangling of the lines, and in mere moments Cruz's family was pulling Kevin to safety. Then Carter.

"So, how was that?" Carter asked as he divested himself of the safety gear.

"Awesome," Kevin said, giving Carter the thumbs-up once his arms were unstrapped from his body. "Freaking awesome."

Down below, Sloane watched everything, and sighed a sigh of relief when both Kevin and Carter were safely inside the helicopter. It hovered for another couple of minutes, until everybody inside was either secure or in a position to respond should Kevin have problems.

"I heard he has PTSD," Mrs. Mallory commented as the rangers led Henry back to his owner and the rest of them cleared the area of the various bits and pieces of medical debris.

"He does."

"And he's allowed to practice?"

Sloane couldn't help but smile, She was so proud of Carter. "Not only is he allowed, he's very much needed."

"Well, what he's done for Kevin goes above and beyond, so I'm glad he's the doctor we got to see. Even something as insignificant as a donkey ride has changed Kevin's life, and that's what his father and I try to do as much as we can. You never know when…"

She choked on tears that couldn't be held back.

"It's difficult living with someone who wants so much but has time for so very little. I hope Doc Carter will stay in touch with Kevin. He'd love that."

"I'm sure he will," Sloane said. She said that because she was getting to know Carter again. And the Carter she knew now would do something like that. She was sure of it.

# CHAPTER TEN

BY THE TIME Sloane woke up it was well into the morning. Something about this place made her relax in ways she'd never relaxed before. Sleeping as late as she had—that wasn't like her.

Her first thought was Carter, of course. He hadn't come back last night, but he had texted to let her know he was going to stay with the Mallory family for as long as they needed him, and that he'd be back first thing this morning.

Which meant he must already be at work.

Yesterday—watching Kevin being airlifted out and seeing Carter dangling from the helicopter in that harness, completely in control—was an awesome thing. Another reason to be proud. The crowds who'd gathered to send them off on the trail had been waving and cheering as the helicopter had flown overhead. And more people had gathered, waiting for news. and stayed gathered well into the night, until the first report on Kevin came back. It was a good one, too. Kevin's setback was only minor and he'd be out of the hospital in a couple of days. And again, the people cheered and partied even farther into the night, toasting the absent Carter off and on the whole time. She only wished he could have been there to see it—to see the impact he'd made in such a short time.

There was such camaraderie here Sloane almost couldn't see Carter working anyplace else now. To her, he'd always been big-city, big-hospital material. Someone who thrived where the odds were greater and the demands harder. But this little area was so—*him*. Every bit of it.

She wondered if he saw that. She hoped so. Because the thing she wanted most for Carter was for him to be happy. Here in Forgeburn, he *was* happy, and Sloane was beginning to see that.

Her phone rang and the identification came up with Carter's name. "You up?" he asked after her hello.

"Barely. People got together last night and, well…"

He chuckled. "Let me guess. You partied with them?"

"A little more than I should have."

"Well, if you're up for a little adventure I've got to make a call about thirty miles away from here—all of it on one of the cowboy roads. There's a hiking party out there and the trail guide's collapsed. He's alert now, but a little disoriented, and definitely not in any condition to bring the people back in. So, I thought one of us could tend to the guide while the other gets the hikers back safely. Are you up for it?"

"Do you know why he collapsed?" she asked, heading toward the shower.

"My guess is he was doing the same thing as you

last night—except you don't ever drink very much, and he did. He's probably dehydrated. I told the man who contacted me to get fluids into the guy, so with any luck by the time we get there the crisis will have been averted."

"And this is in your job description?" She reached into the shower, turned it on, then waited for the water to adjust to the right temperature.

"*Everything* is in my job description. What Matt told me when he hired me is that the diversity is the best part. As good a surgeon as he is, he loves being out here, where one minute he's chasing down a cowboy and the next he's delivering a baby."

"Well, you seem to be thriving here as well."

"Maybe not thriving so much as coming to terms with the idea that I don't belong in a hospital setting anymore. It's not easy when that's all you know. But people change, and I have to accept the fact that I'm one of them."

Carter sounded so good. It was hard to believe that this was the man who'd walked out on her just a little over three months ago.

"You're getting there, Carter," she said, wiggling out of her shorts and top while trying to balance her phone. "Look, let me grab a quick shower, then I'll meet you in the parking lot."

"Gear up," he said.

"As in motorcycle?"

"As in that's the only form of transportation I've got."

She smiled, thinking about riding behind him

again. Maybe it wasn't meant to be sexual, but being in that kind of contact with him was as sexual as it got. And while it was too early in the morning to be having those kinds of thoughts, she couldn't deny them. And she never had, when they'd both awakened together in the morning with the very same thought.

"Great, just great," she said, reaching over to adjust the shower temperature to something a little colder, then bracing herself for the jolt of it. Which came. But, didn't take away those feelings.

So, she hurried through, got dressed, then by the time she opened her hotel door, Carter was standing out in the hall, waiting.

"Something wrong with your back?" she asked, noticing the way he was leaning against the wall, gingerly rubbing his lower lumbar.

"Twisted it a few days ago. Nothing serious. Not even worth getting x-rayed."

"But you're up to another hike into the desert?"

It hurt him worse than he let on. She could see it in his eyes.

"Because I could grab one of the tour guides here and we could go out."

Carter waved her off, then stepped away from the wall.

"Like I said, nothing serious."

"When was the last time you saw a doctor, Carter? Weren't you supposed to be checked every two or three months?"

"I'm fine, Sloane," he said, sounding a little bit annoyed. "Not sick, not injured. Just adjusting to more activity than I've had in a while."

She wasn't convinced, but she wasn't going to argue the point. Why bother, when Carter didn't want that kind of intrusion from her? So, instead of continuing in that direction, she grabbed up her backpack which, little by little, had filled up with medical supplies, and stepped into the hall.

"This is the new me—no mincing of words. It is what it is, Sloane. I don't mean to be harsh, but I don't want to argue about my physical condition, either."

She stopped and simply stared at him for a moment. "It wouldn't hurt you to find a nice comfortable spot in the middle. Especially if you're holding on to any thoughts of staying here."

"I *am* leaning in that direction," Carter said, as he stepped aside to let her through the elevator door first. "A lot of things are hinging on how well I do with the last two parts of my program, so for now nothing is set in stone. I'm still at the stage where I'm getting myself through day by day. But I do like it here."

As the elevator doors closed, he took his place on the opposite side from her, then continued, "It's not easy going from being someone who has his life planned out every step of the way to someone who's only able to take it a day at a time, or one challenge at a time. But I'm working at it. Not always successfully, though."

"What do you mean?"

Carter creased his face into a frown and leaned back against the wall. "I do have this idea—but it may be too far out there to consider. I've been wondering what would happen if I did come back here after I've finished the program, resume practice, maybe even buy it from Matt. Then set up a recovery program much like the one I'm going through, only with horses. Everybody around here has a horse, and there are wild horses everywhere. I know there are a couple programs already working with horses, teaching people how to handle them and even become farriers, and they're getting a lot of notice in the PTSD communities. So why not here, in Forgeburn?"

"That's a whole lot of thinking into the future," she said, reaching behind Carter to push the button. "But it sounds fantastic, provided you can recruit the right people to run it."

She was excited for him, because looking out toward others' needs, and not simply inward at his own, was unlike anything he'd done in the past year. But she had to be reserved about it, rather than plunge in and make plans with him, or try to help the way she always did. Right now, treading lightly with Carter was the way she had to go.

To what end Sloane wasn't sure. She'd come looking for peace and quiet, and yet her hopes were beginning to take over—which wasn't necessarily bad, but also wasn't good, since Carter seemed to be the one with the clearer focus now.

"I hope it works for you."

There were so many other things she wanted to say, like *Can I help you?* and *What does that mean for us?* But she didn't, because she'd been rejected by him once before and she still wasn't over it—and she certainly wasn't ready for yet another rejection.

When the elevator door opened she stepped out and walked on ahead of him without another word,

What was there to say anyway?

Carter's life was going in one direction and hers in another. In a few days she'd be back at her L.A. hospital, doing all the things she'd done before. And Carter—well, his future was wide open, and she doubted it would ever again include routine medicine. No surgical schedules, no surgical follow-ups.

What he had here—this was what he wanted, and it did suit him. It was nothing she would have seen coming. Probably nothing Carter would have seen coming either. But he was growing into a contentment she'd never seen in him before. And a different kind of focus. Something more laid-back and personal. In a way, she envied him.

"So we've got to go thirty miles to give this guy some water for his hangover?" she asked as they approached his motorcycle. "What happens if in the meantime you have a real patient who needs real skills?"

"I make the choice." He got on the bike, then held out his hand to help Sloane climb on the back. "And the people here seem to trust me to do that."

"Your skills as a doctor were never questioned, Carter. Up to and including that day you walked out, I never heard anybody question any medical decision you made."

"Then you weren't listening, Sloane. The criticisms were real—and loud. And they wouldn't let go of me no matter what I did."

"They were in your mind, Carter."

"And your mind is a terrible thing to have turn against you."

"But you're turning it around now. Remember that. You're turning it around."

Sloane fastened her helmet and wrapped her arms around his waist, and as she did so she noticed him jerk slightly to the side.

"Did I hurt you?" she asked.

"Nope. Just making an adjustment."

And that was the last thing he said before they took off. Because their helmets were not in sync for communication, they rode in silence for thirty minutes, but when they got to the site where the questionable trail guide had collapsed no one was there.

"Did we lose our patient?" Sloane asked, once they were stopped.

"Our patient *and* his party."

Carter radioed the lodge hosting the group and discovered that they'd gone on without their guide.

"Except they went in opposite directions. The group is headed to the finish of the trail and they left their guide here, sitting on a rock."

"So maybe he's gone on ahead, too?"

"According to the concierge, Kip—that's his name—was in no shape to walk anywhere. In fact they specifically told him to find another guide, that he was not to lead anyone anywhere."

Carter let out a frustrated sigh, then sat down on the rock.

He looked tired. But then yesterday had done *her* in and she hadn't been involved in that rescue to the extent Carter had been, so maybe this was simply residual tiredness that would be fixed by a good nap.

"So, what's our next option?" she asked. "Because if you want this doctor's opinion, I think you should go back to your place and get some rest. You're not looking good, Carter."

To prove her point, Sloane took him by the wrist to check his pulse—but it seemed fine, which surprised her.

A sly grin crept over his face. "Care to examine any other parts of me? You know I'm not in the least shy about that—as long as it's you doing the exam."

That was definitely the old Carter speaking and she blushed. thinking about how many times she'd given in to his naughty persuasions.

"Yeah, right. Out here in the open, where anybody could see us."

"Look around, Sloane. We're the only ones here."

Laughing, she sat down next to him, wondering why she'd worn such a tight sleeveless T-shirt. It left nothing to the imagination, especially without a bra, and she wasn't wearing one. And what with the sweat it might be a wet T-shirt contest for all the good the stretchy fabric was doing.

Self-consciously, she crossed her hands over her chest and hunched down a little.

"No need to hide from me, Sloane," Carter said.

"I've seen it all—and God knows you know how much I've always liked that aspect of our relationship."

"Except our relationship is over, Carter."

"But the memories linger..." He reached over and traced the line of her collarbone with his index finger. "And they're good ones."

She thought about slapping his hand away, but too much of her wanted this. Wanted his touch and so much more. Because they were good at this. Maybe too good. So many of the other aspects of their years together seemed to fade away, but not those details.

"Were we ever right for each other?" she asked. "I know we had a lot of years, but you were gone for so many of them I'm wondering if we ever got past the physical attraction."

Carter pulled his hand away. "Seriously? You think in all that time that's all we had?"

"I'm at a place right now where I question everything. The way we are now—it's hard to put us together the way we were back then. We did things together all the time, and that was good. But I wonder who were we that you didn't feel inclined to tell me something so important as that you needed space and encouragement, not someone to jump in and take over and try to fix you. So, yes, I do question things now."

Sloane noticed his hands shaking and wondered if he was on the verge of a PTSD incident. Shaking hands was always a giveaway—one that told her to tread very carefully. Was she pushing him into this?

"I don't have an answer for you because I always thought we were good."

"So did I—but were we really good enough? We were almost married by the time you left. My wedding dress is still hanging in the closet."

Carter wiped the sweat off his face, then studied his shaking hands for a moment before he spoke.

"By that time we weren't good. At least I wasn't. And it killed me watching you trying to help me all the time, especially when I knew nothing was working. I never meant to hurt you, Sloane. But, honestly, at the point when I left the only person I could think about was me. I hated seeing you cry, which was happening more and more, and I didn't want to be responsible for that. I didn't want to be responsible for me, either."

He wiped his brow again, then crammed his shaking hands into his pockets.

"Is something going on I should know about?" she asked, her level of concern rising at seeing so many physical symptoms she remembered. Shaking hands. Sweating. Shortness of breath. A relentless restlessness that kept elevating. And his restlessness was definitely elevating. In fact he was so antsy he hopped off the rock and started to pace.

"No, I'm fine."

But he wasn't. And here they were, right back where they'd used to be. He was leaving her out. Something was obviously wrong, and she wasn't being included in it.

"Well, I say we call the rangers and let them worry

about our errant tour guide and his hikers, then we can head back to the hotel."

He stopped for a moment to look at her, but it was a strange look. One that was almost looking right through her.

"Sloane, I—" He stopped. Gasped for breath. Then bit down hard on his lower lip. "I need help…" he gasped.

Then he collapsed into her arms.

Her first reaction was to lower him to the ground. Then feel for a pulse in his neck—it was there, but thready.

"Carter, can you hear me?" She had no idea what this was. Certainly not PTSD. "Carter…?"

Grabbing his medical bag, she pulled out his stethoscope and listened to his chest. It was clear. When she checked his blood pressure it was strong enough. But his ankles were slightly swollen. As were his hands. And his breathing was…labored.

She thought back to his stitch of pain earlier, when she'd climbed on to the motorcycle. And his tiredness. And all the other little things: his shaking hands; his sudden irritability. She thought hard for a moment, running down the list of things she'd observed, things she'd been worried about then, suddenly, it hit her, as did a mammoth bout of nausea.

"Carter!" she said, picking up her phone and hoping she had enough bars out here to ring Cruz.

Because Carter was dying.

She believed his remaining kidney had failed or was in the process of it and, while she wasn't a specialist, she knew that if she was correct, he needed dialysis as fast as possible or the toxins that weren't being filtered due to kidney failure would kill him.

"Hang in there with me, Carter. I think you've got a kidney problem going on." Naturally, she didn't expect him to respond. But she hoped he would.

"Hear you've got a semi-sober trail guide out there," Cruz said after he answered his phone.

"I have a patient in renal failure. I need to get him to the hospital, so can you track me and come get us?"

"I'll be right out to you," he assured her. Then, "Since you went out with Carter—is it him?"

"It is," she said, fighting back the panic and the fear rising in her. "And it's bad. He's unconscious."

"Ten minutes tops."

Which would turn into the ten longest minutes of Sloane's life.

"Look Carter," she said, sitting in the middle of the dry, dusty dirt road with Carter's head in her lap. "I understand why you weren't taking your health seriously. You were fighting such a huge battle and your life was getting better. But to ignore this? Sure, maybe you didn't want another obstacle in your way, but this is your life we're dealing with."

She lifted his limp hand to her lips and kissed it.

"How could you do this to yourself, to me. To us?"

Any other time the tears would have been flowing, but she was in full doctor mode and when she was a doctor, she didn't cry. Never. But she was so close because she was scared. This was the man she'd loved more than life for six years and he was dying in her arms.

"It's not going to happen. I won't allow it." she said, trying to move herself into a position where her body shaded his.

Allow it? Right. As if she had any control over his condition.

"We've come too far, for too long, to end it here, this way, Carter. Whether you want to hear this or not, I've loved you so much and for so long, and while I got frustrated with you so many times this past year. But that didn't mean I didn't love you, because I did. And I still do. Nothing about that has changed. And I'm pretty sure you love me."

Sloane wiped his sweaty brow with the bottom of her shirt.

"I don't know if we can fix things. But I want to try again. I deserve it. *We* deserve it."

She glanced up to see if Cruz was on his way, but the sky was empty.

"And if that means I move to Forgeburn and turn myself into a GP, that's what I'll do. It's called being in love, and somewhere along the way I think you forgot how to do that. But I want it back, Carter. Do you hear me? I want all of it back."

Sloane assessed his vitals again and found there was essentially no change.

"I may not have been forceful enough when we were together before, or maybe I was too forceful—I don't know. But it was because I loved you so much."

Even though the tears were threatening harder

now, she still wasn't going to cry. Carter needed her to be a doctor, needed her to save his life. And the way she was going to do that—he might not approve but, at least, he'd be alive to argue with her about it.

"So here's the plan. Carter. Cruz is going to fly you to the hospital to get you fixed. After that, you and I are going to quit all this avoiding the real situation, and deal with it. Like, how you still love me." She brushed back the damp hair from her face.

"Because I love you, and that's the only way I know how to take care of you. For me, Carter, it's all or nothing. And I want it all."

The distant sound of a motorcycle startled her out of her moment, and she looked up to see Matt coming to a stop. He grabbed an armload of supplies from his storage and came running to her.

"Cruz called me. He's delayed a little longer than he should be, and since I was already in the vicinity…"

"IV," Sloane said, snapping back into doctor mode.

She had a patient to take care of here. The most important patient of her life.

Carter opened his eyes, but nothing came into focus except a white ceiling. He stared up at it for a moment. Then he blinked, wondering if it would go away. But it didn't, which meant it was real. He fixed on the ceiling for a full minute before he finally turned his head and saw the IV line in his arm—a sight with which he was well-acquainted—and the stand-by ventilator next to the bed. There were other monitors too—for blood pressure, heart-rate.

As he twisted a bit, to see what else he was hooked up to, a sharp pain stabbed him in the side. Slowly he twisted left and saw the patient in the bed next to him. He couldn't bring him into focus, though.

"Where are we?" he asked, wondering if his roomie was even awake.

His roomie sat up. That much he could see.

"Carter?"

"Sloane?" Something was off here, and he couldn't even begin to make sense of it. "What's going on?"

"You collapsed. It seems your kidney shut down and you've been suffering from uremia for a while. Uremia, by the way, has symptoms you should have noticed. You know, your back cramps, lack of appetite, excessive tiredness."

"Are you here to nag at me for not diagnosing myself?" Carter asked, so glad to hear her voice that if he could have hopped across to her bed he would have.

"It's a tough job, but…"

"Somebody's got to do it? I know. So what did they do? Dialyze me."

"Too late for that. Your kidney was—let's just say *done*."

They'd removed his kidney? No way in hell. "Seriously, what did they do to me?"

"They couldn't save it, Carter. Your binges for the past year…they took a toll. I'm sorry it happened this way, but there was nothing they could do."

He was so tired. Too much pain. And he simply couldn't take it in. No kidney meant dialysis for the rest of his life. That would take him out of The Recovery Project. Force him to move somewhere close to a dialysis center. End his medical career. End everything he'd fought so hard to get back.

"So, I'll add that to my list, right? No spleen, no kidneys, and I'll never know when my PTSD will trigger. I mean, what's the point? What's the damn point to any of this?"

"You mean what's the point of being so loved by a small community that they're raising funds to give you a proper home there? People *love* you, Carter. They depend on you. You are such a good person—such a good doctor.

"Yeah, well, tell them to skip the home and buy me a dialysis machine. Because that's the way the rest of my life is going to be written."

"Only if you want it to be," she said.

"And what's my alternative?"

"Keep the kidney they transplanted into you healthy. You know…live the better life, do the better thing."

"I—I had a *transplant*?" He looked over at her, his vision slowly returning. But not enough to really see her yet. "How? I wasn't even on the list."

"A perfect match donor came forward."

"And just *gave* me a kidney?" Now he was totally confused. People didn't just give away kidneys. Sure, the body only needed one healthy kidney, but most people opted to hang on to the other one just to be on the safe side.

"Something like that."

"Tell me how it happened. Especially since I didn't consent to it."

"You didn't have to. Remember all those years ago when you joined the Army, and you gave me your power of attorney to make decisions if you couldn't make them yourself? I still have your power of attorney, Carter. You never had it revoked after we split up, and I made the medical decision. There was a kidney available, and because of your condition you went to the top of the list. So—"

"So someone's tragedy saved my life?"

The doctors had talked to him about the possibility of a transplant at some time in the future, if the one kidney he had went bad, and being a surgeon himself there was nothing he didn't know about the whole process from start to end. But he'd never really thought in terms of having a transplant, even though he'd known his existing kidney was fragile. Now that it was done, he wasn't sure what to think.

"Do we know anything about the donor?" he asked, the way any doctor would ask. Hiding behind his medical credentials right now seemed the safest place to be. It was the only place he truly understood.

"We do. It's a woman. About your age. Well-educated. A doctor, in fact."

Carter swallowed hard. "And the match? How close was it?"

"It was a perfect match in all three categories. Blood type was perfect—both you and your donor were type B. I know that's a little bit rare, but you got lucky. The cross-match was perfect as well. And the HLA testing came out just fine. As far as a match goes, you couldn't have done any better."

"When?" he asked. "When did this all happen?

"Late yesterday—a few hours after they got you to the hospital. You were unconscious, because your kidney had bled quite a bit, so the surgery took a while longer than it normally would have. But they put you in intensive care overnight, then brought you up here to this room a few hours ago. Your vitals are stable, your incision is good—everything either of us would want to see in our surgical patients."

"And how long have *you* been here?"

"I flew in with you and haven't left."

"You didn't have to stay."

"Actually, I did. The doctors here wouldn't let me go. Although I will say it was difficult, persuading them to put a man and a woman in the same room. But after I explained how we'd lived together for so many years, and seeing that it was my kidney you were getting…"

"Stop! Did you say *your* kidney?"

"My kidney. Back in Germany, when they removed your first one and told me your second kidney could be living on borrowed time, I had myself tested as a donor just in case it ever came to that."

"And you never told me?"

"I intended to at some point, but the relationship turned so bad it never seemed like the right time. Then, when you left me—well, let's just say that I wasn't giving it a lot of thought because there were other more important things on my mind."

"*Why*, Sloane? Why would you do something like that? Especially with the way I treated you?"

"Love is bigger than any illness, Carter. You don't just stop loving someone because they're ill. Sometimes I thought I didn't love you, but it never really sank in because I knew all along that nothing about the way I felt for you was different. I loved you that very first day and I never stopped. We did get misdirected. But that's fixable. The thing is, I think we both fell into that trap of thinking that hiding the truth from each other was a good way to protect them. But it's not that way. Hiding the truth only hurts more when it's revealed. And eventually most truths *are* revealed.

"I should have told you that I would be the one stepping forward should you ever need a transplant, but I didn't because I was afraid that if you knew that it would change who we were. And you should have told me how your brother has affected your life in so many ways. It would have made a difference in the way I perceived you."

"And you gave me a kidney?"

"You always were difficult to shop for…and you do have a birthday coming up in a few days."

"Don't joke about this, Sloane. You gave up a *kidney.* Do you know what that means?"

"In terms of recovery time—a few weeks."

"In terms of your life, Sloane. *In terms of your life.*"

"It means she loves you more than she loves herself, you idiot," Matt McClain said as he entered the room. "I tried talking her out of it, but the lady is stubborn. She wouldn't listen to me. Wouldn't listen to her dad, either."

"He's here, too?" Carter asked.

"At the hotel right now. But he'll be here in a little while." Matt pulled a chair in between the two hospital beds and sat down. "I can only stay a couple minutes, because Cruz needs to get back. But just listen to this—*both of you*. Sloane, you're an idiot for hanging on to this man. He's put you through hell and you don't deserve that. And, Carter, you're just an idiot, period. Walking away from the best thing you'll ever have in your life... If there's a word stronger than idiot, that's what you are. I love you both, and you know that. But you've got to do better. Because if Carter is going to stay here and continue his practice—and God only knows why the people of Forgeburn want that, but they do—that means Sloane's going to stay here, too, so you're going to have to face up to your problems, then deal with them. So, Sloane, tell the man what you want to say. And, Carter, listen to her. That's all I've got to say."

With that, he stood up, scooted the chair back, and headed for the door.

"Ellie's made up the guestroom for when you get out of here. *One guestroom*. We expect you'll be staying with us for a while, until you're stronger. And, Carter, you still owe me that motorcycle ride into the canyons."

Matt smiled as he left the room.

"It's going to work out," he told Harlan Manning as they passed in the hall. "They've got an awful lot of obstacles right now, but when they come to their senses and figure out they're still together they'll be fine. In the meantime, I think they need some time alone. Care to follow me home? Ellie's fixing enchiladas and Spanish rice tonight."

"Sounds good to me," Harlan said. "But are you sure about Sloane and Carter?"

"I told them they were both idiots. What more is there to say?"

"Now what?" Sloane asked. "We've been avoiding each other for so long I don't even know where to begin."

"Is this where we're supposed to embrace and tell each other everything's going to be all right? Because it won't be, Sloane. I may have a new lease on my physical life, but that has nothing to do with—with the reason I left you in the first place."

"Which is?" she asked, desperately wishing they could embrace.

"I couldn't hurt you anymore. I saw it happen over and over. Saw you brace yourself to take it on the chin, then get back up and take it again. And I saw you crying, Sloane. That was the worst of it. I made you cry so many times."

"It wasn't easy, Carter. Never knowing when something would trigger you. Never knowing when I'd have the real you or have to deal with your PTSD. But I coped. And I tried to help."

"I know that. I could always see it, even when I was in panic or rage mode. I always saw what it was doing to you, but I couldn't control it. It was like someone else was taking me over. Someone I couldn't control. And it scared me. Still does. Which is why

I left. Not because I didn't love you. But because I loved you too much. More than my own life. Sloane, I always have. Always will."

"But you're getting through it, Carter. I called your counselor and told her what had happened, and she told me how hard you're working. They're very optimistic for you, and they'll hold your spot open in the next phase of the program until you're physically able to participate in it."

"Thank you," he said. "Thank you for everything you've done, even when I wasn't being very appreciative."

"That's what you do for your other half, Carter, and you've been my other half since the day we met. And even when you left me."

"I saw how I couldn't live up to the man I used to be, and I knew you wanted him back. After a while I figured you were staying out of pity, and that was the worst—thinking you had going from loving me to pitying me. You needed better than anything I could give you or would ever be able to give you."

"You didn't think your love was enough?" Sloane asked.

"For you, Sloane, I didn't think anything about me was enough."

"I've never stopped loving you, Carter. You've been difficult, but my love has been unconditional through everything. Because when you weren't difficult you were the Carter I fell in love with. I could always see him, even when you couldn't. And I always believed in him. So, how did we get here, Carter?

Loving someone shouldn't be done in fear. But that's all we've had for the last year. I remember the night before you shipped out to Afghanistan, when we talked for hours, made promises. The promise I remember the most was that no matter what happened while you were gone it wouldn't tear us apart. That you'd come home to me and I'd wait for you. But that didn't happen. You never came home to me."

"It's hard losing yourself, Sloane. But what's harder is losing yourself and then getting occasional glimpses of who you are only to have them ripped away from you."

"And you couldn't tell me this?"

"I couldn't tell you anything, because to have done so would have meant it was true, and I didn't want it to be true. I wanted to be *me*, Sloane. I wanted to come back home to the life we had. But I didn't get any of that, and all I had left was a pretty good way to block it out of my mind or deny it when I couldn't. To admit it made it real, and I just couldn't face anything else. Not by myself. And yes, I wanted to talk to you about so many things, including the deterioration in my physical health—my backaches, my lethargy— but that would have dragged you in to it more than you deserved. So, I lied about it to you, and even to myself. And with all that, there was still my PTSD to consider." He shrugged. "I'm overwhelmed right now, Sloane. There's so much to deal with and I'm afraid of getting lost or taking the wrong direction again."

Finally the tears came, but Sloane didn't say anything for a few moments as she took in everything he was telling her. He was scared, she was scared. Yet instead of letting that fear bring them closer together, they'd let it separate them. But maybe they had needed to get here this way, to understand better how love could last through battles.

And love did last. Hers had.

"We're stronger together than we are apart, Carter. That was never addressed in any of the therapy you received when we were still togetehr. In fact, I think it was overlooked in pretty much everything I read. But the fact is you and I may fall into someone's statistical category for the bad things that happen when someone you love suffers from PTSD, but there is no statistical category for the good things. And *we* are the good things. What we were, what we had and still have…"

Sloane shut off her IV, removed the catheter from her vein, then slipped out of her bed and into bed next to Carter. It was a tight fit, but a good fit, especially when he pulled her into his arms and held her."

"I don't want to hurt you," she whispered.

Carter nodded toward one of his IV bags. "I'm covered. But you're not, Sloane. Not in the whole scheme of things."

"Do you love me?" she asked him.

"Of course I do. I've never stopped."

"Do you trust me?"

"I always have."

"Will you take care of me?"

"I've always tried. And I'll never stop trying."

"Then I'm covered." She leaned up and brushed a

light kiss on his lips. "Besides, I made a pretty hefty investment in you yesterday. I think I should stick around and see how that investment pays off."

"Why did you do it?" he asked.

"Would you have done the same for me?"

"I would give my life for you, Sloane. From that first day we met nothing about that has changed."

"And I would do the same. But luckily all you needed was a kidney. As they say, easy-peasy."

And it had been. The instant Sloane had known Carter would lose his only kidney she'd stepped up. No hesitation, no fear. All she'd known was that the man she loved needed something she could give him, so how could she not?

"I'm beginning to remember why I fell so hard for you, so fast," he said, holding on to her as tight as he could, considering his condition.

"Because I'm a catch. I may not always get it right, but when I do it turns out brilliantly."

"As in...?"

"Us. You and me. Carter Holmes and Sloane Manning—meant to be."

"Even in Forgeburn?"

"Even in Forgeburn!"

# EPILOGUE

"I'M GOING TO miss this place," Sloane said, settling into Carter's arms, on the porch swing. "It's so peaceful here. And all those baby bears…"

"Sounds like someone's got a mommy craving."

"Well, I'm not getting any younger…"

Carter chuckled. "We could always bump up the plan. You know how I feel about starting a family."

"But we've broken ground on the hospital already, and you've got all your licenses in line to start your new PTSD program. All that besides our medical practice. Are you going to be OK, Sloane, as a GP? Because the world's losing one of its great heart surgeons."

"I've been tucked up here in the mountains off and on for the past six months with you and nobody's even noticed I was gone."

She'd gone with Carter to the second part of his recovery program and taken advantage of the support offered for families and other loved ones. Occasionally, she'd gone back to Los Angeles, or Forgeburn, to work on their future together—the one where they would build a small, but much needed hospital in Forgeburn. But even a day or two away from him had been tough on her.

But, she'd come to Tennessee to stay on through the third part of his program because what she realized was the help was always there if she wanted it. And she wanted it and needed it almost as much as Carter did. Because she had finally come to understand that she needed it if she and Carter were to make a go of their relationship.

They had to be on the same side, fighting the same battle together, and most of all always knowing what was going on with the other one. There wasn't an easy fix, but with the support of The Recovery Project and other groups like it she was positive she and Carter would make it. There was too much love between them to let their relationship fail.

"Sounds like we're going to be busy."

"Which is why I'd like to buy a cabin up here somewhere, for when we get overwhelmed. Which, by the way, will be in about seven months."

"Seriously?" Carter asked, pulling her T-shirt up to look at her belly.

"Nothing showing. Just took the test the morning."

"So we're expanding in all directions!"

"That seems to be the case. So, are you happy that I bumped up our plan?"

It hadn't been intentional, but it was meant to be. A family of three, or more. It was a promising future, and an exciting one.

Carter grinned and pulled her even tighter. The

rusting chain on the porch swing gave a little, with some creaks and groans, but like Carter and Sloane it wasn't about to give up.

"I think I may have had something to do with bumping up the plan."

"Could be…" she said.

She'd come to love the lazy evenings here. They had their own cabin, and while it wasn't secluded from the rest of the program's facilities it was far enough away that it felt like they were in a world all their own.

Tonight was especially beautiful, with the pink glow over the mountains, the darker blues above it, the lazy call of a hawk out on its evening routine.

For a little while it had been a perfect world for the two of them, and she was going to miss it. But Carter was through his program now, and it was time to get back to real life—which would be hectic and unpredictable and just as beautiful as life here had been.

Sloane laid Carter's hand on her belly. "If it's a girl I think we should name her after your first cub—Buttercup. And if it's a boy we'll name him after your second cub—Napoleon," she said with a grin.

She was so glad Carter was seeing more days of calmness and less of turmoil. And while the next part of their life might be a challenge for him, he wasn't alone in his struggles. He had Matt and Ellie, and Cruz—everybody in Forgeburn. And most of all he had her, and their baby-on-the-way.

PTSD might try to take over, but it wasn't going

to win because Carter was one of the lucky ones. He was loved. So loved.

"Care to dance?" Sloane asked him.

And they did. On the pine needles. On the top of the mountain. In the glow of the setting sun.

\* \* \* \* \*

# MILLS & BOON

## Coming next month

### THEIR NEWBORN BABY GIFT
**Alison Roberts**

*'Give Grace a cuddle from me...'*

Evie's voice seemed to echo in the back of Ryan's head every time he was near the baby. Like now, as he held his stethoscope against that tiny chest to listen to her heart.

He had never 'cuddled' one of his patients.

He never would.

How unprofessional would that be?

It wasn't that he didn't care about them. He couldn't care more about their clinical outcomes. He found enormous satisfaction—joy, even, in a successful outcome and he had been completely gutted more than once when he'd lost a patient despite his best efforts.

But those emotions were about the case, not the person.

And, somehow, that careless remark of Evie's had planted the idea that maybe there was something wrong with him. What if he hadn't been in control for so many years and deliberately choosing to keep his distance from people to avoid the kind of pain that emotions automatically created? What if he wasn't even capable of feeling strongly about someone else?

Would that make him some kind of heartless monster?

The complete opposite of someone like Evie?

The abnormal heart sounds he could hear were getting louder again and Ryan suspected that the blood flow to the baby's lower body wasn't as good as it had been straight after the procedure to widen the narrowed part of the aorta. Grace started crying as he pressed the skin on her big toe to leave a pale spot, looking for evidence of how quickly the blood returned to make it pink again.

Ryan made notes on Grace's chart as her cries got louder and then hung it back on the end of her crib. He looked around to see if someone was also hearing the sound of a baby that needed attention. Feeding, maybe. Or a nappy change.

Or just a cuddle…

Continue reading
THEIR NEWBORN BABY GIFT
Alison Roberts

*Available next month*
www.millsandboon.co.uk

# COMING SOON!

We really hope you enjoyed reading this book. If you're looking for more romance, be sure to head to the shops when new books are available on

# Thursday
# 1st November

To see which titles are coming soon, please visit
**millsandboon.co.uk**

# LET'S TALK
## Romance

For exclusive extracts, competitions
and special offers, find us online:

**f** facebook.com/millsandboon

**◎** @millsandboonuk

**𝕐** @millsandboon

Or get in touch on 0844 844 1351*

For all the latest titles coming soon, visit
millsandboon.co.uk/nextmonth